Praise for
TEN AFTER CLOSING

"Both touching and terrifying. Be careful! You may actually burn your fingers reading *Ten After Closing*. What starts as a spark turns into a raging inferno that you won't be able to put down. Wonderful characters + nail-biting tension = one fantastic book."
—Billy Taylor, author of *Thieving Weasels*

"*Ten After Closing* sinks teeth into you from page one and never lets go. Reading this YA heist-gone-wrong thriller was like being strapped to the front of a Ferrari doing 120mph. Set two alarm clocks—Bayliss has crafted an instant page turner that will have you up way past ten. This book is one. Wild. Ride."
—Matthew Landis, author of *League of American Traitors* and *The Not-So-Boring Letters of Private Nobody*

"When you start *Ten After Closing*, you will ignore friends, family, and everyone else until you've read the last page."
—Shaun Harris, author of *The Hemingway Thief*

"This fast-paced thriller grabs on from the first page and doesn't let go. I felt an urgent need to read Scott and Winny out of danger, yet feared every new page for all the twists and turns. *Ten After Closing* does not disappoint, culminating in a heart-pounding finale that left me feeling breathless."
—Kristina McBride, author of *The Bakersville Dozen* and *A Million Times Goodnight*

"Told in alternating perspectives and timelines, this is one unnerving thriller that's destined to make its mark. "
—Dahlia Adler, for *BN Teen Blog*

TEN AFTER CLOSING

JESSICA BAYLISS

Sky Pony Press
New York

First Edition

This is a work of fiction. Names, characters, places, and incidents are from the author's imagination, and used fictitiously.

Sky Pony Press books may be purchased in bulk at special discounts for sales promotion, corporate gifts, fund-raising, or educational purposes. Special editions can also be created to specifications. For details, contact the Special Sales Department, Sky Pony Press, 307 West 36th Street, 11th Floor, New York, NY 10018 or info@skyhorsepublishing.com.

Sky Pony® is a registered trademark of Skyhorse Publishing, Inc.®, a Delaware corporation.

Visit our website at www.skyponypress.com.

10 9 8 7 6 5 4 3 2 1

Library of Congress Cataloging-in-Publication Data available on file.

Cover illustration by Kevin Tong
Cover design by Kate Gartner

Hardcover ISBN: 978-1-5107-3207-0
Ebook ISBN: 978-1-5107-3211-7

Printed in the United States of America

For Samantha. You believed I could, and so I did.

1

SCOTT

THREE MINUTES AFTER CLOSING

I glance at my watch. Three minutes after ten.

God, how long have I been down here, staring at crates of mustard and bags of non-GMO kale chips? As if that will somehow erase the memory of my girlfriend's words, still a tornado in my mind.

Correction: my ex-girlfriend.

I force my brain to shut the hell up and straighten from my slumped position against the wall. Cool damp has seeped into my shirt from the bedrock lining the basement where Becky just dumped me. The sickly feel of the fabric sends a shiver through me, and I untuck my stained work polo to give my skin some breathing room.

Too bad all my problems aren't as easy to fix.

Stretching my spine, I roll my head. My neck and shoulders are definitely feeling the two hours' worth of work I've done tonight, though not as bad as they'd be after a full shift. And it's not over yet. I head toward the doorway and the creaky stairs beyond, skirting the trapdoor that leads to the sub-basement. After the crack it let out when Becky stood on it before, I'm not taking any chances on it holding my weight. I don't need a broken leg to go with my busted life.

"Hey, Scott. You okay down there?" Sylvie calls from the top of the storeroom stairwell. Not out of anger—she's too much of a softy for that. But if she catches on that something's up with me, it will be just like the time I showed up to work with my wrist wrapped in an ACE bandage; she gave me the worried-mom look for weeks, offering her ear if I wanted to talk. Offering to talk to my parents.

"I just want to help, Scott," she said, when I brushed her off for the umpteenth time.

"If you want to help me, then keep giving me shifts. The more the better."

Her renewed worrying will just make the whole thing worse, which is the last thing I need tonight. First the crap going on at home. Then Becky. And the night is still young—plenty of time left for me to get run over by a car or abducted by aliens.

"Yeah. Be right up!"

"'Kay. You have a visitor. A *special* visitor." The door swishes shut overhead, cutting off what sounds way too much like a giggle.

Could it be Becky, back for round two? Nah, she'd storm

right down here if she still had a piece of her mind left to sling my way. Whoever it is, I'll deal with them, do my work like everything is fine, and then get out of here.

I freeze halfway up the stairs.

And where, exactly, do I think I'm going after work?

Not home, that's for sure. After this afternoon and my mom's voice message, I'm not planning on walking through that door until at least two or three, when he'll be out for the count.

There's still the party, but can I even go now?

Yeah, I can go. If I want to make a scene. Becky'll be raring to start something in front of everyone, especially once she downs a couple of those God-awful hard iced teas. I can see her now, just like the day we had the showdown over the prom. Becky in her cheer uniform, looking hot and cute, with her hip cocked, right hand on her waist. Sweet but feisty. Until you take in her expression. That's where the venom shows.

Have fun working all the time and still being broke.

I don't need that shit. Not Becky's *whatever* face and definitely not my name, acid in her voice. I already got that enough times tonight.

And what if she's with someone else? Ricky Belsen, maybe.

I shake my head. She wouldn't do that, but still, plenty of guys would love a chance to get with her.

My muscles turn to lead, heavy and slow, and my hands

are twin twenty-pounders hanging at the ends of my arms. Any fight I had in me earlier is gone, along with what little stomach for celebration I'd managed to scrounge up. What do I have to celebrate anyway? It's not like I'm allowed to make plans like everyone else. Do I really want to hang with all those drunk assholes as they go on and on about next year? Schools, majors, frats. Sucking it up wasn't so bad with Becky there to distract me, even if I was usually the only straight edge at the party, but no way I'm subjecting myself to that now.

I'm tired of changing the subject when my friends start talking about plans for the future. How the hell do you explain sitting on three college scholarship offers just because you've got a messed-up family? Especially when that family would kind of prefer you go if only they didn't need you to stay? That's a question I'm not willing to answer. Not for anybody. Not even Winny.

But if the party's a no, then what? Doesn't matter right now anyway. I've got a good half hour of work to look forward to. Plus my mystery visitor.

I'd better get going. Everyone else will want to get out of here on a Friday night—like I did twenty minutes ago.

My shitty life will still be there waiting when my shift is over.

I plod the rest of the way up the stairs, but before I even reach the kitchen, I realize something is off.

I pat my pocket. Damn. My phone is still down in the

basement, tucked on the shelf between the plastic forks and knives for our take-out orders. Useless as the busted thing is, I turn back to grab it, but no more than three steps down, a scream stops me. *Sylvie?* I do a jump-spin combo, throwing out a hand to keep from tumbling backward down the stairs. Once I'm sure I'm not going to break my neck, I bolt the rest of the way up and through the door to the empty kitchen. Oscar and I cleaned up in here over an hour ago, when we stopped serving all but soup and pastries.

Shouts. Bangs. Laughter, but not the good kind. Is Sylvie crying? My fists clench.

"You slimy son-of-a-bitch!" That's Oscar. "I don't give a crap if he's your brother!"

"Oscar, no!" Sylvie shouts. "Ryan, please. No, Oscar, stay here! Don't go near them. Please, everyone. Please, just stop!"

A new voice speaks, but softly, and I can't make it out. Everything on the other side of the door goes quiet, too quiet. Now, all I'm getting is mumbling. Can this day get any weirder?

I peer through one of the windows set in the swinging doors, not sure I want to know what flavor of drama is happening out there. "Oh, shit," I whisper, and my warm breath bounces off the glass back into my face.

My special visitor is nowhere to be seen, unless it's one of the three men blocking the way to the café entrance and the quiet street beyond. There's Ryan, his blond hair and freckled complexion almost a perfect match to his sister's. But who the hell are the other two? Something tells me they're not here for a late-night scone. If they're tight with Ryan, they've got to be asshats like him. Whatever went down between Sylvie and her brother in the past, it couldn't have been pretty. His drop-ins, which have gotten more frequent lately, always end with Sylvie in tears, or in a screaming match between her and Oscar, who doesn't like his brother-in-law any more than I do. The tension when Ryan worked here made every shift miserable. I know I wasn't the only one who was glad when he left.

How did Ryan and his friends even get in here? I check my watch. Nine minutes after closing. The doors should have been locked. Oh, right. That's my job, and I've been in the basement, sulking.

This little standoff isn't looking like it'll wrap up any time soon. I should just slip out the back door and jet. But I'm not done with my tasks for the night. If it hadn't been for Becky and her bombshell, I'd be all finished and long gone. Now I'm stuck waiting for this family drama to play out.

As if I don't get enough of that at home.

But I can't leave Oscar and Sylvie alone to deal with this, and it's some major shit, for sure. Sylvie's in full-on sob mode. Oscar is behind the counter near the door to the kitchen, his back to me. The way he's standing behind

Sylvie, with his arms around her waist, brings me back to this afternoon, and memories of a power drill. Only one reason why Oscar would hold his wife that way: he doesn't want her to run toward Ryan and his friends. He's *afraid* she'll run toward Ryan and his friends.

The question is why.

Ryan is ranting about something, but the words die before they reach the kitchen. Only his cold tone slices through the glass and wood. His friends flank him, a shorter guy who's silent and still, and a tall, skinny dude who's antsy as hell.

What's Ryan doing hanging out with those two, anyway? Forget the fact that he's at least five years older than them; they look like he picked them up on the streets. Scabs and sores dot the taller guy's sickly pale face, and he keeps shifting his weight from foot to foot and hiking up the jeans that hang off his narrow hips. The dude is seriously thin. The other guy—stockier, and way cleaner than the tall dude—wears a black leather jacket over a white tee and jeans, even though it's warm enough outside for shorts. And he's got on a pair of aviators, like no one told him the sun went down hours ago. He says something to Ryan, who shoots the guy a glance before returning his attention to his sister.

This is all probably nothing, but best to hang tight, just to be sure. At least whatever's going on will kill some time.

"You heard me!" Ryan shouts, and I jump.

Maybe I'll be calling 911 today, after all. I grope for my phone again, but it's still in the basement. I'm about to head back down to get it when Sylvie screams, "No, no! Please, don't!"

I pause and spin to peer through the window again. Everyone's in motion. Oscar blocks my view of Ryan, but I've got a new angle on his friends. And what his friends have in their hands. Now I know why that dude needed a jacket on a warm June night.

My stomach turns inside out and my heart slams to my ears as I stumble away from the door. "Oh, shit. Oh, motherfucking shit."

That's when I hear the first gunshot.

2

SCOTT

Twelve Minutes Before Closing

Scott stared at his girlfriend of the last six months. The hard line of her jaw. The raised eyebrow. The slight smile edging her sneer, like she was enjoying this, or at least part of her was.

"Are you kidding me?" He rubbed his eyes. "I came in tonight because Josh will give me first dibs on next month's shifts. I'll let you pick my days off." He reached for her elbow, but she jerked away.

"Too little, too late," she said. "This has been over for a long time. Maybe even before it started."

"What's that supposed to mean?"

"Let's just say I'm tired of waiting around for you, okay? I'm frickin' sick of this bullshit." She pointed up toward the ceiling.

"You mean my job? The way I earn *money* so we can do stuff?"

"Oh, please. You give most of that to your mommy, and you know it."

How she could make that one word sound so ugly, he'd never guess.

"I have to work, Becks. And yeah, I help my family out. You used to think that was noble."

"Well, I don't. Not anymore."

"Fine, but not all of us are fortunate enough to have a father who pays for everything."

She lifted her chin and glared at him. "My parents prefer for me to focus on school."

"Yeah." He laughed, an ugly sound. "School. Cheerleading. Dance committee. Yearbook—which, of course, you only joined so your pic would show up as often as possible." If she was going to go there, he would hurl that shit right back at her.

She put her hands on her hips and leaned in. "Is that what you think of me, huh?" She stomped her foot right on the trap door and it rattle-creaked. "You think I'm some spoiled, shallow, rich girl? Say it, Scott." Another stomp, and the old plywood let out a protesting crack.

"Careful!"

She stumbled a few steps toward him. "What is that?"

"Sub-basement. It's a good fall if that thing gives. And it's all tunnels down there, probably filled with rats. Who knows what else."

"I don't get how you can stand this place. And don't change the subject. Say it." Her voice was low, dark.

What were they even talking about? It was too much, and he was finally cracking—maybe it hadn't been the trapdoor making that sound, but something deep inside him, breaking. He'd known this day would come. Becky was just hurrying the process along.

Still, she didn't deserve to be insulted. "No," he said, voice softening. "No, I don't think those things, Becks."

"Stop calling me that."

He couldn't see the tears in her eyes, but they were there in her voice. He was such an asshole.

"I'm sorry." And he meant it. "Please, just come here."

He reached for her again, and this time she let him tuck her head under his chin. Her perfume called up a kaleidoscope of memories: parties, like the one they were supposed to go to tonight—those rare moments when he got to be a regular senior. Her scent, mixed with the less pleasant but perhaps more familiar odor of the old school heating ducts as he and Becky whispered together before homeroom. Sweet skin and silky blonde hair falling over his face and tickling his chest. Her lips.

She'd said their relationship was over before it started. She was part right. If he asked himself, really pressed for the truth, could he say he loved her?

Yes.

But no, too.

He loved her a little, as much as he could, but the beta version of the free app had never developed into the full, paid program. Sure, he was a sucker for her smiles and her perfume on the air. But there was no burning, no pull in his gut, no yearning for her nearness. No lost sleep. He'd wanted to love her the right way, had every expectation of losing himself in her. God, how he wanted to get lost. She'd been a bright glimmer that promised something better than everything else he was stuck with. So yeah, he'd been selfish and kept it up—because losing her was way worse than pretending. Because, even if he and Becky weren't soulmates, their relationship was the one thing he got to have just for himself, and not because he owed it to anyone else.

The one thing his family hadn't ruined.

The way they'd ruined his chances with Winny.

For a moment, the ghost of Winny's white puffy coat haunted his fingertips, and he was back there with her on his front stoop the day of the football game, the January cold prickling his nose. Until the heat of shame elbowed the icy memory away as it always did whenever he thought of the way her brown eyes had met his, full of questions and hurt, but not wavering, not even one tiny bit, as she'd waited quietly for him to explain himself. The gentlest of demands.

Snap out of it. You lost her already. Don't lose Becky, too.

Maybe he and Becky were always destined to end, but hell if he was prepared to let her go tonight. He tightened the hug, and Becky's arms squeezed into the minute space between them so she could rest her palms on his chest.

Then she pushed away.

The strength seeped out of him, and he let his own arms fall to his sides, trying to catch Becky's gaze as she stepped back.

One step.

Two steps.

With the third, a wall slipped into the empty space between their bodies. Though invisible, it carried the heft of lead, separating him from her warmth, blocking the flow of air to his lungs. The reek of basement doubled, and the atmosphere curdled around him, no longer cool and musty, but raw, clammy. Rotten. He marveled that he could still breathe.

"Maybe we should skip the party," he suggested. "Talk this through."

"No."

"So it's all over, then?" His voice came out shaky, weak. "Just like that? Here?"

"I'm done, Scott. Done coming second to everything else in your life. School. Your parents. This place. They call, and you jump. Your mom. Your boss. You jump for everyone except me. You don't even ask questions. You just do what they ask. I'm tired of going out alone, explaining to my friends over and over why you're late or making excuses when you don't show up at all. I'm done with you changing plans at the last minute."

"You know how it is for me."

She nodded, just once. "I know, and I'm sorry, Scott. I really am." Her expression softened, and she caught her bottom lip between her teeth.

Maybe Scott didn't love her the way he should, but he knew her, and she'd just given herself away. If she was uncertain, this could be his last chance.

But in the next second, her face closed off again. She shut her eyes, avoiding his glance. "I can understand it, but I don't have to like it. And I don't have to deal with it anymore."

"Real nice," he said. "Real compassionate."

She shrugged. "Maybe. Whatever. If you want to be everyone's martyr, fine, but I'm done suffering with you."

He clenched his fists—his jaw, too—and forced his next words out. "All right, then. You're leaving for Portland in a couple months. If we're careful, we won't need to see each other again."

"Good." She paused at the bottom of the stairs. "I mean it. Stay away from me." Without another word, she stomped up the steps and out of sight.

He almost followed her, almost chased her into the night out to her car, where he could have tried to convince her to change her mind. He'd have blown off the rest of this shift and gone to Brian's party. Screw Sylvie and Oscar. If they wanted to fire him, fine.

But Oscar and Sylvie were two people in his life who gave as much as they took. Besides, he needed the money. His family needed the money, and this job was the one thing that hadn't blown up in his face.

Yet.

So Scott did what she asked. He stood in the basement, giving her time to stretch the space between them as far as she could before whatever cord still bound them snapped, leaving them alone again.

3

WINNY

I'm not even supposed to be here.

For the tenth time, I scan the room for Scott as the gunshot echoes off the black and white floor tiles.

So loud.

The man fired only once, but my ears ring until the ringing turns into a buzz.

Like a gymnast, Oscar vaults over the counter, scattering organic chocolate bars and flinging a wire basket of apples and bananas to the ground. "Winny, move." He tugs my arm and tries to shove me behind him, but my legs don't want to work, and I almost fall over.

At the register, a woman stands, clutching a paper bag, eyes darting from the men to Oscar and back again. The only other person in the place, an old guy with white hair and a white beard, sits frozen at his table with a book open before him, one finger still resting on a page, a half-drunk

16

mug of tea at his elbow. Chai, I'm pretty sure. Its perfume greeted me when I came in, but now the sulfur stink of gunfire blots out the delicate aroma. The man observes the scene before him like he's watching a movie.

But this is no movie.

Oscar needs to stop these men. Why doesn't he do something? Why doesn't somebody *do* something?

"Everyone stay right where you are." It's the skinny guy, and he's grinning. "Show us your hands," he says with a series of giggles.

I shuffle to stand beside Oscar, but I can't look at the men's faces. If I ignore them, maybe they won't notice me and will leave me alone. Oscar and Sylvie will calm them down, and they'll go. It'll be fine as long as I don't look at them.

I study Sylvie's shirt instead, the same green CAFÉ FLORES polo worn by everyone who works here, but hers is new and crisp. Not faded like Scott's. No lint fuzzies or pilling stuck to the fabric. Only fresh, smooth green cotton.

I let my vision blur and some of the tension melts from my muscles, but the green line of Sylvie's shoulders hitches. She's sobbing. Even from here, it's so obvious. I can't do this, can't watch her cry, even from behind.

The floor can't cry. I stare at the checkerboard at my feet. Much better.

Si ou kouvri dife, w ap gen dife, my mom says inside my head. Always my mom and her Haitian Creole, which she uses mostly so she can pick at my life choices. My mess-ups. *If you cover a fire, you still have a fire.*

I don't care. I stare at the floor anyway.

How can this be happening? And where's Scott? I want him here next to me. I shouldn't want that, though. If I'm his friend, if I care for him, I should want him to be safe, on his way home or to Brian's.

Please, God, let him have gone home.

Please, God, let him still be here, hiding somewhere.

He was here when I arrived; that I know for sure. He answered when Sylvie called down the basement stairs. So where is he now?

I crane my neck to peer behind the counter through the windows in the doors to the kitchen, but it's no good. The glare from the rainbow-swirl shades of the pendant lights obscures the glass.

"Ryan," Sylvie says in a liquid-choked voice. "Please. Don't do this."

"Too late, big sis. You had your chance. You blew it."

"Twitch, check the kitchen," the guy with the sunglasses says.

"Right, Toto." Still giggling, the skinny guy—Twitch—marches by us.

I hunch my shoulders, wrapping my arms tight around my waist. I don't want any of him touching me as he goes by, not even the breeze he makes. It carries a sweet chemical smell that tries to pull a gag from my throat. I turn my head, but the odor lingers in my nose. When the kitchen door swishes shut behind him, I relax my arms and try to take a deep breath, but the air keeps getting stuck halfway down.

Twitch's voice carries from the kitchen. "Look what we have here." More laughter, high and breathy.

My skin crawls. This guy is having fun. This is *fun* to him.

"Let go of me!"

Scott!

Relief rolls through me when I see him. And then a wave of guilt. Scott strains and jerks against Twitch's grasping hands, though it's a wonder the guy can hold him with those bone-thin arms.

Sylvie's still crying, but silently now. "What are you going to do? Please don't hurt anyone."

"You had your chance," Ryan says again in a distant, trailing voice, almost like he's talking to himself. "Two months ago, I came to you with a prime opportunity, but you said no, even though it would have set me up—set both of us up—for a good long time. Then, yesterday, I came to you for help, and you wouldn't give me a dime." Something in his eyes hardens. He turns his gaze on his sister. "You wouldn't give it, so now I have to take it."

"You scumbag." Oscar lunges for Ryan. Ryan can't aim in time, and he knows it; his face tightens as if he's about to jump into a freezing cold swimming pool.

But Toto has his gun ready.

I look from the barrel to his face, and see myself reflected in the mirrors of his sunglasses. When he fires, I scream and jump back, because I know that bullet is coming for me.

But it isn't me the bullet finds.

With the report of the shot still echoing in the small space, Oscar lets out a bark of pain and crumples to the ground. Sylvie is trying to scream, or maybe she's gagging.

"What the fuck, Toto?" Ryan says. "You shot him! Not that I mind seeing this asshole taken down off his high horse, but this puts a real dent in our quick in-and-out plan."

Toto only shrugs. "We have to make sure they know who's in charge." He glares at Oscar, who's too busy eyeing his leg, grimacing in pain, to argue.

Scrubbing his hands through his hair, Ryan paces a five-foot line. "Okay, new plan. We just need a new plan. What are we going to do?" But his attention is snagged by Twitch, who's back behind the counter. "Shit!" Ryan smacks Toto's arm and points. "Look what you've done! He's freaking out."

Eyes glazed over, pupils huge, Twitch raises his gun. "We won't let them get us. We'll show them."

Toto swears under his breath. "Twitch, man. Chill. Don't do anything stupid. Stick to the plan."

"The plan? What part of the plan is *that*?" Ryan asks, flapping his hand in Oscar's direction.

"Shut *up*, Ryan," Toto shouts.

Twitch is still muttering nonsense I can't quite catch. "... ether ... they know ... can't let them ..."

"Twitch, just chill, okay?" But Toto's words come too late, and he's too far away to stop what happens next. Without bothering to aim, Twitch fires off four shots so fast they blur together.

To my left, Scott pulls free and ducks behind the counter. Sylvie drops. Me too, I guess, because I'm on the ground eye-to-eye with the lady by the register, who's now sprawled on the floor next to us. She's still clutching her paper bag as if her hands haven't caught on to the current state of affairs. As if they don't know they can let go now, rest.

Because the woman they belong to is dying from the bullet that tore through her neck.

"Twitch, man! What did you do?" Toto shouts through the painful ringing in my ears. He straightens from his sudden crouch and lunges toward the counter.

"What? What?" Twitch protests. "It was the ether. We had to stop them. You fired, I thought you needed my help."

"You pick today to go all delusional on me? Damn meth heads. Gimme that, you tweaked-out motherfucker." Toto wrestles the gun from Twitch's hand and turns to survey the damage. "Aw, man."

I can't stop staring at the bag. Just a brown paper bag filled with bagels, or maybe a sandwich. It's so normal—until the paper begins turning red. Black dots are swimming in front of my eyes. The floor's not safe anymore, so I search for somewhere else to rest my gaze. But nowhere's safe. The ringing in my ears—I can focus on that. It's dropped in pitch a little, might almost be white noise, like what you use to relax at night before bed.

But everyone is moving and shouting. Everything is chaos, and I can't stop it from breaking through.

Twitch finally sees the dead woman. "Oh, shit," he whispers.

"Maggie!" Sobbing, Sylvie tries to go to her, but Toto is faster. He grabs Sylvie under one arm, hauls her up, and shoves her toward the counter until her back strikes one of the black vinyl-topped bar stools. She ignores the jolt and reaches for Oscar, who's still on the floor, clutching his thigh, red seeping between his fingers.

So much red. It's everywhere.

"Don't move," Toto growls, and Sylvie freezes. He looms over me and Oscar, jerking the muzzle of his gun toward where Sylvie stands. "Up. Over there. Both of you."

I try to stand, but only make it to my knees. Dark pixels sizzle in my vision and mix with the blood coming from Oscar's bullet wound.

A frickin' bullet wound.

Oscar struggles on the floor in front of me. When he lets go of his leg, the blood flows faster, causing the black spots clouding my vision to expand and the floor to tilt under my knees.

"Help him," Ryan barks at me.

"What?" My voice is too loud in my ears, like I'm wearing noise-canceling headphones.

Ryan rolls his eyes and sighs. "Help him up."

Putting his weight on me, Oscar is able to get his uninjured leg underneath him and hobble to the stools. He barely has enough time to lean against one of the spinning discs before Sylvie throws her arms around his neck.

This can't be happening. In real life, people don't have bullets in their legs or lie dead on the floor.

I'm supposed to be with Janey and the rest of my friends at Brian's end-of-the-year party. Or home where my mother told me to stay. These guys don't understand. The door calls to me. I should be out there, on the sidewalk in the humid night. Janey will probably be back any second. She'll realize how dumb she acted and come back for me. I've got to be waiting when she pulls up.

A force yanks my wrist, triggering a jolt that travels all the way to my shoulder. I pull against it, but it won't let go. Hating to slide my gaze away from the door, I twist and see fingers wrapped around my wrist—strong, tan fingers against my brown skin. I follow them with my eyes and find the rest of the hand, then the wrist bones, dark hair trailing up the arm.

"Winsome," Oscar hisses, "what are you doing? Come back here."

But I have to get to the door.

Except the door is blocked by three men with guns. What am I even thinking?

When my legs finally catch up to what my brain is saying, I shuffle to Oscar's side.

"You, behind the counter," Toto says, "stand up. Nice and slow."

Scott! I almost forgot he was here. On the other side of the counter he gets to his feet, hands raised alongside his head.

"Out here where I can see you," Toto orders. "Man, someone close the goddamn blinds. Do I have to do everything myself?"

Ryan rushes to one set of window treatments while Twitch gets the other. I want to cover my ears against the twangy, metallic clang when they crash shut.

"The ones on the door, too," Toto says. "And when you're done with that, we need to lock this place up tight."

"She keeps the keys by the register," Ryan tells Twitch.

Twitch does not look good, and he's not giggling now. Pale to begin with, the rest of the blood has drained from his scabby face. When he finishes with the windows, he grabs the keys and takes care of the front door.

The click of the lock sliding into place makes my eyes prickle with tears.

Pocketing the keys, Twitch stands at the end of the counter closest to the door and the register and stares at the dead woman on the floor. Just stands there, still as a wax figure—all except his hands, which never stop moving. With his thumbs, he taps each finger—pointer to pinky—then back again, over and over, while his stare remains fixed on the woman at his feet.

No matter what, I'm not looking at her. I don't care. I'm not looking at her.

"We've got to get her out of here," Twitch says.

"Oh." Toto throws his arms up, waving the gun in his hand. "Now I'm getting advice from a guy who just killed this lady."

"You're the one who gave him a gun," Ryan shouts. "I told you this would happen. I told you not to bring him."

Toto turns on Ryan. "You also said three people, max." He shoves Ryan in the chest, and he stumbles backward.

"Hey, don't blame me. It was ten after closing. How was I supposed to know they'd still have customers?"

"That was your job, man." Wordlessly, Ryan backs toward the counter as Toto advances. "To scout out the place, learn the routine."

Going so red, his freckles darken, Ryan spits his words right back into Toto's face. "I wanted to watch from the street, but you wouldn't wait. I was right about the cook and sandwich guy being gone, wasn't I?"

"Good for you. You got two out of eight. You want a

trophy now?" Toto stares Ryan down, breathing hard through his nostrils.

"You know where I'm supposed to be right now," Toto says.

Ryan rolls his eyes. "I'm sure Rochelle will wait."

They keep arguing, but it fades into a meaningless drone as I stare at the door. No matter how much I squint, I can't tell if the glow around the closed blinds is from street lights or a business across the way. Or a car—Janey's, maybe.

Moun ki bezwen deyò chache chemen pòt, my mom says in my head. *He who must go out must search for the door.* Yeah, that's super-helpful. The door is right there—*right there*—but totally out of reach.

And I'm not even supposed to be here.

4

WINNY

FIFTEEN MINUTES BEFORE CLOSING

The slam of Becky's car door rang in Winny's eardrum. They were *so* caught.

"Shit!" Janey hissed. "Down! Get down!" Janey tugged at her arm, and Winny fell back across the center console, one leg still dangling out the open door.

"Ouch, you freak!" But Winny's giggles were a perfect match to Janey's.

"Is she gone?"

"Um, lying down here. You look—" Stupid, crappy timing. The last thing Winny needed tonight was for Scott's brand-new ex to find her here, about to swoop in to catch him on the rebound.

"Okay, hold on." Janey squirmed and, using her driver's seat as a shield, peeked around it through the back window.

"You know," Winny said, half-lying and half-sitting in

the passenger seat, "if she did see you, it wouldn't be a big deal. It's me who needs to stay hidden."

"She's just sitting in her car. Oh, God! She's looking this way." Janey ducked behind the seat again. "And I don't want her seeing me, either. She might put two and two together."

Becky's engine roared to life, grew louder, then faded to nothing. They waited a full thirty seconds, just to be safe.

"Holy shit!" Janey said. "That was close. Okay, you ready?"

"Are you serious? How can you still think this is a good idea? Becky is our friend. And they just broke up. Like literally *just* broke up."

"Nothing's changed. Come on." Janey hopped out, circled the car, and attempted to drag Winny from her seat by her arm.

"Stop it!"

"Oh my God, you're so frickin' heavy!"

"Okay, that's just mean."

Nèg di san fè, Winny heard her mother say in her head. Always her mother's voice. Always criticizing. *People talk and don't act*, she reminded Winny now. Though she doubted her mom would ever use that saying when it came to boys. Or any other topic or decision she didn't personally endorse. And the one time Winny did act, it blew up in her face and got her grounded.

"Come on," Janey grunted. "Aren't you ever going to take a risk?"

"Uh, I've taken quite a few risks today, don't you think?"

"Be careful over there, rebel."

"Hey!"

"So, prove it. Prove the new Winny is out to play. You march your hot self in there—"

Winny snorted. "Let's not go overboard here."

"—and get the guy. What would you rather be doing tonight? Moaning about how you and Scott will never hook up, or finding out what kind of gum he likes best?" Janey grinned and wiggled her eyebrows.

"Eww! Definitely not that." But Winny stopped resisting all the same. "Do you really think he likes me?"

"Only one way to find out." Janey finally tugged Winny from the car. "Holy crap, I feel like I just birthed a horse."

"Janey!"

"What? I love horses. Now come on. We are *so* going in there."

Laughing, they half-ran to the café, Winny's heart skip-beating in time with their steps. Janey froze with one hand on the door. "Crap! I left my purse. Hold on."

"No. Let's just get this over with. I'll buy your stupid gum."

"I've got it. I'll just be a sec."

No way was Winny going in alone. She leaned against the building, arms crossed, as Janey scooted into the driver's seat.

And didn't come back out.

Janey's party playlist filled the night as brake lights illuminated the street and sidewalk. She had started the engine. "See you at Brian's!" Waving from the open driver's window, she nudged the car into traffic.

"Janey!" Winny raced after her a few yards, before watching the lights streak away. This had to be a joke. Any second now, Janey's car would come back around the corner. Or maybe she'd trick Winny by coming from behind. But the street remained dark no matter what direction she searched. "I am so going to kill her."

I am SO going to kill you, she keyed into her phone.

No response.

As if she were still here, Winny heard Janey speak in her mind: *It's not safe to text and drive.*

Just like it's not safe to abandon your friend by the side of the road at ten at night. . . . What was she going to do?

A car zoomed by, blaring its horn.

"Okay, getting out of the street is a good start."

Winny knew she wasn't really stranded. She had her phone. But calling her parents was out of the question. Even if her mom's work party wasn't in the city tonight, there was still the little matter of her being grounded. And that's exactly what Janey had been counting on. She expected Winny to go inside, talk to Scott—

And have him drive her to Brian's.

She turned and stared at the rectangle of light on the ground in front of Café Flores.

"Janey is a villainous mastermind," Winny mumbled as she tugged open the door.

Inside the small restaurant, Sylvie smiled at her. "Hey, Winny. Where's your friend?"

"Not here, that's for sure."

Sylvie winced. "Alrighty. Not going there. What can I get you?"

"Is Scott here?"

"He sure is. Give me a minute to finish wrapping these muffins, and I'll go find him."

When three men walked into the café a few minutes later, Winny was so focused on writing a scathing text to Janey and watching the doors for any sign of Scott that she almost didn't see the gun tucked into one of their waistbands.

She stared at it for at least fifteen seconds before her brain turned back on.

Should she tell Oscar or Sylvie? Guns weren't illegal in Connecticut or anything . . . and who was she to butt in on someone else's business?

People talk and don't act, Winny's mother's voice echoed in her head. But she shut that voice right up. She was done taking her mother's orders. Whether this guy had a gun or not was none of Winny's concern, and besides, it was probably fine. She had more important things to worry about, like how she was going to explain her predicament to Scott, the boy who took her out once, but wouldn't let her into his house, then dated someone else for the next six months.

Until tonight.

5

SCOTT

Fifteen Minutes After Closing

Sylvie's cell phone won't stop ringing. At first, I think it's the main café phone, which I expect to start up any second now. Why isn't it ringing? What good is an alarm system if no one responds? Seconds tick by, but the white handset remains quiet, while Sylvie's cell bleats from behind the counter where she keeps it plugged in under the register.

"Shut that thing up right now," Toto orders. "We've got to think. And kill the land line, if they've got one."

Ryan runs behind the counter and grabs the cell, cutting off the incoming call with barely a glance, and shoves it into his pocket. A second later, the crunch of smashing plastic makes me jump. Ryan goes on stomping the remnants of the cordless handset long after the main café phone is beyond saving.

So much for that.

My arm aches where that skinny guy, Twitch, grabbed me. For a little dude, he's crazy strong. Then I see Oscar wince, and a bruised arm feels like less than nothing. He put a clumsy tourniquet on his leg, but he's having a hard time keeping the leather belt in place, and the bloody spot only grows. As a Desert Storm veteran, Oscar was our best shot at fighting off these guys, and now he's out of commission. We're screwed. I should have escaped out the back door when everything started going down, but instead of running, I had to stay—like I'm any help in a situation like this—and here I am, a hostage, clustered together with my bosses and one of our regulars.

"Hey, Scott," the white-haired customer, Pavan, said to me earlier. "The weather in Gainesville, Florida, is perfect today." He's one of the few people who know I've been stalling on my college decision. He thinks tempting me with fun facts about the places I might go will sway me, and I'll finally make up my mind. If I ever told him the *why* behind my delay, he'd know it's way more complicated than cold feet.

But college never felt so far away as it does right now, and poor Pavan is stuck here with the rest of us.

And so is Winny.

What's she doing here?

Wait, was she my special visitor? The one that got Sylvie all giggly before?

My heart nearly stops.

Of all the people who could drop in tonight, it had to be Winny. Not that her coming here is weird. She stops by the café all the time, just like most people from school. More, maybe. But never alone. Did she come here to see me? Maybe to talk about before?

If that's the case, it would have been better if I'd never offered to help and just left her stranded at the art gallery earlier.

Her eyes are messed up, glazed over, and she's got some serious shakes going on. Oscar has one hand on Winny's arm even though he's the one bleeding, and I don't blame him. I've always thought Winny would be the perfect person to have around in a crisis. She's with me in the advanced classes, super smart, and she did that training course last fall—first aid or something like that—but she's so freaked right now, she might do the wrong thing without thinking and get hurt.

And if she gets hurt because she came here to see me . . . I can't even handle that thought.

Who the hell are these guys? I don't know which one I need to worry about most. Twitch mutters to himself like he's about to have a meltdown. That Toto guy is pacing, pausing only to check between the closed blinds, lost in thought, plotting his next step probably. And Ryan—when he worked here, it was always with too much attitude and too little actual effort, but still, he was one of us.

None of that matters now, though. The hunch of his shoulders and the way his face hardens when his gaze settles on us tells me he won't think twice about doing whatever he has to to protect his own interests.

"Ry, search them," Toto says, "in case they've got more phones on them."

"Right. Everyone, empty your pockets. Give me all your cell phones." Ryan stops in front of Sylvie first. He won't meet her gaze and his voice is weird, thick.

"I don't have any pockets." Silent tears roll down her cheeks, and she speaks through clenched teeth. "Which is why my phone was up there." As if on cue, it starts ringing again in Ryan's pocket.

"Fuck." He pulls it out and jabs the screen, and after a second the shrill sound dies.

"Are you going to frisk me now, brother?"

Ryan flinches. "What? No. Don't be dramatic."

"Dramatic? Are you crazy?"

He leans in close to her and whispers, but his voice is intense. "Listen, you want this to go smooth? Then do what we say. It's on you how this ends."

I wait for her to argue, for a patented Sylvie-Ryan showdown, but instead she nods. Just a tiny bow of the head, but it's something. Pavan puts his arm around her and whispers into her ear. The old guy is here every day for a cup of tea and to read, sometimes a paper, sometimes a book like the one lying on the table where he was sitting. I wonder what book it is. I wonder if that will be the last one he ever reads. If he dies, he'll never know how it ends.

Ryan is in front of me now.

"I don't have a phone," I say.

Oscar gives me a puzzled look. *Crap.* He knows I had my cell here earlier, charging on the very same cord Sylvie's was plugged into before Ryan grabbed it.

But these guys can't know that.

Ryan squints at me. "Prove it."

I turn out my pockets, then take off my busboy apron and lift my shirt to show him there's nothing underneath. "I left it in the car." If Oscar or Sylvie give me away I'm screwed. But with the other phones confiscated or busted—though mine might not be much better than the shattered mess on the floor—this may be our one shot.

"If I find out you're lying . . ."

I don't go so far as to smirk in his face, but man do I want to. I've seen that same glint in my father's eyes right before he hauls off on me. At least my dad only uses his fists; these guys are armed, and I suspect Ryan would have no problem shooting me.

I curl my toes inside my shoes. It helps me keep my face calm. When Ryan nods and moves on, I force my breath to stay nice and smooth, rhythmic—as if I'm on the uphill stretch of my morning jog—instead of unloading my lungs in one *whoosh* like I want to.

Oscar gives me a hopeful look, but I can't summon any hope of my own. I may have won a little victory, may have fooled our captors, but that's not important right now because Ryan is standing over Winny. As he squares off before her, she shudders.

"Let me," Oscar says, raising his eyebrow and waiting for Ryan's approval.

Ryan nods, and I give in and let my breath *whoosh* out after all.

"Winsome, sweetie," Oscar says. "Do you have anything in your purse?"

She doesn't answer, or maybe she can't hear him.

"Winsome?" Oscar reaches for her bag, but she jerks away with a sharp cry.

Sylvie's phone goes off again.

Toto stops pacing and clutches his skull with both hands. "If everyone doesn't shut up right now, I swear to God—" With that last word, he tugs off his sunglasses and flings them at the wall. More plastic debris litters the floor.

Spinning, Ryan extends a hand, palm out, in Toto's direction. "I've got this, okay?"

But he doesn't have anything.

When Ryan demands her purse again, Winny just stands there, too shell-shocked to get what's going on. Don't these guys see it? Her blank eyes, tight muscles—she's trembling with tension. She isn't hearing a word they say.

"Damn," I mutter and push myself between Oscar and

Winny, my body nearly touching hers so I can squeeze her hands in mine, hands that were warm only a few hours ago, but have since turned to ice. "Winny, it's just me. Just Scott." I massage her palms with my thumbs and her trembling lessens some. "Good. You've got this. I'm just going to check your purse, okay?"

No response.

This may be a huge mistake, but I let go of one hand and pluck the strap of her bag off her shoulder. "They just want to look inside for your phone." When the bag is free, I pass it behind me to the first set of hands but keep my focus on Winny. I lean in to whisper in her ear, "We're going to get out of this. I promise you. I'll make sure of it."

When I pull back, her eyes focus on my face for the first time. They're so full of trust, of confidence, that her whole body sags.

But for me, it's like stepping into the deep freezer out back. How can I know I can keep my promise? I suck in a breath and smile—the hardest smile I've ever had to pull off. A smile that feels like a lie.

The shrill cellphone ringtone makes her jump and erases whatever calm had settled over her.

"Give me that thing." Toto wrestles Sylvie's cell from Ryan's fingers and swipes it silent. His eyes go wide and he turns to face Ryan. "You didn't look at this? What the hell's wrong with you?"

"What? Oh, shit," Ryan says when he registers what's flashing across the screen.

Toto is vibrating with rage. "Which one of you set it off?"

Oscar and Sylvie look at each other, then us. "Set off what?" Suddenly, Sylvie understands. She squints at the phone, which has started up again.

Toto bellows and smashes the device to the ground, stomping on it with his high-top. He snatches the rest of the phones from Ryan and does the same to them. "Who the fuck pulled the alarm? Did you know about this?" he asks, turning to Ryan.

Eyes wide, Ryan shakes his head. "Must be new."

Bullshit. We've had that setup as long as I've been here. If he hadn't been such a suck-ass employee, maybe he would have remembered a little detail like an alarm system. But even when he showed up, he was barely here.

"Who set it off?" Toto demands again.

"I did." I try to swallow, but there's too much friction in my mouth, like I just chewed a handful of grape skins.

"Turn it off. Now." Toto's lips quiver, spit-foam flying into my face when he shouts. "Do it!"

Scrambling around Sylvie, I bolt for the counter and the alarm keypad hidden beneath it. I thought I was all slick hitting the panic button while I squatted on the ground during Twitch's gunslinger moment, but a lot of good it did. My finger hovers over the keypad as the code surfaces in my mind, drilled into me by Oscar. There's a sham code, too, one that keeps the alert active and silent. What is it? Zero, six, zero, nine, two, zero, zero, nine—their wedding anniversary? Or one, one, zero, five, one, nine, seven, six—Sylvie's birthday? If I get it wrong, the main alarm will sound here in the café and tip Toto off.

"Do it," Toto growls.

I'm out of time.

I hit the disengage code, the signal that we don't need help even though we're in some deep shit.

"What's going to happen?" Ryan asks Oscar.

"The cops are coming." His voice is a choked grunt as he struggles with the pain in his leg, but there's a note of satisfaction there, too.

It makes me smile.

"Toto!" Twitch is by the blinds, and the light out there is brighter and shifting. "Someone's here." He lets the window treatment drop into place, but it doesn't obscure the red and blue swirling lights. His next words are mumbles, but I catch something about the "ether."

"We gotta move the woman." Ryan bends and grabs her feet, but Toto smacks him on the head.

"Quit that, fool. There isn't time. You," he says to Sylvie, "get rid of them. Do not let them in here, you understand? Ryan, help her. If anyone can smooth-talk them, it's you. You're slimy as hell. Get out there. Now." He turns to us. "The rest of you, we'll be back there." He angles his head to the EMPLOYEES ONLY door that leads to the back hall, office, and stairwell to the basement. Before passing through, he glares at Sylvie. "Just remember, if I hear anyone in this place but you two, I'm shooting every last one of them. Starting with this one here." He shoves Oscar, who nearly falls over. "I may not get to them all before the cops stop me, but it'll be close."

As we shuffle toward the door, Winny takes my hand and squeezes. "You did it," she whispers. "They're going to help us. I know it."

"I told you, didn't I?"

The hope lighting up her face does nothing to warm me, not one little bit. Until I see those guys shoved into a cop car, I won't let down my guard. I may have sworn my life away, but I'm not breaking my word to Winny. She wouldn't be here if it weren't for me, so I'll make sure she gets out of here alive, no matter what it takes.

6

SCOTT

TWENTY-FIVE MINUTES BEFORE CLOSING

Stainless steel gleamed under the white rag, which Scott swept across the prep area in long, hypnotic circles. Maybe he should clean more often. He hit the end of the counter with another blast of cleaner, letting the faint lemony undertones soothe him further. Or maybe that was the fumes, making him high. Either way, it worked. In less than an hour, he'd be done and at Brian's party, where he and Becky could chill.

Oscar burst through the door, holding Scott's cell out like an offering. "Hey, man. This just went off. But you may want to plug it back in to Sylvie's charger when you're done. It's still running low on battery power."

The notification read *Mom*. He was about to dial her back, but then his voice mail indicator lit up.

"Scotty," his mom said. "I just wanted to double-check your plans for later, make sure you're still going to that party. You probably shouldn't come home for a while. Dad's . . . well . . ." A deep breath. "You probably shouldn't come home."

The words sounded as dull and flat as an old penny lying in the road, run over by a thousand tires.

"I'm at Aunt Linda's with Evie for the night," she went on. "After you left, I got thinking about that video, and I . . . I couldn't stop shaking. I had to get out of there for some space, some time to think. Dad won't be happy when he wakes up and finds we're gone. Think you can find some-place to crash? That would be . . . easiest."

He'd bet his entire night's pay she'd been about to say "safest."

"If not, come to your aunt's. We'll leave the spare key under the ceramic frog. And Scotty, listen. I'm sorry about before. Really. I don't blame you for anything and you have every right to be upset with him. And me, too. You do a lot for this family. I see it, and some day, your dad will see it, too."

That wiped out some of the tension creeping up his neck, but her next words undid it all.

"You know, this . . . this side of him isn't the real him. He'll snap out of it, you'll see. Once he finds a job. We'll talk more tomorrow. Come up with a plan. I love you, sweetie. See you tomorrow."

Before the message cut off, Scott heard his sister cry-ing in the background, and then his mom's voice. "Oh, baby girl—"

He stared at the grayed towel in his hand. When would this nightmare end? At least this time she'd given him some warning and saved him from a surprise like the one he'd gotten on prom night.

Of course, Scott hadn't gone to prom. No money for a tux rental or a limo or a corsage. Or the damned ticket. No prom didn't mean no after-party though, and Scott had an in at nearly every event. Becky had wanted to go to Brian's, so, at twelve thirty, that's where he'd shown up to wait. The first people had already arrived by the time he got there. After the epic fight he'd had with Becky in the weeks before prom, followed by an even more epic stalemate, he hadn't been sure what kind of mood she'd be in, but by the time she found him in the living room, any lingering crackles of tension between them had died out.

The rest of the night had been just like old times, but his good mood had crumbled as soon as he walked through his front door at four. He'd snicked the door shut as quietly as he could, which hadn't been quiet enough. His dad stumbled from around the corner just as Scott spun to head to the stairs.

"Where-fuh you been?"

Scott had opened his mouth to answer, but his dad's fist cut off his words, and he'd sported a bruised temple for the rest of the school year.

"Hey, Scott," Oscar called from the storeroom behind

the kitchen. "When you're done with that, mind helping me restock the beverage cooler?"

"Yeah. Be right there."

Why'd he have to keep thinking about this stuff? He glanced down at his reflection in the spotless stainless steel where he could just make out the remnants of his dad's prom-night gift, a faint ghost of a smudge near his hairline that might be mistaken for dirt.

In the right light.

Becky used to ask him why they never hung out at his house. He was the king of excuses on that front. Never telling her he'd rather slit his wrists than expose someone he cared about to that scene. Or maybe he didn't want to expose himself, to let her see that her boyfriend was the son of a drunk asshole in four-day-old Levi's and a faded Sox tee, who barely left his chair, let alone the house.

Scott had almost made that mistake with Winny that winter afternoon after the football game. Winny had offered to drive him home, even though he could handle the two-mile walk just fine. When she pulled up to his house, he'd lost his mind for a second.

He'd invited her in.

Maybe the scent he'd come to associate with her—sweet vanilla mixed with cherry, or something fruity like that—had messed up his brain. Maybe it was the flash of her dimple when she smiled or the way she kind of snorted when she laughed really hard. Maybe it was that he was afraid of losing the chance he'd finally gotten to be with her, even if just for a little while.

"I can make you some cocoa," he'd said. "A warm-up, you know, after the cold?"

Her thick, dark lashes had fluttered as she smiled down at her mittened hands. "Yeah. Sure."

As their boots scratched against the sidewalk, he'd felt her behind him, making his neck prickle, making his head hot—not in the ugly lava way, but in a steamy-shower-on-a-cold-day way. It melted the January frost that had frozen his heart.

If it hadn't been for the two panels of glass alongside his front door, he might have actually gone through with it. One glimpse of his dad heading from the kitchen to the living room was all it took to turn off the pleasant warmth.

Scott spun, and she'd been right there. Nearly touching him. So close, she'd jerked back at his sudden movement. Her puffy white jacket had squished in his fingers as he grabbed her arm to keep her from losing her balance and falling down his front stairs.

They'd stood like that, his hand around her elbow, the afternoon sun no match for the cover of clouds, nothing but a hint of a glow above their heads. Winny, so warm. Her gaze on him so firm. So grounded. So here. It had almost been enough to coax him into going through with it anyway . . .

Until he heard his dad call out, "Scotty? That you?" with that familiar booze-flavored drawl.

"You know what, I just realized, we're out of cocoa."

She'd shrugged. "I can drink coffee. Or tea. Or water." She peeked around him, trying to catch a glimpse of the speaker, but Scott had leaned to keep himself squarely between her and the window.

Shuffling footsteps on the other side of the glass drew closer.

Scott shook his head. "We're out of coffee, too."

Something clatter-banged from inside, and his dad had muttered a phrase Winny probably couldn't make out—thank God. Scott recognized it, though, his dad's trade-mark, "son-of-a-bitch-bastard."

"Listen, Winny. I can't. I mean, I just remembered, I promised my dad I'd help . . . I've got stuff to do."

It had taken her a second to process his blindside, then realization settled in her eyes. Crazy how a handful of words could stomp a delicate smile into a cheap counter-feit of itself.

"Is something wrong?"

Footsteps from the other side of the door. "Scotty?"

She leaned around him and she saw. Of course she saw. Cringing, he tried to remember what his dad had been wearing when he'd left the house for the game. Jeans? Those cut-off sweatpants Scott used to wear for runs?

No. It had been just a pair of old boxers.

Scott closed his eyes for a second and commanded his throat muscles to relax. He would not make this worse by hurling all over Winny. When he spoke, his voice was a rasp. "Rain check, okay?"

"Sure." Emotion wrinkled her brow and tugged at the corners of her mouth, and he struggled to decipher their message.

Was that worry? Hurt? Pity? Relief at her close escape?

"See you around, I guess."

He was still holding her arm, but he let it go, feeling stupider than ever. "Yeah, see you around."

Scott had seen her around, had even braved the shame rooted inside to ask her out. Once. Twice. Third time's the charm. Except it hadn't been for Scott. Instead of her cherry-vanilla aura and sunshine smiles, she greeted him with that wrinkled brow and a mouth that turned down at the corners before feeding him excuses about why she couldn't see him. Too busy with school, after-school commitments, like that paramedic training. Too busy for him. She never said it in a mean way—that wasn't how Winny operated—but her message was loud and clear and it hurt all the same.

They'd be friends, that was all.

He'd found a way to settle for that, and he'd done the only thing he could. He'd moved on. Becky might not have been Winny, but she was good and real and what he needed.

Okay, but how did all *that* jibe with what happened in Winny's driveway just a few hours ago?

"Scott? Hey, man, Becky's here to see you."

"Okay. I'll be right there." If he could calm her down fast, he could finish up and they could almost be on time. If not, they'd be late, which she'd probably blame him for even though she was the one interrupting his schedule. He let his eyes rest on the polished stainless steel for a second before shaking himself out of his thoughts. After one last deep breath of lemon-cleaner air, he headed out to face the wrath of Becky.

7

WINNY

Eighteen Minutes After Closing

The cops! Before we take two steps, my muscles go woozy and weak with relief, and my head clears enough for me to squeeze Scott's hand. The cops are here, and they'll fix this, no matter how smooth that guy Ryan thinks he is. When the installers came to set up our home alarm system, they said law enforcement has strict rules about responding to situations like this. They'll go through the proper protocols and realize this is a crisis, and we'll be saved as long as we stay alive a little while longer.

We shuffle toward the EMPLOYEES ONLY door in the little vestibule just past the ladies' room. On the other side, Twitch and Toto hover by the door, while the rest of us cluster to their left. Scott and I are on either side of Oscar to help him stay on his feet.

"You okay, Pavan?" Oscar asks the old man, who takes a spot behind us.

"Don't worry about me," Pavan replies.

"Thanks," Oscar mouths when I let him use my shoulder to balance.

"No problem," I mouth back.

The dim corridor is tight, and I don't like the feel of the gloom at my back. But the real-life monsters are right beside me, spotlighted by the ancient halogen over our heads that sizzles and flickers, making this feel even more like the horror movie this night has become. Not fifteen minutes ago, I thought nothing could be worse than the trouble I'm in with my parents, but my definition of "nothing worse" has had an extreme makeover since then.

Toto leans close to the swinging door, probably to watch for signs of trouble so he can keep his promise to us—his promise about what he'll do if the police enter the café.

"We should try to run," Scott mouths, throwing a thumb over his shoulder.

Three doors open off the corridor in the back. The one to the right looks like it leads into the kitchen. I can't tell where the one to the left goes. And the one all the way at the far end . . . A red-lettered sign glows EXIT.

Tight-lipped and sweaty with pain, Oscar shakes his head. "Just do what they say and shut up."

Maybe Oscar is dealing with more than pain. He could be going into shock. In EMT training, they taught us that shock can be triggered by blood loss, and it's just as fatal as the bullet wound itself. That woman out there is bad enough, but at least she's a stranger. I *know* Oscar and Sylvie. I see them all the time. What would it be like if it were one of them on the floor? Oscar, who always makes sure to put extra whip on my macchiato? Or Sylvie, who never forgets to hide the last lemon scone for me on Wednesdays, because she knows I'll be in after choir practice?

How could someone I know maybe die?

For now, though, Oscar is hanging on.

Twitch's mumbles grow in volume, little by little, until I can make out his words. "The ether. They're coming from the ether. But how?" He's still doing this finger-tapping thing, and he increases the speed as though his anxiety is turbo-charging his motor neurons. "They know, out there, looking for me. The etherkind."

"What?" Scott mouths.

I shake my head.

"That man is not well," Pavan whispers behind us.

"Shut the fuck up with that ether bullshit, man," Toto says to him, but Twitch only giggles once—or was that a whimper?—and goes on mumbling, finger-tapping the whole time. Turning, Toto gets in Twitch's face. "I mean it."

"What's he talking about?" Scott asks. "What ether?"

I can't believe he's talking to a murderer.

"Don't ask me," Toto says. "Some of that is the programmer in there talking, and the other half . . ." He shrugs. "That's the meth, pure and simple."

"Programmer? Like computers?" Scott says.

"Not anymore. Stay away from drugs, kids. That shit will kill you."

"If you don't do it first," Scott mutters.

"That's right, my man. Now shut up, all of you."

Twitch's gaze remains riveted on the door, and his mumbling surges into full-on chanting, his voice growing higher in pitch with every word. "Mean it, seen it, been it."

"They're gonna hear you," Toto says, but it does no good. "Don't make me shut you up myself."

"Hear you, bear you, fear you. Fear them. The etherkind."

"I *will* take you down." Toto lunges, and Twitch screams and stumbles away until his back strikes the wall.

Too much is happening, and I can't process it properly. Oscar's weight seems to double against me as Scott releases his hold. Twitch screams again, loud. Loud enough for the cops to hear?

Please, please.

And Scott, he takes a step backward. What's he doing?

But I know the answer. Scott is going to bolt. And that's good, but if Scott runs, what will Toto do to us?

I could tell Scott not to leave, but I can't take my eyes off Toto and his gun.

It's aimed at Twitch's head, but Twitch doesn't see it. Not the gun, and not Toto. Nothing but the door. Or maybe he sees something we don't. His fingers tap faster and faster and faster, and his monologue is nothing but a steady whimpering ramble now.

"I said—" Toto takes a step closer to Twitch—"shut." He presses the gun barrel to Twitch's temple. "Up."

I can't look, but I can't not look. My muscles seize until they hurt, and I can't move. Twitch is a killer, but I don't want to see his head blown off right here, four feet in front of me.

Finally, the skinny guy's rabbit eyes roll upward and take in the gray muzzle of the handgun. "Oh shit! Don't shoot! Don't do it, Toto. Don't do it, man!"

Finally, I pull my eyes away, focusing on Scott, and he takes another step toward the back exit.

"Scott, don't be stupid." Oscar's hissed words are drowned out by Twitch's shouting.

Scott's focus never wavers from the door. "This may be our only chance."

"Just great." Ryan's shout echoes from the café.

Footsteps. Coming our way.

The cops?

They didn't fall for Ryan's lies. Any second now, they'll open that door, and we'll be okay.

This whole thing is going to be over. All over.

But what if it's not the police?

It could be Sylvie and Ryan, or even worse, just Ryan. I close my eyes and shake my head. I can't see, don't want to know. The end to this terrible night might be waiting for us behind this door. Or it could be more of the same hell. If that's not the police, I don't think I can handle it.

The door bursts open with a whoosh of air that tickles my face.

"They're gone," Ryan says.

No.

No!

It can't be. I clench my eyes even tighter. I won't look. If I don't look, it won't be real. I'm crying, but that doesn't matter as long as I don't look.

If you cover a fire, you still have a fire.

My eyes betray me, flying open as Oscar totters and nearly goes down, threatening to take me with him.

Toto grasps Scott's arm, and they eye each other— Toto's expression full of swagger and Scott's full of hate. A slow grin spreads across Toto's face. "You tried, I'll give you that. Too bad your ass failed. Now get back in there." He points at the café door.

Sylvie's already helping Oscar to a stool at the counter, and Scott flies against her when Toto shoves him.

From out in the back hall, Ryan calls from the doorway. "I'm going to cut the phone lines so we won't have another alarm incident."

White-faced, Sylvie gestures at the wound in Oscar's leg, and he nods. Despite the gentleness of her probing, he still throws his head back, hissing, and draws Toto's attention.

"He needs a doctor," Sylvie pleads. "He's lost so much blood."

"No one's going anywhere." Toto comes toward us and

throws a quick glance at Oscar's leg, then goes around the counter. "Here. You can use these." He tosses a clean stack of bar towels at Sylvie.

She flinches, but reflexively throws up her hands and catches the towels. "This is going to hurt," she says to her husband.

Oscar nods, but stays quiet when she presses the stained white towel against his leg. It's going to leave lint in the wound, could maybe even cause an infection if it wasn't properly cleaned, but I don't say anything. Why bother when we could be dead any minute anyway?

"No one's calling out," Ryan says as he emerges from the employee hall. "We need to regroup."

I let the rest of his words fade. We were so close. The people who were supposed to save us were right out there, and now they're gone.

Chwal ki gen dis mèt mouri nan poto. A horse with ten masters will die tied to its post.

I can't even argue with the mom-voice this time, because she's right. Waiting for someone else to fix this could kill us. Only problem is, every time I try to think of what to do, my heart rate speeds up, and my skin gets too hot, and my head spins too much. The gloom of the back hallway wasn't fun, but being in here with the bright lights—and what they reveal—makes everything worse.

The woman on the floor.

The blood.

Just breathe, Winny.

Someone will do something. Someone will come. They have to.

A horse with ten masters . . .

This can't be happening.

But the red staining the rags on the floor at Sylvie's feet is real enough, and so is the red on the fresh towel she's using to sop up the blood still oozing from Oscar's bullet wound.

I shake my head, and the trembling threatens to overtake me again. I have to grit my teeth and clench all my muscles to stop it.

"Winny."

I jump, then realize Scott is right next to me, his lips almost touching my ear.

"Don't say anything. Just listen."

I nod, a motion that might be mistaken for a fresh burst of trembling. And maybe it is, a little.

"My phone's downstairs. In the basement storeroom. We need to get it."

Toto and Ryan are arguing.

"We should be on our way to see the Chef's man, Aaron, right now," Toto says. "Rochelle is waiting for me at her place."

Ryan's response is lost, drowned out by Twitch's rambling, which has grown frenzied again. He's having a conversation with some invisible guy standing behind him. He keeps mumbling, regularly throwing clipped comments over his shoulder. I don't want to be here. The promise of a cozy daze calls to me from la-la land, and it takes every ounce of effort I have left to keep my attention focused on the words feathering my ear. The words riding Scott's warm breath.

"You can get it," he says.

"What? No!"

"Shh! All you have to do is use the ladies' room. When you go in there, you can slip out to the hallway and run downstairs, grab the phone, then slip back in. It will take, like, forty-five seconds."

"But . . . I can't."

A horse with ten masters . . .

"You can," he whispers.

"Why not you?"

"Because the door to the men's room is in plain sight from here. They're too busy arguing to notice something hidden in the vestibule, but not something right here in the same room. Pretend you've got to pee. Or, better, that you're going to throw up."

"Scott." I pivot and tilt my head to look up into his face. He's already got a tan from jogging all spring, and scruff that wasn't there this afternoon shadows his jaw. His hazel eyes are intent, lips hovering so close to mine.

Close enough to kiss.

The way his gaze flicks up and down makes me wonder if he's thinking the same thing.

What the hell is wrong with you, Winsome? It's like I can't even be around him anymore without my thoughts getting all wonky.

I close my eyes for a second then fix them firmly on his. "I'm scared."

"Me, too."

Oscar is listening now, and I can tell he likes this plan. "It's worth a try," he murmurs. "We'll keep them distracted. Don't worry."

Sure. No problem.

The old man quietly observes our exchange, brain churning behind his sharp expression. Sylvie is too focused on the towels and the blood to pay attention.

So much red.

The room spins, but Scott's voice in my ear grounds me.

"The phone's right next to the plastic cutlery. Once you're back upstairs in the bathroom, use it to dial 911. It won't work down there. Too much rock."

"What if they say no?" What if they don't?

The vestibule is too much like a dark mouth, waiting to swallow me up.

Stop that. It's just a hallway, a short, three-foot hallway that leads to the door you just went through and came back out of again not five minutes ago.

And what if I can really do it? I can end this, maybe.

I risk a quick glance at the men. Toto shouts at Ryan, who just stands there, taking it all in, almost bored, like he knows he has to let Toto get this tantrum out of his system. Twitch is still talking to himself.

Scott and Oscar are right. If there's ever a time to try something, it's now. I take several deep breaths.

"Don't ask them for permission," Oscar says. "Just go."

Sylvie finally catches up with the conversation. "No." She shakes her head. "Let's just wait. Ryan will figure out something."

"Are you out of your mind, Silv? He's the cause of this. He's not going to help us. We've got to help ourselves."

A horse with ten masters . . .

Sylvie and Oscar are still arguing, so are Ryan and Toto, but I'm done listening.

After one last deep breath I'm on the move before I can think twice. "Oh my God, I'm gonna puke!" I clap my hand over my mouth and bolt for the vestibule and the ladies' room door.

8

WINNY

TWENTY-FIVE MINUTES BEFORE CLOSING

Janey's car stereo blasted, and she sang at the top of her lungs, dancing behind the wheel. Winny was familiar with that glint in her best friend's eyes; nothing would bring Janey down tonight. And why should it? Weren't they free? Free from high school, poised to move on and become whatever they wanted. Free to go to Brian's tonight and let the bass bounce and jiggle their insides while illegal beer fizzled their brains.

Correction: Janey was free. Janey with her plans for next year all set—an acceptance to her first-choice college filed with the university admissions board right on schedule—and out tonight without any of the covert maneuvers Winny had to perform. Janey's parents let her choose for herself—let her live. She thought about the family portrait that hung in her dining room.

"He *looks* like a doctor," Janey had said of Winny's father the first time she saw it.

And Winny's mother looked like a lawyer. If her parents had their way, Winny would be an exact replica of them. They were prepared to encourage and insist and coerce until she fulfilled all their visions for her future.

If not for her mom's note this afternoon, they might have been successful.

Winny tried to lose herself in the shifting swirls of street lights illuminating the sticky night, but with no success. Her psych teacher's voice echoed in her memory: *White Bear Phenomenon, whereby the act of telling yourself not to think about something requires that you bring it to mind in order to give yourself the command.*

Winny was white-bearing all over the place tonight.

"Hey!" Janey shouted over the music.

"What?"

"Detour!" She made a right followed by a left a street later.

Letting her head sag backward slightly, Winny let out a pained sigh. "Please tell me you're not doing what I think you're doing."

Janey cut the music. Far from looking repentant, her expression was barely even sheepish.

"Janey . . ."

"Yes, Winsome, my love?"

"Where are we going?"

Janey shrugged. "I need some gum."

"I have no intention of standing between you and your gum, especially if it's that grape-lemon kind, but please tell me we're not going there."

"What? It's practically on the way."

"Oh, please. Like we didn't just pass two gas stations and a mini-mart. This is about Scott, and you know it." Winny stared at her knees, which peeked out from beneath the hem of her white ruffled peasant dress.

"Maybe I don't want to get my gum from any old gas station or mini-mart. I happen to like Café Flores. They buy from Connecticut farms, and you're the one always going on about supporting local agriculture."

"Because gum is a local agricultural commodity. We don't even know if the rumors are true."

"Oh, they're totally true. I heard it from Simone who heard it from Jackson who heard it from Rachel who heard it from Becky herself."

"You'd think she would have said something to one of us, then."

Janey shrugged. "You know how it goes. Girl meets guy. Girl gets guy. Girl stops confiding in her friends."

"Still. Until we know for sure, we should just act normal and stay cool."

"Like how you acted this afternoon?"

Winny's face burned. "No. Definitely not cool like that."

Janey turned on to Milne Avenue and pulled into the

first empty spot on the street in front of Café Flores. "Too late. We're here." The brakes screeched under Janey's hot pink sandal and she let loose a hearty laugh, head thrown back. That laugh always meant trouble.

"Why do you sound like some villainous mastermind from a silent movie?"

"First off, 'villainous mastermind' and 'best friend' aren't necessarily different things. Second, how could anything sound like anything in a silent movie?"

"You know what I mean."

"I need to save you from yourself. I'm only saying this because I'm your friend. You can't even try to pretend you're not still totally into him, not after what you told me on the phone. What the hell are you waiting for?"

"Let's see," Winny said, counting on her fingers. "Confirmation that the guy's actually single. For the dust to settle. Who wants Mr. Rebound City?"

"You're all set to move into Rebound City, and you know it."

"And how about some indication that he actually likes me? Like, one little bit."

"Oh, come on. You know he likes you."

"Could have fooled me. I mean, how do you go from asking one girl out to asking out someone completely different the very next day?"

"Yawn. I'm so tired of hearing you whine about that. And technically, she asked him out."

"But he was the one who said yes."

"Get over it already. Cut the guy some slack. You *did* turn him down three times. I mean, come on, what would you have thought if you were him?"

Winny groaned. "But I was legitimately busy."

"You're always busy."

"I know. I know. I'm such an idiot."

"Forget it. You guys have gotten along great since then—better than great. You can't fool me. I've seen those longing glances you've been throwing back and forth, like, all the time. Today seals the deal as far as I'm concerned."

"What happened today may have been a huge mess-up, though. *My* mess-up. *Ugh.*" A little shiver ran through Winny as she recalled Scott's lips against hers. But what had happened after, the expression on his face. Had it been longing or regret? "It's like he's Mixed Signal Man. Dating Becky, but putting out these vibes . . ."

"Everyone deserves a second chance, Win. And he probably needs a friend right now. A friend who can pick him up, brush him off—"

"And kiss the shit out of him?"

"That's my girl."

"But—"

Janey held out a palm. "*Shush!* We'll just go inside, grab some gum, chat him up a bit, and see what's what. And, most importantly, we'll let him know you'll be at Brian's." She raised an eyebrow.

"Everyone's going to be at Brian's. That's not exactly news."

"Ten minutes, tops, okay? Then we'll hit the road."

Winny cracked open her car door and sighed. "Fine." She'd placed one foot on the sidewalk when, three storefronts down, the door to Café Flores burst open. "Shit!" Winny froze as a familiar blonde stomped onto the sidewalk, beelining for a Honda right in front of the café.

"Becky's still here," Winny whispered, ducking back inside Janey's car.

9

SCOTT

O h my God, she's doing it.

"Hey!" Toto shouts as Winny streaks by me.

My heart might explode, like literally explode. I was supposed to keep her safe, and here I am sending her into more danger. What the fuck is wrong with me?

But she makes it. The bathroom door swings shut with a small sigh of hinges that need a hit of WD-40.

"Young man," Pavan calls to Toto in his almost musical accent. "Why don't you let the girl be for a minute? She's feeling very ill, and it will only make everyone feel worse if we have vomit on the floor to mix with the blood, don't you think?"

Pursing his lips, Toto gazes toward the short hallway and takes a step in that direction, but Ryan puts a hand on his shoulder. "Come on. Let her be for a minute. There're no windows in there. She can't go anywhere. We need to stay focused."

My chest burns from holding my breath, but I can't seem to exhale until Toto turns away. "Yeah. Right." He and Ryan cluster together again.

They're trying to talk quietly, but they're too worked up to keep their voices down. My brain ping-pongs between their words and thinking about Winny. I want to watch the vestibule like a hawk, but it might give her away, so I try to focus on Toto and Ryan instead.

"You two are amateurs, man," Toto is complaining. "I can't believe this shit." He makes huge movements, waving around the gun he's still holding. I flinch each time the barrel points in my direction.

Maybe focusing on the vestibule is a better idea after all.

A tiny squeak tells me that Winny has opened the bathroom door. Damn it! I was supposed to grease those hinges two days ago, but I kept forgetting. Ryan and Toto don't seem to notice the sound, though. When I can't stand it anymore, I risk a glance.

Nothing.

No sign of her.

A warm hand settles on my shoulder. "She's through," Pavan says in my ear.

"Thank God." I'm too loud, maybe, but Twitch is getting amped up again, and his ranting is good cover. Breathing slowly and steadily, I count out the seconds—*one, two, three*. Forty-five. That's how long I told her it would take.

"I'm sorry, Toto," Twitch mumbles. "I'm sorry I'm sorry I'm sorry."

Seven. Eight. Nine.

"Will you shut up?" Toto raises the back of his hand, and Twitch immediately goes quiet.

"We need to help you find a response to anger that doesn't involve physical threats," Ryan says.

"Do you think you're being funny right now?"

"No. Sorry." He sighs and rubs his temples. "Okay. Our original plan—quick in and out—is no good now. We need to figure out what to do about her." He gestures at the dead woman.

Thirteen. Fourteen.

Toto looks over at the body splayed out on the floor, and I do, too, getting my first really good glimpse of her from this side of the counter.

Oh, God, I know her.

I'm jogged out of my counting for a moment, but I get it together again a breath later.

Sixteen.

Though my brain keeps generating numbers, it's harder to stay on top of them. Her name is Maggie Hightower or Highsmith, something like that. She comes in two or three nights a week near closing for the old baked goods. Sylvie always throws in extras for her, since Maggie is on a limited income.

Was on a limited income.

Without fail, Maggie would always make a big deal, protesting she couldn't accept the charity, but Sylvie convinced her to take the extra muffins and bagels every time. *They'll just end up in the trash, otherwise.* A lie, of course. Sylvie and Oscar always take the unsellable leftovers home. If we all get through this, will Sylvie and Oscar want them anymore? Will they be able to stand looking at pastries sitting there on their kitchen table or counter or wherever, knowing they got their friend killed?

"I'm sorry I'm sorry I'm sorry," Twitch starts up again.

"There's no way they're not reporting this, Ry," Toto whispers. "Maybe your sister would cover for you over some paper from the register, but this is different. And if she takes him to the hospital, you know they're gonna ask questions."

Ryan's glare bores into Sylvie. "Yeah." He rubs his face. "You're right."

"Fuck yeah, I'm right. We were supposed to come in here, flash some chrome, get the money, and book it. Now we've got a situation. What are we gonna do about it?"

Twenty.

"Don't even." Ryan takes two steps toward Toto, but pivots at the last second, like he's thinking better of it. When he's a safe distance from the other guy, he turns again. "Don't even try to blame this on me. You know how I felt about—" He shoots a glance at Twitch, still smack dab in the middle of his meltdown. "I told you something like this would happen."

Pavan, who'd been standing this entire time, back set in a rigid line, drops to a stool. "We're in trouble," he says to no one in particular.

Twenty-five.

"We need a plan," Toto says.

"We need a plan," Oscar says.

"We've got a plan." Pavan cuts his eyes toward the vestibule. "Now is the time for patience." He sighs. "How I wish I had a fresh cup of tea."

Ryan sure looks like he could use a soothing drink or maybe a shot of whiskey. He paces and throws out words around the thumbnail he hasn't stopped chewing since he came out of the back. "I know we need a plan. I just need to think a minute. Will you shut up?" he bellows at Twitch who's changed from his chant of *I'm sorry* to something I can't quite make out.

Twitch jumps, then falls silent, but he's still staring at Maggie.

"Just let me think," Ryan says.

"So, their original plan," I whisper to Sylvie. "They were going to rob you?"

She doesn't acknowledge me. Oscar shakes his head. "You know what this is," he says.

"Please, Oscar," Sylvie says. "Not now."

"It's always *not now*. When are you going to face reality about your brother?"

"Maybe if you hadn't fired him—"

"He was selling drugs out of the shop."

Pavan's eyes widen, and I bite back the *holy fuck* that wants to escape my lips.

"Not. Now," Sylvie says.

My head spins as I try to take it all in. I always thought Ryan was slimy, but this is next-level shit. As if he can feel my gaze on him, Ryan looks at me, and for one moment his eyes meet mine. They widen as he takes in what Toto is whispering into his ear, and he casts them down, looking anywhere but at us.

I forget what number comes after thirty.

They're talking about what to do with us. Their hostages. The witnesses.

Shaking his head, Ryan backs away from Toto a step, but Toto sticks tight to him. "You know I'm telling the truth," Toto nearly shouts, which gets Twitch muttering again.

Thirty-three.

Oscar angles his head my way. "Scott, ease down."

"What?"

"Chill, dude." Oscar points at my hands. "They'll know something's up."

He's right. I relax my fisted fingers and focus on the counting and the breathing. It helps me let go of a little of the anger surging through me. Anger at Becky, my parents, these maniacs. Releasing a huge breath, I let my shoulders sag and roll my head. Better, but only for a second.

Forty.

I can't stop checking the friggin' vestibule. Ryan and Toto haven't stopped arguing. Toto throws glances at Twitch every couple seconds.

"Will you just shut up?" Toto asks when Twitch's mumbles turn into whining moans.

"Toto, man," he says. "You got a little shard? I need one. Or else the ether will get in."

Forty-three.

Toto's brow wrinkles in disgust and he sucks his teeth. "Fuck, man. If you're gonna bug me all day. Here, have yourself a party." He hands the skinny guy a baggie. Without missing a beat, Twitch pulls a glass apparatus out of his pocket along with a lighter.

Drugs. He's going to do drugs right here. First Maggie, dead, and now this.

"Twitch, you asshole. Don't be doing that by me." Toto shoos him to a table in the far corner.

"Oh dear," Pavan whispers as he watches Twitch select his party spot.

"Holy shit," Oscar adds.

Forty-five.

I exhale the last breath and though the numbers continue to climb in my head, I forget to inhale again until the floor tilts under my feet. Ryan and Toto are still in the perfect spot for Winny to keep her cover, but where Twitch has parked to enjoy his fix gives him the only direct sight-line into the vestibule and ladies' room door.

And Winny's not back yet.

Anger may be a liability, but it's better than the fear. I stop resisting and let the anger flow. Oscar will just have to suck it up.

"What are we going to do?" I whisper to him.

"Shh." He winces and clutches his leg above the tear the bullet made in his flesh.

Fifty-one.

"We need to warn her," I whisper. "Stop her from open-ing that door." I tilt my head toward Twitch. "He'll see."

"I know," Oscar says, scrubbing a hand through his hair. "It's the *how* I'm stuck on right now, okay? And don't blame me. This was your idea, remember."

God, how I remember.

Sylvie tosses a blood-soaked towel to the floor. "What did you guys do? What's going on?"

Throwing a fast glance at Toto and Ryan, Pavan leans in close to her. "The girl went downstairs to get Scott's cellphone."

"Are you crazy?" Her glare catches all of us, but lingers longest on me. "If this gets her hurt . . ."

Oscar bites his lip against the pain as Sylvie increases the pressure on his wound. "Ow, Silv."

"Well, dear husband, I don't want you bleeding to death, do I?"

"I'm sorry, but it was worth the risk," he says. "We need help."

"Worth the risk? This isn't Fallujah, Oscar. These kids aren't your soldiers to command."

"I'm a marine, not a soldier."

"You know what I mean."

"Baby." He runs a hand up and down her arm. "Think. We are witnesses to murder. We have to figure a way out of this."

I swear, she's about to smack him with one of the bloody towels. "Look." I stand between them. "Someone needs to warn her. Sneak back there. Intercept her."

Seventy.

"If she can't get out because that goon has a direct sightline to the door," Oscar says, "how the hell are you getting out?"

Hands in my pockets, I kick a jelly packet someone dropped under the counter. "I don't know, but we need to do something. Those guys aren't going to stay in that corner arguing forever."

"No," Sylvie says. "It's bad enough we put one kid's life in danger."

"Hey!" Ryan shouts as Toto shoves past him to glare at us around the beverage cooler. "What the hell do you all have to be talking about?"

We all freeze.

"That's better." He grabs Ryan by the collar and pulls him back to the corner where their own hushed conversation continues.

"Sylvie, my dear," Pavan whispers, "all our lives are in danger."

She glances at Maggie, still on the floor where she fell. Sylvie's eyes fill with tears.

How long since this messed-up circus started? I would have sworn it was a lifetime ago that these men intruded on my mundane haven, but the clock tells me it hasn't been fifteen minutes. How is that even possible?

"Maybe we can distract them, somehow," Pavan whispers. "Make noise or something, so if she comes out, they won't be focused in that direction?"

"But what can we do?" Sylvie asks. "And who should do it?"

Eighty-eight.

"Whatever it is, we need to act fast," I say. "She's been gone a minute and a half. She'll be coming out any second now."

We stand there, circled around Oscar, each exerting so much self-control to keep from looking at the vestibule that we collectively vibrate.

We're out of time. Any minute now, those guys are going to remember Winny is gone and wonder what the hell she's doing.

Should I just wait and see how it plays out? How can I even consider that when I'm the one who put her in this mess? I can't let her down.

Technically, I already did—that day after the football game.

I don't have time to be thinking about that. We've got enough on our plate without me dragging old regrets onto the menu. This indecision can just bite me. The plan was my idea—and if Winny hadn't come here to see me tonight . . . If anyone's getting hurt to help Winny, it's going to be me.

Maybe I even deserve it.

"Scott," Sylvie says, "whatever you're thinking, stop it right now."

"Screw that," I whisper. Then at a normal volume I announce, "I'm going to check on Winny."

"Oh, you are?" Toto starts to come at me, but Ryan gets in his way.

"Forget the goddamn kids! We've got some serious people waiting to hear from us tonight, or did you forget? The clock is ticking."

Toto glares at me, then checks his watch. "Fine. You've got five minutes. If you aren't out here by then, we're coming in. I don't care if she's puking, passed out, her panties all around her ankles, whatever. You drag her ass out here if you have to."

"You bet." Five fast strides and I'm there. With my right hand pressed to push open the ladies' room door, I catch the faintest flash of movement as the employee door cracks an inch.

Even with just a strip of her showing, she's the most beautiful girl I've ever seen in person, and it nearly makes me freeze. But I don't stop. In a smooth movement, I hold up one finger and mouth *wait* before I slip inside the bathroom. Back against the door, I bend over, head by my knees, and try to catch my breath.

I made it all right. Only problem is, now we're both trapped.

Cracking the door, I peek out at the café. The one pro of this whole deal is that I have just as good a view of Twitch as he has of the door I'm standing behind. At least I have a view of the door shielding Winny, too. As I watch, she cracks it again and catches my eye. I smile at her, but of course, she probably can't tell. I hold up one finger and see her nod from the shadows.

We just need to wait for the right moment, then I can usher her in.

Twitch is no longer messing with the baggie Toto gave him. His chair is angled in our direction, so if we move, it's sure to catch his eye.

I check my watch. Almost a minute down already. Crap, he might stay like that all night. The dude is talking to himself again, each sentence punctuated with a series of giggles. And then he tilts his head over his right shoulder, away from us, like he's listening to someone. A smile spreads across his face, as though whatever his invisible pal just said makes him happy. Mouth full of words I can't hear, he places his fingertips on the tabletop and taps them like he's typing on a keyboard. God, he really must have been a computer programmer. The whole time he works on his nonexistent desktop, he cocks his head to catch the data being fed to him by his invisible friend.

There's a rhythm to it. *Tap tap tap taptaptap, tap*, followed by a word thrown over his shoulder. *Tap tap tap taptaptap*, followed by a giggle aimed at his hands. *Tap tap tap taptaptap, tap*. Another word for his imaginary friend.

This might be our shot. I hold up three fingers for Winny and breathe the taps along with Twitch's manic digits as I count down.

10

SCOTT

Two Hours and Thirty-Five Minutes Before Closing

The run had been a major mistake.

Gut burning, Scott kicked off his running shoes and shoved them as far back in his closet as possible, although that would do little to prevent their stench from infiltrating his room in a matter of minutes. Another reason he should have just stayed put. He needed an airtight container, or better yet, he should burn the sneakers and just get a new pair. He scoffed and wiped sweat off his face with the tee he'd just removed. Yeah, like that would happen. His paycheck was sucked up as fast as he could collect it. He'd probably develop quite the case of arthritis in his knees if he kept running with this old pair, but he needed the exercise to keep him going. To deal with the stress.

On his way to the bathroom for a shower, he ran into his mom in the hallway. She moved past him like a ghost, one finger held up to her lips, a gesture that could only mean one thing: his dad was out cold.

For now.

Scott passed the living room doorway and paused to study the sleeping man's face. He still didn't get how this new-and-not-improved version was the same person he'd idolized as a kid, the epitome of safety and of know-how. Everyone changed—no surprise there—but he'd always assumed when people did change, it was for the better. Who knew how little it would take to totally derail a life?

"Scott!" his mom whispered at his back.

He jumped. "Shit, Ma."

"Don't wake him. Please. I finally got Evie down and I need this quiet time."

Scott felt an urge to laugh, because he knew what she really meant. Safe time was more like it. But when his mother eyed his dad like he was some kind of sleeping predator, the urge died away. How the fuck did a normal, working-class man turn into someone his family tiptoed around out of fear? In his dad's case, all it had taken was losing his job of twenty years and the inability to find another one. That, and all the liquor he could drink. As the weeks and weeks ticked by, turning into years, his dad had grown increasingly helpless, demoralized, and outright depressed.

"We'll help him, right, Scotty?" his mom had said when the telltale signs of a man on the edge had started to show up for breakfast.

That had been two years ago, and Scott still didn't know if he'd ever see his real dad again.

When that guy finally showed up, the version of the son he'd left behind might be gone for good.

"Scott, come on." His mom tugged his arm, urging him out of the living room doorway.

✽

As he got dressed after his shower, his phone went off and he snatched it up. The chance his cell could be heard in here from the living room were slim, but his mom's pleading expression—her dull eyes and limp hair—haunted him. Scott would be getting out of here in a little while, and probably wouldn't be back until morning, knowing the way Brian's parties usually went, but she'd be stuck here all night. With *him*. No matter how pissed Scott still was, he couldn't risk her getting hurt because of something he did. So far, that was a line his dad hadn't crossed. Scott wanted to keep it that way.

He brought the phone to his ear. "Yeah."

"Scott, hey man. Glad I caught you."

"Josh, what's up?"

"Listen, I'm here at Flores, but I just got a call. My buddy is over at this bar in New Haven. Turns out their band just canceled, like totally left them in the lurch. So my friend, he's like, hey man, I know some guys who could bail you out."

"He got you a gig?"

"I'd have to head over there right now. No time to even change out of my Flores shirt." Josh laughed. "I'll tell Sylvie her place will be getting free advertising."

"You need me to cover?"

"You're the best!"

"Hold up. I didn't say yes. I'm picking Becky up in less than an hour—"

"Don't make me beg. This could be huge for us. If the owner likes us, he'll book us outright. Come on, Scott. It's only for like two hours."

Scott checked the clock and sighed.

"I'll give you my pay for the entire shift—"

"Josh—"

"And give you first dibs on next month's schedule."

Scott rubbed his brow, because Josh knew him and was totally using that knowledge to hook him. With first shot at the shifts, Scott could be sure to have off the night of Becky's annual pool party. That would make her happy. "Fine. Give me a half hour." He checked the battery, but only a sliver of charge had soaked in since he'd plugged his phone in before his run.

The morning's fiasco had fucked it up good.

*

A golden light showed beneath his parents' bedroom door. Scott knocked lightly. His mom opened the door, book still in hand, and ushered Scott in. Evie slept in her portable crib next to the bed.

"Can I take the car?" he asked.

"What, you're asking now? I don't recall you getting our permission when you ran out of here before and then trashed it. As it is, you're lucky it was me who went outside for the drill bits and not your dad. If he'd seen what you did to the interior—"

"Mom, it was just a little tear in the trunk. Who cares about the trunk? It's where you put your shit. Besides, this time I need the car for work. The bus will take too long, and Josh needs me there now. Besides, Becky's going to have to go to Brian's without me, and I'll need a way to meet up with her."

His mom stared at the floor and chewed her lip. "Fine, but if you can get someone to follow you home to return it, that would be good."

"I'll try."

On the way to Café Flores, he deliberated over whether he should call Becky. She'd be royally pissed about the change of plans, and he'd already pushed his luck with her with the whole prom thing. He'd never forget the look on her face the day he told her they couldn't go as a couple.

She'd come in after cheer practice, still in her uniform, and she'd pulled out a fabric swatch and laid it on the table next to the remnants of his late lunch.

"This is my dress."

He'd eyed the square of gauzy peach material. "It's a little small, but fine by me."

She shook her head. "Ha ha ha. No, silly, it's the *color* of my dress. For prom. So you can match your tux and the flowers and stuff."

Playing with a fragment of straw paper, he'd stared at the tabletop so he wouldn't have to meet her gaze. "Becky, I can't go to prom."

"You can't be serious."

"I don't have the . . . you know how it is for me."

A lava flow, starting in his gut, had burst through his chest into his throat. He'd avoided her gaze for as long as he could, but when the silence kept building, he had no choice but to look up. First, there had been only a flat stare, then she furrowed her brow, and finally, her eyes glassed over and melted into tears that slipped down her cheeks.

He'd tipped his head toward the ceiling and sighed. "Look, I'm sorry, okay."

"There's got to be a way," she'd said. "What if . . . what if—"

"There just isn't."

"I'll ask my dad."

"I can't let you do that."

"How can you not have anything saved up? Isn't that

why you've been wasting your free time in this frickin' place?" She waved her hand in the air over her head.

"Is that what you thought?"

She knew it was bad at home, but not *how* bad. Was that because she couldn't comprehend a world where wanting something means you don't get to have it? Or was it because he hadn't let her get close enough to him to actually see his world?

Both, probably.

What did it say about her that she could be so oblivious? What did it say about him that he let her stay in the dark?

He'd toyed with his uneaten crusts. "No, I don't have anything saved." The lava flooded his skull, filling the space behind his eyeballs, burning into his brain.

That's when Becky's savage temper had hit. "So, what? I'm supposed to *miss* my senior prom?"

Scott was back to staring at the table again. "No. I can't go, but that doesn't mean you can't."

"Alone? What about the pictures? What about having someone to dance with at the *dance*? You can not be serious."

"What? You want to go with someone else?"

"Maybe I do."

He pushed back from the table, chair legs squealing against the floor, the skin-crawling sensation reverberating through him all the way to his gums. With one knuckle he massaged them through his lips as he picked his way between the tables. "Then that's what you should do. Ask someone else."

"Where the hell are you going?"

"Work."

"Seriously?" She'd gaped at him, one eyebrow raised, a hand on her cocked hip. When he didn't return to the table, she slapped the top with an open palm. "Whatever. Go ahead. Have fun working all the time and still being broke." Then she'd stormed out onto the street.

It could have been worse. The café room had been empty except for Pavan with his cup of chai, and Sylvie, of course.

They hadn't spoken for three whole days after that, but eventually Becky answered his messages, and they'd found a compromise. She'd go to prom with Ricky Belsen, and Scott would meet up with her at Brian's for the after-party.

The night had been torture, waiting for her to come back, imagining what might be happening between Ricky and his girlfriend, but by the time she'd made it to Brian's, that look of impatience she got when she was annoyed was all over her face.

Impatience to be away from Ricky. Impatience to be with Scott.

That was all he'd needed to put everything back to rights.

The party had been like all of Brian's other parties, and

Scott forgot every messed-up thing in his life as he chilled with his friends. He even managed to convince himself he hadn't just missed the main event. Becky had never looked more beautiful than that night, dressed in shimmery peach. Strands from her fancy hair had shaken loose and were dangling around her face, brushing her creamy shoulders when she'd parted the crowd in Brian's living room to find him.

And then Scott had gone home to find his dad waiting up to greet him with his fists, and the peach night turned red.

✿

Scott pulled into the back employees' lot at Café Flores and turned off the car. Now that things had returned to an even keel with Becky, he didn't want to risk another fight, so he settled on a text message.

Becks, change of plans. Will meet you at Brian's. Figure on 10:45ish.

He hadn't so much as settled his time card back in its slot when his phone pinged.

Where r u?

He considered lying. Screw that. It was just for a couple of hours. She probably wouldn't be ready much before ten anyway.

Seconds after he hit SEND, he received a new message: *I'm coming there. We need to talk. Be there around closing.*

He kicked the garbage can. "Fuck."

Whatever she wanted to talk about, it couldn't be good.

11

WINNY

I have no idea what Scott is looking at, but all I can do is trust him. The cell is a sickly weight tugging at the skirt of my dress. I don't know how I'm going to tell them it's useless, but I'll worry about that when I make it back out there.

If I make it back out there.

Scott's palm appears in the slit of light coming from the ladies' room and I tighten my grip on the door handle as my heart skips a beat. His palm is replaced by three fingers.

He folds one down.

Then the second.

And the third.

I pull the door open, smashing it against my hip in my rush, but I don't care because all that matters is making it to the door and Scott, which are both only two-and-a-half steps away. I clench my eyes, readying for a gunshot and the flash of pain that will signal the men saw and our plan failed, but the only thing I feel is warmth wrap my body. Gentle strong warmth that pulls me against it.

Scott's arm around my waist.

Scott's body pressing against mine.

When I open my eyes, it's his shoulder I see, clad in his green Café Flores polo, and I lay my head against him as his hands smooth up and down my back.

"I'm so sorry, Winny. I'm so sorry. I never should have suggested—" He buries his face against my neck and shakes his head from side-to-side, his misery a caress to my skin, and when his lips move, they flutter against my pulse.

"I'm so sorry."

"It's okay." My breath hitches, but I manage to coax out the rest of the words. "I made it."

He pulls back to study my face, one hand skimming over my back and up to my neck, the other resting against my cheek. "Are you sure?"

I nod and he rests his forehead against mine. His heat ignites the cologne and soap lingering on his skin, and I breathe him in, letting my muscles relax when I exhale. "I wish we could just stay in here, lock ourselves in, and forget everything else."

"Yeah. Me, too."

Even though at least two inches of air separates us, I can feel his lips when he speaks, can feel them brushing mine in a ghost of a caress. In a memory.

Or maybe a promise.

He withdraws a second later. "Shit!" he hisses, glancing at his watch. The door bursts open, and we both jump.

"I said five minutes." Toto grabs my arm and drags me from the restroom.

"I can walk." I tug out of his grasp.

"You can? Then how come you didn't walk your ass out here ten minutes ago?"

"I was . . . sick."

"Well, you best be feeling better, because no one's leaving my sight again."

Toto's words sink into my brain like a prediction instead of a threat, a dark pledge to vanquish the last spark of hope I held.

Before I reach the stools, Sylvie rushes me, practically knocking me over with her hug. "Don't you ever do that again. Promise?"

"Okay. I'll never use the bathroom again."

She's crying and laughing at the same time. "Good."

"That was a very brave thing you did, young lady." The corner of the old man's eyes crinkle when he smiles.

Oscar half hugs me with one arm, using the gesture as a fake-out so he can whisper in my ear. "Did you get it?"

I nod and take a deep breath, because the words don't want to come. Right this second, these people are holding on to hope that they're the survivors in this story, but what

I have to tell them will turn them back into hostages in a hopeless situation. "There's just one problem."

"We didn't have time to make the call," Scott says.

"That's okay." Oscar lays a hand on my shoulder. "You guys did good. We'll get our chance."

"No, that's not it."

I'm pinned by their stares. Making sure our captors are focused on something other than me, I pull the phone from my pocket and show everyone the blank LED screen.

Scott's back goes rigid.

"But you had it on my charger under the counter for two hours," Sylvie says.

He thrusts his hands in his pockets and kicks at nothing on the floor. "It's a piece of shit. Damn!"

I want so much to hold him the way he held me in the ladies' room. The way he looked at me, it made everything okay for a little. I want to do the same for him.

"Not now," Oscar says "Winny, hide that!"

I jam the phone back into my pocket, its cold weight pulling at the skirt of my dress.

It's Ryan, he's coming.

And he's looking right at me. He knows. Oh my God, he knows. The phone seems to grow heavier. Can he see it? Does my skirt look uneven where the phone's weight drags it down? Can he see the black case through the white cotton? I clench my hands together so they won't betray me and feel for the cell through the eyelet fabric. Or do something worse: hand it over, turn myself in, face the consequences.

Ryan stops right in front of me. "What are you talking about over here?"

Sylvie checks Oscar's wound again. "Oh, let's see. We're just trying to figure out how to keep your brother-in-law from dying on the café floor."

Ryan rolls his eyes. "That thing still bleeding?" He doesn't even bother to try to sound concerned. But at least he's not looking at me anymore. He's bending over Oscar, acting like he knows what's going on with the injury. Suddenly, I want to laugh. Who'd have ever thought I'd be the go-to girl? *Call Winsome Sommervil for all your bullet wound needs.* This situation has just hit a new level of surreal.

But it hits me. I'm calmer, more grounded, and way less scared than I was before.

If you need a way out, search for the door yourself.

I'd never tell her so, but my mom's right. It's better to do something, stay moving, than just sit around and wait for someone else to fix my problems.

"It's slowing down," Oscar says. "Don't worry, Silv. The bullet is still in there. It's helping."

It may be, but any bleeding is too much. Sylvie has at least two of those white bar towels by her feet and a third in her hands, and they're all soaked in blood. I won't look at her hands. The wound is one thing, but Oscar's blood on Sylvie's palms, under her fingernails . . .

"Looks fine to me," Ryan says.

"It's not *fine*." Everyone jumps, as though they've forgotten I know how to speak. "Well, it's not. If it's been bleeding like that this whole time, he's only minutes away from passing out."

Toto lifts his chin to peer over the counter from his corner by the main entrance.

"Do you have a first aid kit?" I ask.

Ryan returns to Sylvie's side, and—totally weird—he talks to her, not me, like I'm invisible. "I said, he looks fine."

"Ryan, please—"

"And I've had EMT training." I hate to cut Sylvie off, but I have an idea, and if I'm going to try it, I just want to get it over with. I may not be panicking anymore, but my hands tremble, and when I speak next there's a tremble in my voice, too. "I can stop the blood, but I need a few things. First aid kit. Plastic wrap."

"No." This time Ryan aims his words at me, and they're a full-on growl.

"Think about it, young man," Pavan says.

"It's okay, man. I'll be fine," Oscar says.

"No, this is important." Tension marks Pavan's age-lined face. "What if we need to move again suddenly? If this man is immobilized . . ."

Ryan sighs. "We'll have two stiffs to deal with."

"Ryan! What the hell is wrong with you?" Sylvie gapes at him, and I can't believe that anything he says can surprise her at this point.

Would I react with excuses and denial if it were my family here—my mom or dad, or my cousin Gracie—holding the guns, barking out orders? Maybe. Then again, how someone can deny a problem that has literally drenched her hands with blood is beyond me. "If you cover a fire, you still have a fire," I mumble.

Sylvie's crying again. "What?"

I shake my head. "Nothing."

"Let me get the supplies to help him." Sylvie reaches toward Ryan almost as if she wants to give him comfort. "Please."

"The girl can do it," he says. "I'm not letting you back there. You might pull something."

Oscar's large, warm hand cups my shoulder. "The first aid kit is under the counter," he slurs, struggling to force the words out, and it's no wonder with all the blood he's lost.

"Okay." Scott's cellphone is a reassuring weight in my pocket.

"You've got three minutes," Toto says.

The way behind the counter is a narrow passage, mere feet from the vestibule. I skirt the counter and slip between the wall and the black stone counter top.

A lump lodges in my throat, one I can't swallow down

because, phone aside, if I can't stop Oscar's bleeding, he might die.

"One thing at a time," I whisper as I squat down to examine the contents of the shelves.

"You see it?" Sylvie sounds near panic, but she needs to keep it together so I can do this.

"Not yet," I call.

"Let her focus," Oscar says.

I find the kit right away, but pretend I'm still looking. I need to find the phone charger. As I move along the counter, I push the kit with me. Okay, we've got plenty of take-out containers. I dig through the items, inspecting the wall at the back of the shelf for the tell-tale outlet plate. More towels, plates, bowls, a huge box of plastic wrap. I tug that out and stand to plop it on the counter. Squatting again, I find some silverware, including old-school wood-handled steak knives. Should I grab one? It'll be too long to fit in my pocket without sticking out, and with a pang of despair, I let the idea go. I snag a few pairs of rubber gloves, shoving them in my empty pocket with one hand while the other caresses the lump of plastic I need to plug in. Then I grab some scissors and a few bottles of water from the cooler.

"Still not finding it." Hopefully someone will realize that I'm really asking about the charger.

"Try closer to the register," Oscar calls.

There it is! But I need to stay calm. "Let's see." I let my voice trail as though I'm not sure what I'm looking at. A glance at the men could give me away, though not looking makes my skin squirm as though there are eyes all over me. Doesn't matter though, my front is shielded by my crouched position and the shelf itself. If I move fast enough, they'll never see, even if they do happen to be looking my way.

My hand has already crept into my pocket, and I close my fingers over the plastic. It's warmed slightly from being so close to my skin. So I can be certain where the plug goes, I rub my thumb along the sides and edges while I use my free hand to rifle through the objects on the shelf to mimic a search.

"Hurry up back there," Toto says. A squeak tells me he's wandered nearer the beverage cooler by the front window. Not a bad vantage point if he wants to check out what I'm doing.

I need to be fast. Closing my hand in a fist around the phone, I whip it from my pocket and thrust it into the shadows under the shelves. "I think I found it," I say to keep Toto from getting any closer. When I tug the thin wire, a cup with extra pens topples, and the contents scatter on the tile floor. "Shit," I hiss, but the plug end comes into view. I maneuver it, but at first it just skitters around the opening in the phone, scratching the plastic. Finally, it slips home with a *click*.

"I said—"

"I've got it!" Reaching for the kit, I shove the cell to the far back of the shelf behind a box of business cards, just in case they decide to check, and bounce to my feet so fast, not enough blood makes it to my head, and I have to grab the counter to keep from losing my balance.

"Then get back here," Toto snaps.

After a second, the dots fade from my vision, and I grab the plastic wrap and the other items I placed on the counter before scooting through the pass-through to rejoin the others.

"You ready?" I ask Oscar.

"You sure you know what you're doing?"

"I've never tended a gunshot victim, but I think I can manage." I dig in my brain for the steps, and find they're there waiting for me. I can do this. "Among the blind, the one-eyed is king."

"What?"

"Just something my mother says. Trust me."

Then I get to work.

12

WINNY

Two Hours and Fifty-Two Minutes Before Closing

Winny scanned the street beyond her bedroom window again. Dark and quiet. Janey wouldn't be coming for over an hour, not until after Winny texted her that the coast was clear. Winny's parents still hadn't left yet, though she expected them to any time now. She sighed and flopped back onto her pillow. The stack of acceptance letters still sat on her desk. She hadn't been able to bring herself to throw them away, and they glared at her from across the room, whispering warnings to her in voices that sounded too much like her mother's:

The world is a dangerous place, Winny.

You won't have us to take care of you.

We've always supported you, but we don't have to, you know.

Winny had been itching to get out of here an hour ago. Her only plans for the evening were to avoid any more family time, so she'd been hiding out in her room since her parents went to get ready for her mom's work party. She snorted. *Family time.* Translation: listen to her parents talk about everything wrong with her life choices and why Winny would be a failure.

She clicked to a new track on her playlist and cranked up the volume, trying to relax and get in the mood for a party, but she couldn't keep still. The evening's lecture had blown her mom's from this morning out of the water. The words kept playing in her head.

"I still can't believe you didn't follow through with the second part of the EMT training," her dad had said after her mom filled him in. "You did such a good job in the first course."

Yeah, until she almost passed out on the last day. So much blood, it had been everywhere—a bike accident victim. The guy's calf had been shredded, and it had totally undone her, but she'd never told her parents, because for them, there was no such thing as *can't.*

"I wanted to do something different, okay? I'm sorry I lied."

"Your father and I work very hard for you to have those opportunities. First, you let us believe you sent in an acceptance to Johns Hopkins, now this. *Ou wè sa ou genyen, ou pa konn sa ou rete. Bourik swe pou chwal dekore ak dantèl.*"

Super, Winny was in for her mom's snark. Could this day get any worse?

"Jeannette, don't," her dad had said.

"David, she can't even begin university until the spring, and here she is, wasting time with painting."

"Thanks, Mom. I guess you're right. I'm just a lazy freeloader who isn't good at anything."

Her dad had slammed his coffee mug onto the counter. "Now, come on. You know that's not how we feel."

"That's basically what she said this morning. When she threatened to kick me out."

"Winsome, I merely said—"

But Winny had stormed out of the kitchen and away from whatever explanation her mom was going to try to use to downplay her threats, and she'd been hiding in her room ever since. They'd be gone soon, and when they left, she'd text Janey. Until then, she just needed to chill and get rid of her jitters.

Maybe she should dance; that usually worked. She hopped to her feet and checked her reflection in the full-length mirror. Just sweats for now, though her hair and makeup were all set. The white sundress waited for her in the closet.

"All right," she said. "Let's get ready to party."

She searched for a good song, made sure her earbuds were in tight, and hit it. This had been the right choice. The music was loud enough to drown out her mother's voice, and when it started to seep in again, Winny simply clicked the volume up a few more notches.

If only everything could be this simple: get moving, close your eyes, and follow the music until the song ended.

That's how it had been up until now. Everything all laid out, everything decided—as easy as listening to the rhythm and keeping up with the beat—but now it felt totally different. Too many songs to choose among and everyone around her shouting out dance steps she couldn't quite hear, and if she did, she couldn't quite do them. Decisions to be made. Plans to outline. Goals to set—

And to reach.

Everyone else's goals. No one bothered to find out what Winny wanted, and on the rare occasion she made her preferences known, all she got was disapproval.

Wè jodi a, men sonje demen. Live today but plan for tomorrow.

"Shut up, Mom!"

The track approached its climax, and she spun on one foot like back in ballet class, but struck something warm and solid before she completed her rotation. The earbud was ripped from her right ear, and the world outside her head returned.

"Winsome!" Throwing out her hands, her mother caught herself on the desk, knocking the stack of letters off it into the wastebasket.

"Oh my God, Mom! Don't scare me like that."

"Well, if you'd heard me the first dozen times I called . . ."

Panic flared when Winny realized her mom hadn't changed. "I thought you were leaving soon."

"It's a long train ride. I wanted to wait for the last

minute so I won't spoil my dress." She rested one oh-so-elegant hand—with its French manicure and flashy, but tasteful, rings—against her collarbone, wrinkling the silk of her blouse, and setting off the gems in her jewelry against a backdrop of petal pink. So posh. So proper. Here it was, after dinnertime, and her mother was still dressed for the office. She wouldn't remove her daily uniform until it was time to put on her cocktail dress for the party. Not a hair out of place, her makeup still fresh as the morning, right down to the lipstick she reapplied each night, without fail, right after dinner.

When Winny was younger, she wanted to be just like her mom.

Now she didn't know who she wanted to be.

Or who she was.

"We'll be leaving in a little while. Don't expect us home before one. You are to stay here." She put a little more mom menace into her voice. "We will discuss the rest of your punishment tomorrow."

"Isn't grounding enough?"

"Not even close."

Winny pulled her remaining earbud free and flopped back onto her bed. "Fine."

"Aren't you forgetting something?"

Winny scanned the room. "I don't think so."

Shaking her head, Winny's mom strode to the

wastebasket and plucked out the envelopes. She laid them atop the desk in a neat stack.

"Oh, right." Although as far as Winny was concerned, those acceptances could stay in the trash. The one that mattered was on its way to its final destination, the only one of her little secrets her mother hadn't snooped out.

"Have you responded to any of these programs?"

"I already told you, I haven't made up my mind." Total lie, but her mom didn't know that. Yet.

Arms crossed, her mother leveled her narrowed eyes at Winny. "These schools have deadlines—"

"I know," Winny huffed.

"—and you *will* meet them and start college in the spring. I'll be looking up the information tomorrow. You will not pull the same stunt as you did with the fall deadlines."

Winny plastered a sickly sweet smile on her face. "You've said it a million times. College is a very big and important decision. I wouldn't want to mess it up."

Her mother stood by in silence, expression never changing. "I've got to get dressed. You remember what I said. You'd better be here, in bed, when we get home."

Then she was gone, but the ghost of her heavy perfume lingered. God, Winny couldn't wait to get out of this place. She'd go far enough away that her mom's philosophy wouldn't find her. Maybe, eventually, it would fade from her head altogether. Only problem was, Winny had no idea where she'd go. Finally deciding on school was one thing, but that still left everything else, and she had no idea what to do.

Winny's life was a played-out song list. She needed to change the track, but her options sucked, and she couldn't decide what to put on next.

She could confess to her mom and dad, explain what her choice was and why it was the right one for her. Sure, and all she'd get from that would be another lecture on being a responsible adult. Or worse, they might decide to override her decision and choose for her, the way her dad had threatened to do three weeks ago when she'd informed him that she never actually sent in her acceptance to his *alma mater*. No way was she doing premed. Tears threatened, but she turned on her music again and blocked everything out except the rhythm of her feet on her bedroom carpet.

She'd focus on tonight's party and the fun she'd have. She'd focus on the rumor Janey had texted her, about how Scott and Becky might have broken up.

Finally.

But that was a dangerous line of thought, too, especially after what had happened between her and Scott earlier that day. What if she'd caused the breakup? Another notch or two on the volume drove those worries from her head as well.

By the time the song was over, she'd almost forgotten that, at seventeen, her life was already a hot mess.

13

SCOTT

THIRTY-SEVEN MINUTES AFTER CLOSING

Scott, you're loosening the tourniquet." Winny points a latex-covered finger at the apron tie she'd improvised to replace Oscar's leather belt and to help stop the bleeding.

"Oh, sorry!" During her foraging mission under the counter, she'd grabbed a metal butter knife, and she tied the knot around it now.

Shifting my grip on the setup, all I have to do is twist the knife one full circle to increase the tension on the vessel leaking blood from Oscar's leg. At least, that's what I hope I'm doing, but it's hard to focus, because our captors aren't happy.

"Look," Toto replies, not bothering to lower his voice. "It's getting late. We need to deal with Aaron and the Chef first, then we can figure this mess out."

I can't figure out what I should focus on: the shouts, the trickle of red from Oscar's bullet wound, the char of drugs wafting our way from the corner. What is it Twitch is smoking in that pipe of his? Crack? Meth? I've seen enough *Intervention* to know it's one of the two. The fact that Winny can concentrate through this is incredible.

Oscar bites his lip but doesn't say anything as Winny uses the scissors Sylvie keeps behind the counter to cut away the khaki material of his pants for a better look.

"Oh, God," Sylvie whispers when she catches sight of the wound.

Winny closes her eyes. "Just breathe. Just breathe." Her whole body tenses, hands clenching into fists at her sides. She releases the tension, then tightens her muscles again.

"You okay there, Win?" Oscar asks.

"Applied pressure technique. I sort of pass out at the sight of blood."

"Then why the heck are you doing this?" Sylvie asks.

"Don't worry," Winny says. "It's passing." She opens her eyes and lets out a shaky breath. "I'm okay. Just wait till it's clean. It will look way better." She grabs a water bottle and uses it to rinse the wound, her mouth set in a line of determination.

I can't believe I almost kissed her in the girls' bathroom. Again. Here we are, maybe about to die, and I'm thinking about hooking up. I shake my head.

"Scott," Winny says.

"Crap!" I tighten the knot again, but my ears tune into the conversation between Toto and Ryan. I'd rather think about kissing Winny, but I need to stay focused. Something's going down.

"Makes sense." Nodding, Ryan takes a deep breath before turning to us. "Right. First things first. Sylvie, I need you to empty the money out of the register."

She's been standing slumped behind Oscar so he can lean against her as Winny works. Now she straightens. "What?"

"Open your ears!" He closes the distance, striding up to his sister. "Get me the money. Now."

"Fine. I need my keys back."

Ryan holds out his arm and snaps his fingers. "Twitch. Keys."

"Holy crap," I whisper when I follow Ryan's gaze.

Twitch drops his pipe onto the table and stands in a jerky, unbalanced motion. "Yeah, Ry." He sways at the waist and taps his fingers faster than ever.

"Fuck, man," Toto says. "Did you do the whole thing?"

"No. Nononono. I didn't. See." Twitch holds out the baggie, which isn't one hundred percent empty, but close enough.

Toto darts across the room and snatches it from him, almost knocking the guy over. "No more. You gotta keep focused."

"Give me the keys, Twitch," Ryan says again.

"Sure, Ry. Sure, sure. Here you go, Ry. Here you go. Here—"

Ryan snatches the keys away and drops them into Sylvie's hand. "Now clean it out. I want all of it."

"It's clean," Winny says.

For a second, I think she means the register, but then I realize she's looking at Oscar's leg.

"And look, the bleeding's stopped. Good job, Scott."

She's right. A clean hole—angry red-purple, but free from that red, crusted mess—marks the center of Oscar's thigh. It's smaller than I expected. I don't know what I expected.

"The bullet can't have hit the main femoral artery," she says. "Probably a larger vessel, but not the biggie. I can't do anything about the bullet, though. It's lodged in the femur, I think. They'll have to remove it at the hospital when . . ."

She can't finish, and I get it.

None of us has any idea what's coming next.

"We'll have to settle for sanitizing the wound." She pulls her mouth into a wince. "This will sting." The small can of spray sounds nearly full when she shakes it, and she gives the wound a good long spritz.

Oscar can't hold back a grunt of pain.

Wincing, Winny bites her lip. "Sorry."

"Please," he says. "What kind of marine am I if I can't handle the handiwork of a field medic? You're doing great, Win."

She smiles at that. I do, too.

She *is* doing great. *She* is great.

"Just a little ointment, and we're done." She fills the

wound entirely and is laying the first gauze pad over it as the register slides shut with a *clack.*

Sylvie makes her way back to Ryan, the stack of bills clenched in her hand. "Here."

Mumbling, he shuffles through the money. When he's done counting, I expect him to look relieved, but if anything, he's the opposite. He starts from the top again, and the expression on his face grows darker with every bill he transfers from one hand to the other. Sylvie stands before him, her stance like a little girl who knows she's going to be punished, but doesn't know what that punishment will be.

"Scott, can you cut some tape for me?"

Oscar takes over tourniquet duty so I can use the scissors on the medical tape.

"Okay." Winny takes a shaky breath but smiles at Oscar. "This might sound weird, but one more step." She wraps his entire thigh in a tight layer of plastic wrap. "Compression and protection at the same time. They keep this stuff on ambulances especially for burns, but it works here, too. Plus we can see if the bleeding starts up again."

She packs up the supplies and lines everything up neatly on the counter, all except the scissors, which I tuck into the waistband of my khakis. The only person who notices I palmed them is Pavan. Hopefully the guys are too busy to catch on. The tips kiss my back with cold pressure, but I don't care. We need some kind of weapon.

Oscar pulls Winny into a hug. From the way her brow wrinkles and the corners of her mouth turn down, I can tell she's close to losing it. Now that the work is done, the fear and doubt are cracking through, but she wrangles it back under control and comes to stand by my side.

Ryan counts the wad one more time before fanning the bills and waving them in Sylvie's face. She blinks, and I'm suddenly back in the kitchen, a video playing on my still-intact phone—a video showing my baby sister blinking the same way at a flapping dishtowel that barely misses her eyes.

"What the fuck is this?" Ryan bellows.

Sylvie winces as the paper smacks her.

"I said, I want it all. Everything."

"That *is* everything, Ryan. Go check for yourself if you don't believe me."

"What about the safe?" he asks.

"The safe's empty."

"Since when do you finish out the week with only five hundred and twenty-one dollars in the register?"

Sylvie's eyes flood with tears, and she gapes, swiveling her gaze from Ryan to Oscar.

Oscar's face crumples as realization hits him. "Shit."

"Aunt Phyllis," Sylvie says.

"What are you talking about?" Ryan asks.

Sylvie takes a deep breath, and when she speaks again, it sounds like she's exercising every ounce of control to keep her voice level, but her fury pokes through the tension anyway. "Tomorrow is Aunt Phyllis's birthday party, which you were invited to, may I remind you. It's at one. We're closing early so we can go, but we didn't want to cut it too close so—"

"So I made the second bank run today instead of tomorrow," Oscar finishes.

"Are you kidding me?" Sweat pours from Ryan's brow, and a drop hangs in the little divot above his upper lip. His face has already bypassed red and is well on its way to purple.

Toto moves in, snatches the money out of Ryan's hand, and begins to count it for himself.

"You've killed me, Silv." Ryan thrusts his face into hers. "You know that? I'm dead, and it's your fault."

She sobs, hands over her eyes.

Finished with his accounting, Toto steps between them. "This isn't enough."

"You think I don't know that?" Ryan pivots and paces a few steps before turning back. "We're so screwed, man. So screwed."

"Shut up," Toto snaps at Sylvie, who's still sobbing. "I said shut up!" Now Winny is crying, too.

"I said—" Toto raises a hand, but I step in the way. Staggering, I absorb the blow, then right myself. The pain is nothing compared to what my old man gave me this morning. For a second, I wonder who would win in a fight—Toto or Dad—and almost laugh. After a deep breath, the impulse passes. I focus on getting Sylvie and myself out of the line of fire before Toto decides to come at us for real.

My dad may pack more punch, but these guys have guns.

For a second, Toto's expression hardens. His hands clench, and he leans into me like I'm in for a full-body tackle.

Ryan puts a hand on his shoulder. "Come on. This isn't helping. We need to figure something else out."

Twitch watches this whole exchange with a faint smile painted on his pale lips. The guy is seriously out of it.

"We are in major trouble," I say as soon as their backs are turned.

"Oh my God. Scott!" Winny reaches up to my cheek but hesitates before her fingers can brush my skin. "Does that hurt?"

"Huh? Oh!" I touch the place Toto got me. "No, it's fine."

"But it's already bruising. You need ice."

I shake my head. "Forget it. We've got more important things to focus on. If we can't come up with a way out of this mess, a little bruise will seem like nothing."

"Don't say that!" Sylvie says. "There's no reason to think they'll do anything—"

"What?" I say. "Drastic? You've got to face facts. We all do. You heard them. Their whole plan is messed up."

Pavan puts a hand on her shoulder. "I'm afraid he's right. From what I can tell, they came for the money, and they expected only you two would be here. Perhaps Scott, too."

"Right, but I'm usually out back at closing time, so maybe I would have missed the whole deal."

"Only, to their surprise," Pavan goes on, "there were several customers here. In my case, I was avoiding my empty apartment."

"Oh, Pavan." Sylvie takes his hand. She regards us, one at a time. "So instead of an empty café, we've got a room full of hostages, and now Maggie's dead. And the register is empty."

"Yeah," I say. "Do you really think they're just going to let us walk out of here?"

"Someone will come," Winny says. Her eyes are wide, but her voice is firm. "Won't they? The cops? Someone."

"They were here, and they left," I point out. "No reason for them to come back. Wait a minute. Could someone around here have heard the gunshots and reported them?"

Sylvie shakes her head. "We're the only restaurant on this block. The retail shops closed hours ago."

"What about you, Pavan?" Oscar asks. "Anyone at home waiting for you? Someone who'll sound the alarm if you don't show up?"

Pavan sighs. "No. I'm afraid my wife is dead."

"I'm supposed to be at a party," Winny says.

"Scott?" Sylvie asks.

My mom's voice echoes in my head: *Just double-checking*

your plans haven't changed. Listen, Scotty. Don't come home for a while.

"I'm supposed to be at the same party as Winny."

"I believe we're on our own," Pavan says.

"My brother won't hurt us." Sylvie shakes her head. "He may be a drug dealer, but he's no murderer. I know him."

"Do you, Silv?" Oscar says. "Think, hon, the last two years, how he's manipulated you, borrowing money left and right. Then asking for a job, which we gave him even though we didn't need the help or have the budget for another employee. If I hadn't caught him with his 'client' out back, who knows how long he would have played us."

"He said it was only that one time," Sylvie protests.

I laugh, but press my lips together at Oscar's glare. Truth was, I saw Ryan running his side business too. I didn't know what was really going on, not then. I thought he was just slacking off with his friends. But now, I can put two and two together. No point filling them in, though. Oscar knows what's what, and it won't make a difference with Sylvie.

"Ryan banked on you not ratting on him," Oscar goes on, "even if that meant flashing his gun to get what he wanted. Because that's what you do. You protect him."

"They thought they had it all figured out. The perfect plan." I point at the dead woman lying in a pool of her own blood. "But it's a whole new game now."

14

WINNY

Two Hours and Fifty-Five Minutes Before Closing

Never before had the sage-green walls of Winny's room felt so much like prison bars, but they wouldn't be for long. She stood before her closet—which might only be her closet for another few hours—sliding hangers back and forth, the wood and plastic clacking with each movement.

"You can't be grounded," Janey said on the other side of the phone line.

"Yes, I can."

"I can't go to Brian's party alone tonight."

"Please. All our friends will be there."

"You know what I mean."

"Listen, I've got something to tell you. When you didn't show, Scott gave me a ride home from the gallery."

"Scott . . . came? Now I'm glad I got stuck talking to the school nurse about the dangers of the Coxsackie virus and why total isolation is a must. What the hell kind of name is that for a disease, anyway?"

"Focus, please. That's not all. I . . . uh . . . sort of . . ." Winny flopped onto her bed and pulled a pillow over her burning face.

Janey's voice cut through the wad of fabric like a fire alarm. "What? What! You're literally killing me right now."

"I kind of kissed him." Winny squeezed her eyes shut and awaited Janey's ear-shattering squeal.

Janey didn't disappoint. "Are you shitting me?" The drool in her voice practically seeped through the phone.

"I'd never shit you, Janey my dear."

"Like, you kissed him, kissed him? Full-on lips and tongue and everything?"

"Eww. No! It was just a little kiss. Fast. But . . . *sigh* . . . it . . . was . . . nice."

There was more squealing on the other side of the line.

"This is bad. I mean, what kind of person am I? I kissed my friend's boyfriend. He must hate me for real now. The fact that he'll even still talk to me after what happened last winter, after all those times he asked me out—"

"That's ancient history."

But it wasn't, not to Winny. The memory of the third time she picked her EMT class over a date with Scott wouldn't stop playing in her brain—the way his face had gone flat and how he'd sucked in that tiny breath, like she'd struck him.

"Winny! After the kiss, what did he say? What did he do?"

"Nothing, not really. I kind of freaked and ran into the house."

"Ran? Dragging that huge-ass painting?"

Winny wanted to hide under her comforter and never come out. She'd tripped and huffed the whole way to the door—with Scott watching. As if she hadn't already made a total fool of herself. "Exactly. It was a super-graceful exit."

"I bet. Your life has taken some very interesting turns today."

Winny grunted into her pillow. "When I woke up, everything was totally normal, I swear."

"And you're stuck in the house after all that? So not fair."

"It doesn't matter." Winny got up and returned to her closet, where she pulled a white eyelet lace sundress from the rack. She'd been saving it for a special occasion, and she couldn't think of a more special occasion than the night she stopped being her parents' obedient daughter. If she really confessed, she'd stopped being that Winny months ago. Her image in the family portrait was blurred and dull from too many coats of paint thinner. When her parents kicked her out for disobeying them, they might make her leave all her stuff. This could be her last chance to wear this dress, and she wanted to fill in that blurred space with something beautiful and festive and maybe even a little sexy. Even if just for tonight.

Tomorrow she'd worry about everything else.

"What do you mean, it doesn't matter?" Janey asked. "Of course it matters."

"It doesn't matter if I'm grounded, because I'm coming to the party anyway."

"Holy shit! No! Winsome Sommervil is going to sneak out?"

"Shh! Don't say it so loud."

"What? Am I on speaker or something? Are they in the room?"

Winny giggled, then snorted. "No. Oh my God, I literally suck at this."

"Yes!" Clapping and the squeak of bedsprings told Winny that Janey was jumping on her bed now. "OMG, this is going to be an epic party. I heard a very interesting rumor. A very important rumor. You think your life changed today, tonight will blow you away."

"Might as well pile it on. You'll pick me up?"

"Just don't tell your mom I helped you sneak out."

Winny's mother's footsteps sounded in the hallway. Winny shoved the dress into the closet and slid the other hangers around so it wouldn't look like she'd been messing with it. It wasn't like her mom could figure out her plan from the way her clothes were arranged in her closet. Then again, Winny wouldn't put anything past her mother. But, instead, the footsteps passed by her door without stopping. Winny flopped back against her pillows, then hopped up again, unable to sit still. The next couple of hours were going to feel like forever. "So what's this rumor that's going to change my life?"

"Hold up. I'm getting info as we speak," Janey said. "I refuse to disclose what I know until it's confirmed."

Winny rolled her eyes. "Dramatic much?"

"Yup. Besides, look who's talking."

Winny's hair was still up in its bun from earlier, and she pulled out the pins, letting it fall over her shoulders. The twist had given it a smooth wave. It would be perfect with the spaghetti straps of her dress. Add her silver sandals with the tiny buckles and a pair of turquoise earrings, and she'd be set. Janey's rumor could turn out to be nothing. Winny might not have a chance to see Scott, but it didn't matter. None of that mattered.

She was calling the shots now, and if everything in her life was going to be different tomorrow, she would make tonight count.

15

SCOTT

FORTY-SEVEN MINUTES AFTER CLOSING

When Ryan and Toto slip into the kitchen to talk, I expect to breathe a little easier, but that's impossible. It may not have felt like much when I took the blow, but the bruise on my cheek grows more painful by the minute. Winny and Sylvie keep glancing at it, Winny with worry all over her face, Sylvie with guilt. It's the same expression she gets when she looks at her brother. On the other hand, maybe I should be happy that Sylvie cares, that she's upset that I took a hit in her place.

I'm used to it. My mother seems to be quite willing to let me be the official whipping boy of the family.

Between the throbbing in my cheek and Twitch's never-ending soliloquy, I'm having trouble thinking. Twitch is supposed to be watching us, but he can't seem to keep his eyes off Maggie's body.

"Guys, let's focus here," Oscar whispers, leaning low. We

all move closer and form a tight circle. "This is our chance to come up with a plan."

"Your phone has been plugged in for a few minutes," Winny says to me. "You think it's charged enough for a call? I can pretend I need something else from behind the counter."

My face burns—which is not helping the throbbing—but I don't know if my embarrassment is because of my broken phone or how it got broken in the first place. For a moment, the image of a box of generic cereal fills my mind. "It will take a while. It sort of took a flight across the room this morning." We should have left the useless thing in the basement. "The basement," I whisper.

"You okay, Scott?" Sylvie has that motherly look on her face again.

"I'm fine, and I think I have an idea."

"What idea?" Pavan leans closer.

"The tunnels. What if we can get out that way?"

"The tunnels?" Oscar asks.

"Maybe we can take the passages to another building. Bust our way through. If we set off someone else's alarm, even better."

"Shit. Maybe," Oscar says.

"Maybe nothing." Sylvie glares at him. "We're not all marines, and Scott is just a kid."

"So you want us to just sit here? Do nothing?"

She turns to me. "Sometimes it's better to wait, to sit

quiet, than to rush into something just for the sake of action. Scott, we have no idea what's down there."

I know she's right. I wish I'd checked out those passages before today, but the idea of some dark, underground, musty space just doesn't do it for me. Who knows what's down there? Flooded walkways; rats; sewage pipes, maybe busted and seeping I-don't-want-to-know-what onto packed dirt floors. "But if it's our only shot, we need to try."

Pavan shakes his head. "I'm afraid Sylvie is right. We cannot get out that way."

"Well, so far, it's the only idea we have," Oscar grumbles.

"When they converted the factory space across the street into condos a few years ago, I was an engineer on the project," Pavan says.

"That's right." Sylvie smiles. "You used to come in on your lunch break when we first opened."

"So you've been down there?" I ask.

"Not me. They filled in the sub-basement space with cement before I was hired. I can't say about the tunnels below the other buildings on the street, but we were told that many of them had caved in over the years. Think about it, they are hundreds of years old."

"That settles it," Sylvie says. "The tunnels are out of the question. Too dangerous."

I point at the dead woman. "What, more dangerous than men with guns?"

The door from the kitchen swishes open as Toto and Ryan emerge from their private meeting.

"Twitch!" Toto shouts. "Will you shut the hell up? We could hear your ass all the way back there, man."

Twitch is still riveted by the body. And then it hits me. He shot her. It must be messing him up. Removing her from the café may be our key to getting downstairs.

"It's Maggie," I pipe up.

"Scott!" Sylvie hisses, but I drop a hand on her arm.

"I know what I'm doing." At least, I hope I do.

"What?" Toto says.

I motion to the body. "Maggie. She's getting him worked up. Us, too." I try for a sheepish, scared smile. Let this guy think I'm freaked out. Freaked out and embarrassed about it. "What if we move her downstairs, out of sight? It's cool down there. She'll . . . keep."

"Scott, don't be stupid. Just sit quiet," Sylvie commands. "Doing nothing isn't always a bad thing."

I can tell from the way Oscar's brow wrinkles that he's torn. Then Becky's voice from earlier is in my head: *They call and you jump.*

Maybe Sylvie is right, and this is a huge mistake. Maybe it *is* better to wait, to be patient. Do I really think I can just rush in and fix everything?

"Fuck, yeah," Toto says. "Anything to shut him up." He turns and shouts the last part in Twitch's face, but the guy is either too high or too spooked to notice.

I give Sylvie a shrug. For better or for worse, the decision is out of our hands now.

"I'm not carrying a body," Ryan complains. "It's not my mess."

It. Mess. How can he talk about another human that way?

"Twitch can do it," Toto says with a smirk. "Serves him right for making the mess to begin with."

But Twitch's babbling only grows louder.

"Are you kidding?" Ryan asks. "He's on the verge of a breakdown. Isn't the whole point to get the body farther away from him before he loses it?"

"If you ask me," Oscar whispers, "he's way beyond that point already."

"Shh!" Sylvie smacks his shoulder.

Rubbing his forehead, Toto kicks a chair leg, causing it to screech across the tile before it crashes into a table. "Fine." He turns to survey us. "Don't all volunteer at once."

"I'll go," Sylvie says.

But Toto just laughs. "You're staying here."

I take a hesitant step toward Maggie.

"Scott, no," Sylvie protests.

"Then who? Oscar can't carry anyone." Pavan stares at Maggie, frowning. He doesn't want to do this anymore than I do.

Maggie's corpse. I just volunteered to carry Maggie's corpse.

I feel a small pressure on my arm. Winny's hand. But

I can't focus on that because from this angle, I can see Maggie's face. It's as though someone turned on one of those digital camera filters—everything grays out around me, except where Maggie's lying. The world is too sharp, too bright. I know that woman. *Knew* her. Now she's dead. And I'm going to carry her corpse—Maggie's corpse.

The body. I'll call her *the body*. It'll be easier. Then Ryan's words come back to me: *It's not my mess.* No. I'll call her Maggie. She deserves that.

"Someone's getting himself an A-plus tonight." Toto waves at me to get a move on.

"I can't do it alone." I turn back to the group. "Anyone?"

"I said, I'll help," Sylvie hisses through gritted teeth.

Toto spins our way again. "And I said, not you. I'm not letting you out of my sight. She can do it."

Winny's eyes go wide and she clutches my arm. "I can't touch a dead person, Scott. I can't do it."

I move so I'm directly in front of her and take her by the elbows. "You can, Win. I know you can. You just kicked ass in patching Oscar up. This will be nothing compared to that."

"Blood was one thing, but a body . . ."

"Winny, we *have* to. You know why," I add in the softest whisper I can manage.

She swallows hard, and stares off into space for a second, muttering something I don't catch, but a second later she's back.

She nods. "I'll do it. I'll be okay."

I give her a fast hug and inhale her cherry-vanilla scent like it's the last beautiful thing in the world.

No, that's not true. Nothing and no one is more beautiful than Winny.

God, I hope I'm right about this, because I'm not the only one who will pay if we mess up. Not like at home.

We're all at risk here.

16

SCOTT

THREE HOURS BEFORE CLOSING

Scott's mother pounced on him as soon as he stepped through the door. "Where have you been?"

He shrugged. "Just out. Helping a friend." Except helping a friend didn't usually involve kissing.

"Dad's been calling you for hours." Waving Scott the rest of the way inside, she closed the front door with a practiced movement, making barely a sound. Not that his dad would have been able to hear it over the TV blaring from the living room. "He's been in one of his moods since you left," she said, glancing over her shoulder.

"When are you going to stop doing that?" Scott asked.

"What?"

"One of his moods? Is it his Johnnie Walker mood or his Smirnoff mood?"

"Shh, Scott! He'll hear you. He's already pissed about

that damned video and it didn't help that he couldn't get you on your cell."

Scott dug the shatter-faced phone out of his pocket and held it up to her. "Dead. Maybe if he hadn't broken it, I could have charged it." He wasn't technically lying. She didn't need to know that he'd seen the calls, and ignored them, *before* the phone died. "I guess I'll just run out to the store and get a new one. But, jeez, I'm flat broke." He scratched his head. "Now why would that be? Oh, right. I have to hand my pay over to my parents."

"After everything we've done for you, you'd think you could help out a little and not throw it in our faces all the time."

"Help a *little*?"

His mother shook her head and plodded down the hall to the kitchen. Scott followed, and the racket from the living room grew louder. The TV was on full blast, some talk show audience going crazy over today's guest or some new product. But there was also the whir of the . . .

"Is that the electric drill?"

His mom threw him a sharp glance, then she tilted her head to better catch the timbre of the sound. She winced. "Dammit. I told him to just leave it alone."

"What?" Scott called after her as she turned toward the living room.

"The leg splintered off the coffee table this afternoon

after he . . . bumped it. That's why he was calling. His tool-box is in the trunk with the rest of his drill bits."

"Sounds like he's got it under control."

"He does *not*. He's blotto. He'll cut off a finger or set the house on fire. Or worse."

Yeah. Worse. But she wouldn't have to experience *worse*. *Worse* was for Scott and Scott alone.

"And if you hadn't set him off, he wouldn't have taken a drink at noon, and maybe he wouldn't have kicked the damned table."

"Right, because it's all my fault."

"Jack?"

"Mom, just leave it." Scott hooked an arm around her waist. "Come on. We'll go upstairs until he's over this."

She threw off Scott's hold and stopped in the living room doorway. "What are you doing? Scott's home now. You can get your tools."

The whirring stopped. "It's about fucking time." His dad rounded the corner, red-faced, hair mussed, the cordless power drill still clenched in his fist.

Scott's mom jumped back, retreating deeper into the hallway.

"I called you at least ten times. You think you could pick up once."

"My phone was dead."

"Why can't you fucking keep it charged? I pay good money—"

"*You* pay?"

"Scott," his mom warned. He couldn't see her. The shadows in the hall were too deep and his dad too tall, but her tone said he'd crossed the line. Again.

He didn't care.

"*You?*" Scott spat.

His dad leaned back, face wrinkling in confusion.

"How about the truth, huh?" Scott took another step in his dad's direction. "Because if we want the truth, then we have to call it like it is, right? And the truth is that *I*"—he smacked his own chest—"paid for this phone. Just like *I* help Mom pay for the landline and the electricity."

"Scott!" His mom was crying now. He still didn't care. He'd been bottling up his anger too long.

"Because the truth of it is, *Father*"—he made sure to put a little extra asshole into that word—"that ever since you got your ass fired, you've been good for nothing but figuring out how high a man can raise his alcohol tolerance." Scott leaned in closer and closer, until his face, now just as red as his old man's, was right up in his dad's.

Scott never saw the blow coming.

One minute he was drawing in a breath to spew another volley of verbal punches, and the next, he was gasping to suck in any air at all. The actual pain from the punch to his gut took an extra second to register, and then it hit him all at once—huge and flavored with coppery acid.

"Jack!" Scott's mom pulled at her husband's arm, but he

yanked it from her grip, still strong even with half a gallon of the hard stuff in him.

"Shut up!" he shouted.

"Jack, please, just leave him alone."

"I said, shut—"

"No!" Scott launched at his dad. "*You* shut up." He grabbed his dad by the collar, just like the tough guys did in those old movies.

"Stop it, both of you!" His mom was sobbing, but even that didn't break through the volcano spewing hot filth up from his aching gut. Tears stopped being shocking when they were practically an everyday occurrence.

A shrill baby's cry came from upstairs. His mother sniffled. "Evie."

His baby sister's helpless voice hit Scott like an ice bath. He remembered her tiny eyelids fluttering as she flinched away from a damp dishtowel with faded Christmas trees on it. His face went slack and he dropped his right arm. His left still clenched the jersey of his dad's old tee, but he could barely feel his fingers. What the hell was he doing? Scott released the fabric and stumbled past his parents, up the stairs, and to his room.

Brian's party wasn't for a couple more hours, but Scott knew if he didn't get out of the house soon, he'd lose it. Fresh folded laundry lay in a pile on his bed. He pulled his basketball shorts from the middle of the stack, knocking the rest over in his rush. His breath still came in ragged gasps; he'd go for a run anyway. Maybe he'd pass out. Hell, maybe he'd die and his family would get to see what things were like without Scott to keep the shit from hitting the fan.

Maybe they'd even care.

17

WINNY

FIFTY-ONE MINUTES AFTER CLOSING

We're really going to do this, carry a body. I have to do a little dance to keep from stepping in the pool of blood as I take up a position near her. "Oh, God." My throat clenches, and I close my eyes and swallow hard. If I have to look, I'm going to puke. Even in the dark behind my eyelids, little flickers dance and swoop. I cannot pass out. I tense my muscles, just like before, and the threat of unconsciousness fades, but more slowly this time.

"You okay?" Scott's breath in my ear jolts my eyes open again. His worried face is right there, and a light sheen of sweat coats his pale brow. He's trying to keep it together just as much as I am.

"I guess it's my turn to help you carry something, huh?" That earns me a small smile. "Do you want the head or the feet?"

Toto turns our way again, amusement painted across his face. I take another deep breath and try to ignore him.

I can do this.

"Hold up." Scott grabs the knee-length busboy apron he'd been wearing earlier. "This'll help." Once he's draped the apron over the woman's face, he hooks her under the arms. "You take the feet. You ready?"

I nod. Tears blur my vision, but I don't bother to wipe them away. Maybe it's better this way, witnessing the world through a blurry shield. While I grab an ankle in each hand, Scott adjusts his hold. Almost immediately, one ankle slips from my grip, splashing into a puddle of blood, some of which lands, thick and cold, onto my bare shin and spatters the bottom of my dress.

Depi ou nan labatwa, fòk ou aksepte san vole sou ou. Enter the slaughterhouse, and you're going to get blood on you, my mom reminds me.

"Yeah, but I didn't think you meant literally," I mutter.

"What?"

I shake my head. "Nothing." I'm going to have to look at the woman to grab her ankle again, even though I wish I could keep my eyes closed forever. Familiar silver leather encases her foot. "Oh."

Scott freezes. "What's wrong?"

"We have on the same shoes." She might have gotten them at the same store I did, maybe even on the same day. What if we were there at the same time, at the department store in the mall, sitting on the drab sofas? Wrestling with the little slip-on nylon peds that never go on right and always pop off as soon as you take a single step. Did she like the shoes as much as I do? That is, like I did. When I get home—

If I get home.

—I'm throwing them away.

"Winny. Winsome," Scott says in a firmer tone when I don't respond.

I force my gaze to his face.

"Winny, you ready?"

I shake my head, catching another glimpse of her sandals, but I can't let myself get lost in my head again. "Yeah. Let's get this over with."

"Good. On three. Use your core when you stand. She'll be . . . I mean . . . A body is heavier than you think."

I giggle, the sound totally inappropriate, but I can't help it. "Like you have so much experience moving bodies."

He gives me a wry smile. "Right. I know."

Another burst of laughter forces its way up through my chest. "I think I'm cracking up, Scott."

"Yeah. Me, too. Ready?"

"On three. One."

"Two."

"Three," we say together as we push to our feet. Even after Scott's warning, the weight takes me by surprise, and I almost drop her again, but this time I manage to tighten my grip. I won't let her fall. I won't dishonor her that way. I'm still alive. I still have a chance. And the least I can do is see that this woman's remains are handled with respect.

Scott and I begin the shuffle to the door.

"Doesn't it sort of feel like we did this once already today?" he asks.

"Yeah. At least we don't have to try to wedge her in your trunk." Another hysterical giggle bursts from my throat, but I choke it down when Toto's laughter—a dark and ugly sound—joins mine.

He points to the clock over the espresso station. "You've got ten minutes. If you aren't back—"

"Ten minutes." Scott grunts. "Don't worry. We will be. Winny, I'll go backward." He pivots so he's the one facing the room.

"Going backward *is* a risky move," I mumble.

"Right." He winks. "But I'm pretty manly."

I try to smile, but it's hard with the prickles racing up and down my neck. Those men could be doing anything back there, creeping up on us, readying to attack. Scott's lips are a flat line, jaw tense, like he's ready to drop our burden and rush at them in a heartbeat.

"Hurry, Scott," I huff out. If I can get beyond that door, I'll be okay.

His back strikes the swinging door and a second later, he's through. The woman's body bridges us and keeps it from swinging shut again, from cutting off my view of him. From leaving me alone—even for a split second—with this room full of near-strangers and mad men. *Thank you, dead woman, whoever you are. I'll make sure we don't bang you around too much, I promise.* In another three seconds, I'm through, too. The door swishes shut and, with a sigh, the tension floods from my body. So much so that I nearly break my promise and drop her.

"Careful."

"I'm good. Which way to the stairs?"

The door swings before coming to a rest behind me. Just before it does, I hear, "She's going back to the ether! Zero, one, zero, one, one, one. Zero. That's how it goes."

I jump and duck my head like Twitch's words can physically touch me.

"Easy, Winny," Scott says.

"What's wrong with him?"

Scott raises his knee and uses it to adjust the weight of the dead woman. "Strung out. Did you see his face? The scars and scabs?"

I stare off, letting my vision fix on a poster that reads KEEP FLOORS FREE FROM SPILLS AT ALL TIMES TO AVOID FALLS, accompanied by a stick figure lying flat on the floor, arms thrown out, as though it just fell victim to accidental sloshes of coffee or puddles of green smoothie.

Or a drug-crazed murderer's bullet.

"Winny?"

"Right, scabs. Scars. I saw them. Meth? Toto said something about meth."

He nods. "Probably."

"I guess I just didn't realize it could do that, that it was . . . that bad."

"Forget him. We don't have much time." Scott and I shuffle to the left toward the stairwell. "We'll go slow. Ready?"

Sweat blooms on my face, erasing the tear tracks, but I nod. "Let's get this over with."

The air feels colder as we make our way down, slow step by slow step. There's a faint glow to guide us, but it barely cuts through the shadows. Goose bumps pop up on my bare arms, and the sweat sheening them turns cold. I shiver as I reach the last stair, almost losing my grip again.

"You okay?"

"Hold on one sec." I raise a leg to adjust my grip on the woman's silver-clad feet. Her sandal moves, giving me a view of the number stamped on the insole. I wonder if we're the same size. Tilting my head, I twist and turn her right ankle just a bit, and the gap between her arch and the shoe grows wider.

"Winny?"

I force my gaze to Scott's face. "I'm fine." The walls around us are lined with shelves. Boxes of inventory stacked all over, mops, buckets, brooms resting in one corner. "Okay, so where do we leave her? We have to make it at least a little nice."

"Let's just put her down for a minute, okay? I can't hold her anymore."

As if his words have turned up the volume on the world, my muscles are suddenly burning, and it's all I can do to keep from dropping her.

"Right here. Ready? One, two—"

"Three." I squat and lean forward, trying to keep the motion as controlled as possible. *I promise, we won't hurt you. We'll be gentle.* At the last second, I can't balance the weight, and I let her fall, but it's only a couple of inches. Not too much. She should be okay.

The tears start again. I did my best. I really did.

"Deep breaths, Winny. It's okay. We did it." Scott's voice is a little too shaky to be comforting.

"We're not done yet. We can't just leave her on the floor."

"There's nowhere else."

"Can't we at least cover her or something?" The shelves are brimming with stuff. Rifling through boxes and crates, I pass over useless crap—ketchup packets, coupons for the Flores Fiesta Sylvie and Oscar hold every May in honor of Cinco De Mayo, when they offer spiced cocoas half off, coffee filters—but there's nothing I can use to honor her.

"Winny, we don't have—"

"Help me, Scott. Please. There's time. We need to make time."

He lets out a huff of air. "Hold up. I've got something." From a shelf out of my reach, he snags a plastic bin, but the weight must be tricky because it shifts, threatening to crash onto his head.

I scoot in and help him catch it, wedging myself between him and the shelf.

"Thanks," he says.

"No problem."

He freezes for a moment, hazel eyes locked onto mine, our arms tangled over our heads. "We better hurry," he finally whispers.

"Right."

But he doesn't move. I don't, either. I wish we had time to talk about what happened last winter. I wish I could apologize, once and for all. If we survive, I'm doing it. I don't care if I end up looking like a fool. I don't think that's what will happen anyway. Scott may have been with Becky all these months, but the way his face lights up when he's with me—the way it's lit up right now—has to mean something. It *has* to, because when he looks at me like this, I can't breathe.

But then his eyes narrow as they shift to something over my shoulder.

The body.

Suddenly, I'm slammed back to reality. The weight of the bin doubles and my arms, gone noodle-y from carrying her, ache. "We'd better hurry."

"I've got the bin now. You can let go."

He maneuvers the container to the ground, pops off the lid, and unfurls a white cloth. "Extra tablecloths."

Once the woman is draped in white, I take a deep breath. *You deserve better, but we did what we could.*

"Now, the tunnels," I say.

"The tunnels." He spins, moving a few steps farther into the darkness before squatting down near the ground. "Here's the trapdoor."

If you need a way out, you'd better search for the door yourself.

This time, I've found it.

18

WINNY

Four Hours and Five Minutes Before Closing

I t has a window seat," the real estate agent had pro-claimed the day she showed the Sommervils the house in Orange, Connecticut, that would become theirs. Winny had only been eight when her family moved there from New York, and she'd squealed and run to the little nook with its huge window that looked out on the cherry tree in the front yard.

"Our daughter loves to read," her mom had said. "I'm sure she will make great use of this space."

The thing about the window seat, though, was that it was never really comfortable. The idea was nice—leisure, romance, fantasy, and escape—but no matter what cushion they bought or what pillows they arranged on the sides, Winny had never found peaceful, literary bliss there.

The older she got, the more her entire existence began to feel like that window seat. Every new expectation and

rule was just another uncomfortable corner of wood, digging into her shoulder or the back of her thigh, forcing her
to twist and bend and shift just to keep her legs from falling
asleep and her back muscles from cramping.

Soon, her parents would learn what she'd done, all
of it: the details of the parts they already knew and the
parts that they were still totally clueless about. When it all
came out, they might kick her out, but maybe it was for
the best. Winny didn't belong here anymore. Would it be
scary? Definitely. Traumatic? Probably. But she could make
it work. She had to.

She hit SEND on her cell and gazed round her room as
the phone rang, taking in the sage green walls, the shelves
holding all her treasures—her favorite books, trophies
from the science fair in junior high, the stuffed animals she
hadn't been able to part with. The little girl toys and these
walls weren't the real her. But that didn't mean leaving
them behind would be easy.

"Bella Arts and Framing," a woman said on the other
end of the line.

"Hey, it's Winny." She sat on her awkward window seat,
knees drawn up to her chest. "Listen, I was wondering . . . I
know you said summer hours would be tight, but is there
anything you can do?"

On the other end Sue, Winny's boss and the owner of
the art supply shop where she worked, sighed. "Jeez, I don't
think so, Win. I'm sorry, but we're stretched pretty tight.

Able is back from college, and I've got to make sure he gets in some shifts, too. You know how it is."

Art supplies were pricey, which had made Winny's job there, and the employee discount Sue had given her, the perfect solution to her dilemma of how to fund her gallery project without help from her parents. Her job was yet another of the things she'd been keeping from them.

"Of course," Winny said, forcing a smile into her tight voice. "If anything opens up though . . ."

"I'll call you first. So what's up?"

"Up?"

"Hello? To what do you attribute your sudden need for an increase in cash flow? Are you planning another big canvas?" The excitement in Sue's voice when they talked art usually gave Winny a thrill, but not today. "You know I'm a huge Winsome Sommervil fan. Hey! How'd your show go?"

"It was good. Really good. People seemed to like my piece."

"Of course they did. What are you working on next?"

"Nothing. It's nothing like that. I just have some . . . expenses coming up, that's all."

Sue sighed again. "You and me both. I'll let you know if any shifts open up. Promise."

19

WINNY

FIFTY-FIVE MINUTES AFTER CLOSING

The trapdoor is nothing but a hole—a black square—at Scott's feet. "Be careful not to step on it," he says. "The plywood's pretty dry. I thought it was going to give way when Becky stood on it before."

Oh, God. Becky. I almost forgot. Did I really come here tonight to see if I could start something with Scott, literally minutes after his breakup? A nausea-tinged laugh tries to burst from my throat. I sure started something all right . . . but in all the ways the scenario had played out in my head, I'd never dreamed up alone time in a basement with a dead body.

"We're really going down there, huh?" Scott asks.

"It was your idea."

He scrubs a hand through his hair. "Yeah. I'm not a huge fan of enclosed spaces."

"You don't even hesitate when it comes to carrying a corpse, but you're worried about a dark hallway?"

"A dark *underground* hallway."

I roll my eyes but manage a smile. "Why don't I go first?"

The opening reveals a ladder similar to the pull-down we use to get to our attic at home, but this one is way more rickety. The whole thing shivers as I descend rung by rung. "You sure this is safe?"

Scott's face is a silhouette in the square of yellow light above me. "Should be."

"Should be?"

He shrugs. "I only go down there when absolutely necessary, which is almost never."

"Super encouraging." With each step, the ladder protests less and less until my foot touches what can only be a dirt floor.

"There's a light fixture overhead. Feel for the pull-cord. It should only be a couple of steps from the foot of the ladder."

I spin and take two steps, but when I wave my hand, there's no sign of the string. The longer I stand here in the dark, the heavier it feels, like it's growing around me. "I can't find the cord." My voice has a hysterical quality I don't like.

"Take another couple steps. You're shorter than me."

"Okay." I let out a shrill cry as something brushes my face.

"What is it?"

"Oh, for crying out loud. Found it." The room bursts into view around me, every nook and cranny illuminated.

A second later, Scott's beside me. "There it is."

Another black opening yawns before us—the entryway to the tunnels.

"Is there a light in there?"

"It's not wired for electricity past this room, but Oscar keeps a flashlight for when he sets mousetraps. Here it is."

"Mice?" I hop away from the doorway.

"Let's hope there's still juice in the batteries." Scott gives the flashlight a shake, then clicks it on.

"How far in do you think we need to go?"

"I don't know."

"Still freaked about the enclosed space?"

"No . . . I don't think so." He smiles, mocking himself.

I hold out a hand for the flashlight. "Give it up." Without even pausing to think, I plunge into the tunnel, and it's not so bad. With armed criminals two floors up and a body above us, a stone corridor with some rodents feels like kid stuff. I keep up a fast clip, Scott tight at my heels. The first time we encounter a bend, I freeze and he bumps into me.

"Sorry," he says.

Craning my neck to peer around the corner, I aim the light into the gloom ahead, a mirror of the gloom at our backs. "I guess we keep going. How long do we have?" And how much time has passed? It feels like both hours and mere seconds.

"Five minutes. We'd better hurry."

Scott and I make six turns. The farther we go, the faster my pace. Every time we come to another bend, I expect to find the way blocked by a fall of rock or dirt or both. Every time the path stretches clear before us, a new flare of hope ignites within me. Before long we're jogging.

We're going to make it. We're going to get out, get to a phone, call for help. Save the day.

"Nine one one. Please state your emergency," the dispatcher will say. A woman. It will be a woman who answers.

I rehearse my words so I don't waste a single precious second. Later, when the cops replay the recorded conversation, they'll marvel at how clearly, concisely, and calmly I communicated the information they needed.

The passage shifts to the left, then climbs uphill.

This is it. We're almost there.

"Winny, slow down. Be careful."

I don't listen. Another corner and three steps later, I skid to a stop.

A wall of cracked concrete, fallen stone, collapsed dirt, and tangled roots blocks our path.

"No. Nononono," I whisper, but I'm not giving up. I aim my light at the barricade. "Maybe it's not too thick. Maybe we can shift some of this debris and make an opening." The beam can no more penetrate the avalanche than I can, but I sweep it back and forth, checking for a break in the mass, starting at the top where a foot-high gap separates the pile from the tunnel's stone ceiling all the way to the ground. Nothing. The opening up top is the only gap.

"That's it, then. It's over. We have to go back."

"No! What if we can squeeze through?"

"Even if you fit, those rocks could shift. You could get crushed or trapped."

"Or I can go back up there and get shot." I glare at him, daring him to try to stop me even though the thought of trying this craziness causes my throat to tighten and my chest to lock up. The tunnel is one thing, but crawling in a narrow passage of rock is totally different. I don't watch shows about cave explorers because it makes me so claustrophobic. Still, there's no way we're going back without at least checking.

"Win—"

"I said no!" My sandals aren't great climbing shoes, but I search for footholds and gain an inch, then a few more. The mound shifts beneath my feet when I'm halfway to the ceiling, and I skid down several inches, scraping my elbow on some jagged rock.

"God! Careful."

"Almost there." Arm burning, I make it the last few feet and peer into the opening.

"What do you see?"

Although the gap offers close to two feet of space at this end, it narrows down to only a couple of inches in several places before the way is blocked entirely. The mound must come to an end at some point. It could be just beyond the glow of my light or miles from here. Either way, it's too far for us to reach.

There's no choice. We have to go back. What was any of it for? Sneaking away for the phone? Moving the poor dead woman?

Scott pulls me into a hug when I reach the ground. "You tried. At least now we know."

I hug him back like there's no such thing as rejection and angry ex-girlfriends. What do those things matter with death hanging around upstairs? And right now I need this, to feel close to someone, cared for. Maybe because this may be my last chance ever, the pull to raise my head and brush my lips against his is almost too strong to resist. His hands move over my back, and he brushes the nape of my neck with his thumb, making me shiver.

"We'd better head back. We can't wait any longer." Scott tightens his arms around me.

He's right. We're running out of time. For Toto's deadline. For everything. Around us, the minutes tick faster and faster, and they drag us along with them, my future growing shorter and shorter. Forever doesn't even exist anymore. I've wasted enough of my life, wasted chances. The explanation I've been waiting to give him dances at the tip of my tongue. "Scott?"

"Yeah?"

I suck in a breath to say the words that have been

hounding me since the winter, then hesitate. What if I've been reading all of his signals wrong and his feelings for me are truly gone? Sure, he and Becky are broken up now, but I could still be too late.

Again.

Scott's not mine, but I can't lose him, not now. Not during this nightmare.

Greet the Devil, and he'll eat you. Don't greet him, and he'll eat you, anyway, my mom says in my head.

Before I make up my mind, he drops his arm. "Seriously, we'd better hurry. They'll come looking to see what's taking so long soon."

"Yeah." I nod and point the flashlight back toward the darkness we came through, the darkness that will lead us to the last place in the world I want to go.

As we retrace our steps, the hope that had grown nearly to bursting fizzles out, replaced by dread that oozes and seeps into the crevices of my soul, drowning any remaining belief that we can survive this night.

Barely bothering to aim the flashlight, I stumble along, bouncing off the centuries-old stone. I nearly miss a bend and careen into a wall, but I catch myself and change course before I can do any real damage.

"Here. Let me go first." Scott gently takes the flashlight from my hand.

When I straighten my fingers, my muscles ache, and I realize I've been clutching the barrel like my life depended on it. And then I want to laugh, because my life *does* depend on it.

The trip down the tunnels had felt like it stretched for ages, but the return one is over before I'm ready. Not that I'll ever be ready. The light from the room at the bottom of the ladder comes into view as we round the last bend, and we're back.

Scott pauses, one hand on the ladder, and cocks his head. "Shit!"

"What?" But I hear it, too. Toto's voice.

Calling us.

If any of those guys comes down to the basement and finds it empty—except the body, of course—who knows what they'll do.

Scott pulls himself through the opening and reaches to help me up. By the time we lower the trapdoor back into place—the hinges letting out a tortured creak—Toto is at the top of the stairs. His voice carries to us, loud and clear.

"We're coming!" Scott calls.

"Get your asses up here." His glare greets us from the top of the stairwell.

"I told you," Scott says, "we're coming."

I flinch away from Toto's grasp when I reach the ground floor. "Don't touch me." Pushing past him, I make my way into the café, back to where this whole nightmare started.

20

SCOTT

Four Hours and Five Minutes Before Closing

"Y ou're kidding me, man," Scott said to the sweaty thirty-something standing across the counter from him.

"Sorry." The tech shrugged. "It's cheaper to replace one of these than fix it." He shook Scott's pitiful phone, and an ominous rattle sounded from within. "Hear that? It takes a major event to knock something loose in there. These things have no moving parts at all." The phone buzzed in the guy's hand and he passed it back to Scott. "Looks like you're getting a call. At least the phone function still works."

"Yeah, I'm a lucky guy." His dad was calling. Again. Scott swiped it to voice mail. "So, we're in agreement that it's well and truly fucked, but what about data stored on it? Is there any way to retrieve something that got erased when the thing got damaged? I mean, they're always warning people that nothing is ever one hundred percent deleted on these things, right?"

"Was that file open when it fell?"

Scott didn't bother to correct the guy and inform him that it had been hurled across the room or that it had landed on a tile floor. "Yeah, it was playing."

The bell over the door rang as a trio of kids came in and clustered around the counter. "You guys have the new Galaxy?" a boy no older than thirteen asked.

The hot lava tried to flood Scott's brain. "So, the video?"

"Be right with you kids," the tech said before turning back to Scott. "You have two options. You could send it back to the manufacturer and see if there's anything they can do for you, but they can't, so don't bother."

Scott forced his voice to stay calm. "Okay, then we'll go with option number two. Which is?"

"There are a few different apps you can try. They retrieve lost files. If your video was running when the phone was damaged, it could be that it just got deleted. Maybe when your fingers slipped, they hit the wrong button. That's the best I can do, dude. Sorry."

"No, I understand. Thanks. What are those apps?"

The guy scribbled a few names on a sticky note, and Scott shoved it into his pocket as he headed out the door and back to his car.

"Please let these be free," Scott said as he searched the app store for the first one on the tech dude's list. His battery was getting low, and as the program downloaded and installed, the charge dropped from twenty-seven percent to twenty-four. His dad called again. Scott ignored it—again—and ran the first video-retrieval scan. After about ninety seconds, his display lit up with random images and GIFs, but not the video he was looking for. His charge dropped another couple units. He tried the next app. And the next. With his power hovering at seven percent, he waited for the last scan to run then checked the results.

More GIFs. A dog video Becky had sent him the week before. And there it was. A screenshot containing the image of a box of generic rice puffs.

"Holy shit!" Scott tapped the icon and a dialog box popped up, asking him for $24.99 to pull the video from wherever data hid when it went missing. "Fuck." Did he have enough in his account to cover that? Back inside the store, a kid barely into puberty was shelling out bucks for an upgrade, and Scott wasn't sure he could make an in-app purchase.

He hit AUTHORIZE PAYMENT and held his breath.

A green box and a check mark appeared.

He had it! Just to be sure, he hit the GALLERY icon and there it was, in the video folder. A slow smile spread across his face. Scott was back in business.

Then a red battery flashed on his screen. *Warning, battery is critically low.* No problem. He'd go home and charge this bad boy up. It was all good.

And then the whole display went dark.

21

SCOTT

ONE HOUR AND EIGHT MINUTES AFTER CLOSING

Something must have happened while we were exploring the tunnels, because Toto is losing it with Ryan. "This is your fault, man. All your fault!"

Ryan holds up his hands. "Just calm down, okay? Will you listen to me for a minute?"

"We're dead, you realize that? Nah. Not me. *You're* dead. *You*, motherfucker, cause when those guys come in here, I'm telling them who they're really after."

"Toto. For God's sake . . ."

They continue arguing.

"What happened?" I ask Oscar as I slip onto one of the stools.

"He called the dudes he owes," Oscar whispers from the corner of his mouth. "Asked if he can get them the money tomorrow."

"So he has another way of getting it? Other than your register?"

"Yeah." Oscar gives a dark laugh. "He has my bank account. But it sounds like those guys didn't go for it."

"Why?" Winny asks.

"They don't want to wait until tomorrow, I think," Oscar says.

"What about an ATM?" Winny asks.

Oscar laughs. "Sweetie, you can't get the kind of money they need from an ATM. The guy did give them a little more time tonight, though."

"Instead of midnight, they now have until 3 a.m.," Pavan says.

"More time, but that's good, isn't it?" Winny asks. "They can maybe get their money some other way?"

"I don't think it matters to them, I'm afraid," Pavan says.

None of us dare to look at our captors, but they're not even trying to keep their discussion under wraps now.

"I just don't get it," Ryan is saying. "I mean, if they can have the money they want, why not give us the extra time?"

"'Cause they think we're bluffing. And hey, either we give it to them, or they get rid of us and put someone better in our place."

"They wouldn't do that."

"They wouldn't, huh? They've been looking for an excuse to get rid of us ever since you got your ass fired from this place and our revenues dropped."

"But we've still got plenty of clients," Ryan says. "Twitch's college friends—computer geeks—and the yoga moms, doing their shopping at the all-natural grocery store."

"If that was enough, why do you think they've been all over you to get your sister to sell this place? We were raking it in back then. I'm telling you, man, we've been on the outs with the Chef and Aaron for a while. Why do you think Shell and I are skipping town?"

"What does it mean," I whisper to Oscar, "that they're saying all this in front of us?"

He shakes his head, then stares at the floor again.

We are seriously low on options at this point. We can't get out through the tunnels and our captors have the only exit from the café blocked. There's the door off the back hall, but it's not like they're just going to let us saunter out that way. Even if we made a run for it, they'd be on us in two ticks. Our final hope is my wrecked lump of plastic sluggishly charging below the register.

"Fuck," I mutter.

"Fuck," Toto echoes.

Ryan holds up his hands. "Will you just listen? I've got a plan, okay."

"What plan?"

Ryan's face is red; both men are sweating. Hell, we're all sweating, with the exception of Winny and Sylvie. Twitch, who hasn't budged from his spot in the corner, is drenched.

Then again, he's done a shit-ton of meth, so I guess he's the only one with a real excuse.

"Okay, what's this plan?" Toto asks.

Ryan pulls him around the corner of the L-shaped counter, where they're partially obscured by a tall display shelf that faces the front door. If we can't see them, they can't see us. I hope.

I slip off my stool and duck.

"What are you doing?" Sylvie mouths, eyes wide.

"My cell," I mouth back.

Ryan and Toto remain focused on their conversation. So far, so good. I crawl behind the counter from the far-end pass-through, giving me a perfect profile view of their show, and giving them a full view of me if either one of them so much as glances in my direction. The tighter I stay pressed against the counter, the better.

"Listen," Ryan says. "Why don't we use this situation to our advantage?"

I wince when the floor creaks under my knee, but neither seems to notice.

"How?" Toto asks.

"You want a clean break, right?"

"You know I do."

"Think about it. Even if we get the Chef and Aaron their money, what guarantee do we have that they'll just let us walk out the door?"

Toto clenches his jaw and flares his nostrils as he takes a shaky breath. "If we do what we're supposed to do, then the Chef has no reason *not* to let us walk out that door. They think we're still working for them. By the time they're any wiser, Shell and me will be gone."

"And where does that leave me?"

"You can keep sucking up to them and do your thing, man. You don't need me."

"True, but that doesn't mean they'll like seeing you go. And you don't think they can't track you down?" Ryan gives Toto a long, hard stare. "Think this through. Take your time. I can wait."

"You can't know that."

"True, I can't know anything for sure, but . . ."

"But it could be. Motherfucker." Toto knocks a glass sugar jar off the counter, which explodes against the black and white tile like a bomb going off. To my right, Winny lets out a small scream, and I scramble back in case Toto spotted me. I get lucky. This time.

I need to move, to finish what I crawled back here to do, so I can get out of the danger zone.

I reach the section of the counter below the register. Staying low, I grope for my phone. A moment later, the familiar plastic casing rests in my hand, but the display shows no signs of life.

Nothing.

It's off, stupid. I'll have to power it back up, but that means a start-up tone. The guys will hear it from here.

"If you want to be sure, to be really, truly sure you and Rochelle will be safe," Ryan says, "you need to follow through on this. You know it, and I know it."

"So, let's say you're right. What are you thinking?" Toto asks.

"Call Aaron back, tell him that you've got his boss's money, but he needs to come here to collect. Tell him it's nice and private, no chance of being seen. Hell, make him think if he wants to bump us off, that you're giving him the perfect location to do it."

"What's to stop him from doing just that?" Toto says. "And don't say 'bump off.' This isn't the mafia."

"We'll be ready to ambush him when he gets here," Ryan insists.

"You know damn well he isn't coming without backup."

"And we'll have our own backup."

"What backup?"

"Them," Ryan says.

Them? Them. Us.

They drop their voices to a whisper, and I strain to catch anything more. It's no good. I inch farther along the counter, just a little closer, while letting my thumb hover over the tiny plastic button that might mean the difference between getting out of here alive or not getting out of here at all.

"Are you really prepared to do that?" Toto asks. "Your own blood?"

Ryan's response is nothing more than a mumble.

I need to decide. Wincing, I dig my thumbnail into the button while using my hands to insulate the phone speaker.

". . . if it works . . ." Toto is saying.

"Of course it will work," Ryan replies.

Though I was afraid the electronic tune would be a dead giveaway—literally—the lack of any tone at all makes my knees give out, nearly spilling me from my crouch. I check the display again.

For the first time tonight, it's me who wants to cry.

The phone's still dead.

More time. It just needs more time. That's what I tell myself, anyway. I nestle it back among the junk Sylvie has amassed in the five or so years she's owned this place and prepare for the return trip.

"If we agree on this, we have to go through with it, no matter what," Toto says. "There's no changing your mind at the last minute."

My time is running out. I need to move, slip back around to the front before these assholes notice me, but I'm just as riveted by Ryan's speech as Toto is. They're literally deciding our fate right now. I can't get my legs to budge.

"What the . . . ?"

Ryan's seen me. They both have.

"Oh my God, Scott!" Sylvie shouts.

I don't even manage to get to my feet before Toto has his gun aimed in my direction. "Get out here or die."

Every muscle in my body goes numb and my entire world is reduced to one black point, the dark eye of the gun barrel staring me down.

Becky's voice plays in my mind: *If you want to be everyone's martyr, fine, but I'm done suffering with you.*

"You're really asking for it tonight, aren't you?" Toto lowers the gun. Inclining his head toward Ryan, he says, "You've got him to thank for being alive right now, because I swear to God, if I didn't need your ass . . . Now, get back over there."

Winny wraps her arms around me when I rejoin them. She's trembling. "I thought he was going to kill you."

"Any luck?" Oscar asks.

I shake my head. "But I know what their plan is," I whisper. *You just jump . . . everyone's martyr.*

"We only caught snatches," Oscar says. "What are they going to do? It didn't sound good."

Before I answer, Toto and Ryan are back.

"Okay, let's do it," Toto says. "We need more firepower, though." He turns toward our group huddled in the corner. "You got any guns around here?"

"What?" Sylvie cries. "No!"

"No," Oscar agrees, but something about the tone of his voice makes me wonder. He catches me studying his face and nods, sharp and fast.

"What about Rochelle's dad?" Ryan asks Toto.

"What do you think? Man, I'm supposed to be getting *out*, and now you're talking about pulling Shell *in*? She's going to be pissed as hell. And her dad won't do it for nothing."

"We have the cash from the register. It's not enough, but it's something. We can get the rest to him later."

Toto considers and nods. "It's the best we've got. All right, then. We have ourselves a plan."

"What plan?" Pavan asks me.

Sylvie's crying again. Or maybe she never stopped.

"Scott, what did they say?" Oscar hisses into my ear.

"They're going to use us." All eyes are on me, but it's Winny's that I lock on. Winny to whom I deliver this news, though my skin crawls at the thought of laying this on her shoulders.

"What?" Oscar asks.

"As their army. Against their enemy or rival or whatever."

"What's wrong with you?" Sylvie shouts at her brother.

"Shh, Sylvie!" Oscar puts a hand on her shoulder, but she throws it off.

"Why bother being quiet? They won't kill us now anyway. They need us to be their henchmen."

"So you heard?" Toto says with a grin. "Welcome to the crew. You're gonna have our backs. Or, I should say, our fronts, cause you're gonna be on the forward line when the Chef and his men get here to collect. I'm expanding my business, and you're my helpers. And who knows, if you don't get killed, I might let you live. We'll see."

"This is ridiculous," Sylvie says. "We don't know how to use guns. This will never work."

"Your hubby there is ex-military," Ryan says.

"And he can barely stand because of you," she says through gritted teeth.

"We'll prop him up, don't worry," Toto says.

"What about the rest of us? We're not exactly trained here."

"At such close range, you'll do better than you think," Toto says with a smirk. "Besides, all you've got to do is keep them distracted long enough for Ryan and me to do the real work."

"Ryan, you don't have to do this," Sylvie says. "We can figure something out. Just end this now. You're not this person. You're not a killer. Not yet. Please, you've got to snap out of it, or else you're no better than our father. If you don't, you're worse than he ever was."

For a second, Ryan pauses, and a blank expression drops over his face, first flat, then . . . scared? Uncertain? He glances around the room, taking in the splotch of blood on the floor, Twitch still holding court in his corner, before landing on Winny's wide-eyed face. Doubt. He's doubting his plan, this whole situation. Toto must see it because he tenses and leans toward Ryan, taking a breath like he's about to say something more. The five-year-old in me, the one who wrote Christmas lists to Santa and believed that everything would be just fine because Mommy and Daddy wouldn't let anything bad happen to little Scotty—ever—whispers in my ear that there's hope. They won't really do it, and we'll walk out of here.

It'll be over.

But the grown-up Scott snags that little twerp by the shoulder and lays down the brutal truth: dreams don't come true, only nightmares.

When I see Ryan staring at Sylvie again, I know the decision's been made. I know, because I've seen this expression before. It visits me in my own bathroom mirror whenever I have a run-in with my dad.

"Hey, Silv. I took a hit for something you did way back in the day. And I've been taking that hit over and over ever since." Ryan's voice is ice. "I guess it's your turn now. As they say, payback's a bitch."

22

WINNY

With Scott's car still idling in her driveway, Winny lugged her painting toward the house, head spinning and stomach churning. With every scrape of canvas on cement, every click of her heels, she chanted a song of guilt: *I kissed Scott. I kissed Scott.*

Janey was always on her to take matters into her own hands, but even Janey wouldn't have suggested she kiss another girl's boyfriend. What the hell had she been thinking? Nothing, that's what. He'd done something so nice for her, and she repaid him by crossing the line.

That must be her new MO these days.

But under the guilt was something else, a fluttery warmth. Had he felt what she felt? What she'd been feeling all these months since the day they went to the game together?

His gaze burned the back of her neck, and she wanted

to look back, to read the expression on his face, and figure out what this all meant. But she tripped again, and now she imagined him laughing at her. *There goes Winny with her frumpy bun and her professional suit and the frickin' huge-ass painting that keeps slipping from her sweaty hands.*

Like *that girl* could compete with a cheerleader. Of course he'd chosen Becky, with her long blonde waves and blue eyes and perfect boobs.

But when they'd kissed . . . The fluttery warmth returned. He must have felt it, too. He had to have.

When Winny reached the top of the steps, the pull to look back won out, but the driveway was empty. He was gone. The fire in her straining neck muscles spread to her face.

She'd waited too long, and now she'd never know. Just like when he asked her out. As far as Scott was concerned, Winny was always too damned late.

Wiping sweat from her brow, she shoved the door open and dragged the canvas inside, where she left it propped up against the coat closet door. No point hiding it now. That cat had shredded the bag to bits. She kicked off her heels and shuffled to the kitchen on throbbing feet. It took more effort than it should have to move her leaden limbs, yet her brain raced, and her nerves jostled together like birds of prey around some choice roadside pickings.

She needed something to help her out of this funk—coffee and a workout or tea and a nap. She could just stand here and stare at the wall, but that would never wipe the memory of her reckless behavior a minute before from her mind or put her in the right mood for Brian's party tonight.

Okay, tea for sure and probably the nap.

She paused on the way to the stove and the kettle, spotting a sheet of paper lying on the gray granite counter top. When she wasn't experiencing the most intense adrenaline crash ever, that was the first place she checked when she got home. How many pieces of bad news had she received via notes deposited there for her to find in unsuspecting moments? Including her parents' verdict from several months back on her request to try for a spot in the art show today, the one she'd participated in even though they'd said no.

For a moment, she debated simply not reading it, but that wouldn't work. Not knowing would be worse, somehow.

Winsome, her mother had written in her blocky handwriting. *After our talk earlier, I began to wonder how you managed to find time for your EMT course, your gallery project, and your other school commitments. We know the outcome of your studies and school activities, so that just left the EMT course. I inquired with the administrator and she told me that you never signed up for the second part of the series. I have two words for you: you're grounded.*

Grounded? They had to be kidding her with this.

"No more," Winny said, slapping her palm against the

counter top. Sure, she'd lied to her parents and disobeyed their orders, but they'd forced her to do it. They treated her like a little kid, like someone who couldn't make her own decisions. Like someone without goals or passions of her own. Or a brain. As if they didn't even see her as a real person.

Winny stomped out of the kitchen and upstairs to her room. She shuffled past a pile of letters—exactly eleven— sitting on top of her desk. Eleven letters of acceptance from eleven schools her parents deemed worthy of their daughter and her future career. But she ignored those, going instead for the letter waiting in her top desk drawer. The one her parents hadn't seen. The crisp white paper was addressed with the proper postage already fixed in place.

No thoughts flickered through Winny's mind as she made her way back downstairs. No thoughts could fit in there with her anger elbowing out every other thing. She didn't hesitate, not even once, as she marched down the street, her flip-flops smacking the pavement. Only when she reached the mailbox did she pause, her hand, clutching the letter, trembling over the slot.

Cold fear diluted her anger. If she dropped this letter in the box, that would be it. She'd be cut off. On her own. No college tuition, room and board gone. No car to borrow and no one to pick her up if she needed a ride.

No place to live.

"I don't care," she announced to the empty street.

Her future, her way, was in this envelope, and there was only one way to make sure she got there to live it.

Before the letter disappeared into the dark mouth of the mailbox, she caught sight of her own sweeping script: *Dean Hollis*. The flap snapped back into place with a satisfying clunk.

Smiling, she hummed "Für Elise" all the way home.

23

WINNY

Ryan, this is between me and you," Sylvie says. "Please don't punish them for my mistake. I left you, I get it. Dad was a monster, and I wasn't there to protect you, but you don't get what it was like for me, living in that house every day."

"What are they talking about?" I ask Oscar, but he only shakes his head.

"I don't know? I don't *know*?" Ryan spits in Sylvie's face. "Did you really think you could just leave like that and Dad wouldn't take it out on someone?"

"I thought, maybe if I was gone, it would . . . he would . . . things would be better for everyone. I was wrong. I'm sorry."

"Yeah, I'd say you were wrong. First off, he beat me because you left. Like that was my fault. Then, any time the wind so much as blew wrong, I got it again. Do you know what that's like?"

I try to imagine Ryan as a kid, little, vulnerable, the victim. I try to imagine him feeling like I feel right now or with the bruise Scott bears on his cheek from when Toto hit him, put there by someone bigger and stronger than him, but I can't. All I see is his rage-reddened face and the way his fist tightens around the gun as he breathes hard into his sister's face.

"I'm so, *so* sorry," Sylvie says.

"Sorry doesn't even come close to being good enough. But, you can make it up to me now. Last time pays for all, right, sis?"

"You scumbag asshole!" Oscar bolts to his feet and manages a single step before Ryan has his gun on him.

"Go ahead, Oscar. Tempt me. Make me do it." Rage wrinkles his forehead, but Oscar stands down, and I let my muscles relax.

Ryan turns to Sylvie. "Too bad. If you ask me, your dear husband is on his last leg, anyway. Killing him might be a mercy."

"I stood up for you!" she shouts. "I made excuses. All these years."

"Maybe if you hadn't fired me, we wouldn't be here."

"Are you kidding me?" she asks. "Oscar was going to call the cops when he found your stash here, but I talked him out of it."

Ryan puts his hands over his heart. "And I'm touched. Really I am."

"Shut it, all of you," Toto says. "We don't have all night."

"You go for the guns, and I'll stay here and keep watch over these guys," Ryan suggests.

"Who's in charge here? No way I'm leaving you behind. How do I know you're not gonna run away the minute I'm out that door?"

"You know I wouldn't turn on you."

"Really?" Toto smirks and raises an eyebrow. "Last time I checked, you're the guy who came up with the brilliant plan to let his sister fight his battles for him. How can I trust a guy who'd do something like that?"

"Toto—"

"I said no. You're coming with me."

"Okay, and who's going to make sure they stay put?"

Toto shoots his glance toward Twitch, who looks like he's starting to nod off. "Oh, hell no." He crosses the room and bats the sleeping guy's shoulder.

Ryan gapes at the pair. "Are you even thinking right now?"

"Come on, Twitch. Wake up," Toto says, ignoring Ryan.

Twitch startles awake, shoving the table in front of him a couple of inches in his rush to get to his feet. "Yeah. Yeah, Toto. I'm here. What do you need? I got you. No worries."

Toto grins at Ryan. "See? No worries."

"And how do we know these guys won't pull anything while we're gone? It's not like he's at his best right now."

Twitch has started up a game on his cell and seems way into it.

"Twitch," Toto barks, "put that thing away and focus."

"Sure, sure." Twitch fiddles with his phone, and the electronic beeps stop.

At least, some of them do. The beeps continue, but not from Twitch's phone. The little tune is coming from near the register.

"Now what?" Toto storms toward the noise. "Are you kidding me with this?"

"Shit," Scott mutters.

Toto emerges from behind the counter with Scott's phone in his hand, a grin on his face. "Looks like someone is in the doghouse with his daddy. 'You good for nothing, you better call me now,'" Toto reads. "Dang! Listen to this one. 'If you think I'm supporting your lazy ass anymore, you're mistaken. Get home or you're out on the street.'"

Scott's face goes red, and he clenches his fists. I want to do something for him, but I have no idea how to help.

"Scott, my boy," Pavan says so softly, it's barely a whisper. "Just let it go. Relax."

It was all for nothing. Sneaking downstairs. My mission to plug the phone in. Carrying that poor woman. I stare at the blotch of blood that splashed on my skirt when I let her foot slip from my grasp. My cardigan is almost long enough to cover the stain. It might if I pull it all the way down. But as soon as I move, the sweater shifts and the blood leers at me again, mocking me for ever thinking we could escape.

"They didn't call anyone, did they?" Ryan tries to read the display over Toto's shoulder.

"No calls for the last couple of hours. We're good." Toto tucks the phone into his pocket, then claps his hands together. "All right. Do we have any volunteers?"

"Volunteers for what?" Pavan asks.

"Who wants to go for a little ride?"

"Aw, Toto," Ryan says. "I don't think that's a good idea."

"You said it yourself. We need to make sure these guys don't try anything. We'll take someone along for insurance. If anything happens to Twitch while we're gone, their guy will get it."

The pair regard us all clustered together. I try to make myself as small as possible, but Toto's eyes land on me anyway.

"You," he says, coming toward me.

"Winny!" Scott tries to pull me back, but Toto tugs me out of his grasp.

"Just sit back down, kid," Ryan says.

"Please, take me instead," Sylvie pleads. "You're pissed at me, right? I'll go."

"We'll take the girl." Toto's fingers dig into my skin. I think about struggling, but then I see the gun tucked in the waistband of his jeans and let him lead me away.

Electronic music I recognize from a popular game app

comes from Twitch's corner. I can't wrap my brain around how a guy who killed someone a mere hour ago can be sitting here now, playing a game with candy and hearts and sparkly fireworks.

"I told you, put that thing away." Toto snatches Twitch's phone.

"Sorry, Toto. Sorry. Sorry. Sorrysorrysorry."

While Toto is busy with Twitch, I retreat to Scott's side. "I don't think I can do this." My teeth are chattering. "I can't go with them."

"Just do whatever they tell you to, okay?" Oscar says. "But if you have a chance to run, you take it, Winny. You run. Don't stop until you're sure they're off your tail, okay?"

"I can't."

"Listen." Oscar maneuvers me to face him, both hands on my shoulders. "I'm going to try something while you're gone."

"What?" Sylvie looks like she might burst with tension. "No one's trying anything. Please. I can't take anyone else getting hurt."

He shushes her. "Winny, when you get back, there's a chance we will have taken Twitch out. Be ready for that, okay? Be ready to run or duck or hide."

"What are you saying?" Pavan asks.

"I'm saying I have a gun hidden in the office. If we can get to it, we may be able to take Twitch out. He's barely even here. I think we can do it."

"That will work," Ryan says to Toto, before they return their attention to our group. I try to shrink behind Scott and Pavan.

"Get her," Toto orders Ryan. "Now, all of you, listen to me. We're going to call every ten minutes. If Twitch tells us you tried anything, the girl's dead. You understand? If he doesn't answer by the time the voice message comes on, the girl's dead. If anyone else answers, the girl's dead."

"How do we know you won't just kill her as soon as you walk out that door?" Scott snaps.

A gold glint flashes from within Toto's cocky smile. "Because we need her. You're all official members of my gang, remember? Your membership might be short, but it sure won't be boring. Don't forget, when I call, if anything's not as it should be . . ."

"But you took my phone," Twitch points out. "Can I have it back?"

"I don't trust you with this thing. You can have this one." Toto shoves Scott's phone across the table.

Twitch frowns at the cracked screen. "This thing's on its last legs. I bet I can't even get anything good to work on it."

"Exactly. Kid, write down your number for me."

"Okay. I need a pen and paper. There's some by the register."

"Go ahead," Toto says, "but be quick."

Behind the counter, Scott bends low to scribble something. He tears the sheet and comes back around and hands the paper to Toto. A second later, Scott's phone rings when Toto tries the number. "Good. You keep doing just what we say like that, and maybe you'll be okay." He turns to Ryan. "Are we ready?"

Scott wraps his arms around me as though he's hugging me, shoring me up. "If you see anyone who can help," he whispers in my ear, "give them that."

"Okay," Toto says. "Enough of that little lovefest. Let's go get us some guns."

As I follow Toto and Ryan out the door, my hand sneaks into my pocket and I find a little reassurance as my fingers brush a slip of paper Scott put there.

A horse with ten masters will die tied to its post.

Except where I'm going, there are no other masters. From now on, I'm on my own.

24

SCOTT

D on't worry," Winny said. "It's not heavy."

"If you say so." Scott eyed the canvas doubtfully.

"If we carry it together, it won't be too bad."

"If you say so."

"Stop saying that!" She laughed.

"Fine. Okay, seriously. Let's do this."

They each took an end of the painting. A rainbow of colors swirled across the stiff fabric. That's what he always liked about Winny's art; she used color, a lot of it, and texture. His fingertips rested against raised clumps of paint.

"It gives the piece depth," she'd explained once.

"Be careful," she said now. "The doorway."

He almost dropped his end as she jerked hers sideways. "Shit! It might not be heavy, but it's awkward as hell." Readjusting his grip, he just missed slamming his end into the polished molding of the gallery door and ended up cracking his elbow against it instead. He hissed with pain.

She peeked around the frame. "Sorry! You okay?"

"I'll live. Going backward is a risky move, but I'm pretty manly."

Giggling, she said, "I was going to offer to swap, but not now."

After bumping into a dude passing by the storefront, and Winny tripping over a crack in the sidewalk, they managed to carry the painting the remaining three feet to Scott's car.

"It may be a little big," he said, eying his family's mid-sized sedan.

"Does the backseat fold down? I bet we can get it in that way."

"Yeah, hold on."

"It still looks tight," she said when the trunk had been prepped. "I guess there's only one way to tell if it will fit."

"I'll go inside and pull," he said. "You push from out here."

Despite their twisting and turning, the painting kept getting lodged where the wheel well narrowed the space.

"Maybe Jackie can give us some twine or something. We can tie it to the roof."

"Nah, we've got this. Push really hard. Dig in with your feet."

"I am." She grunted. Turning around, she leaned in with her back, shoving as hard as she could with her heels. Then something shifted, and Winny flew backward.

Scott shouted from inside the car as she slammed against the edge of the canvas with a thump.

"Ow." Her cry of pain turned into a stream of laughter. And one snort. She clamped her hands over her mouth.

"You said it," Scott muttered.

"Oh my God. That really hurt." She was still laughing as she regained her balance. "Is it in? I'm afraid to look."

"It's in. Now, we just have to figure out how to get it out again."

"Are you okay?" she asked as she settled into the passenger seat.

"Just banged my head a little."

"Oh no!" She shot out a hand, resting it on his. He tried to hide his intake of breath at her touch, at her warmth.

Get it together, Bradley, his track coach chimed in.

He gave her hand a quick squeeze and forced himself to break the contact. "I'm fine, Win. No worries. But I'll say this, you pack a lot of power."

She cracked up again. Her giggles finally tapered off into awkward silence as they rode along. Scott searched for something to talk about, but the only words swimming in his head were *I'm sorry*. Though he had no idea why he felt the need to apologize. Maybe because he'd blown her off that day after the football game? Or because he'd asked her out when she was clearly not interested? Or because he'd decided to date Becky?

Winny's house was quiet when they pulled up in front, the two-story structure welcoming them proudly from its spot in the sun as though it had nothing to hide. In there, closet doors were probably all closed—totally free from skeletons—no hangers sticking out at odd angles, no clothes in a pile on the floor or on the bed or still in the dryer waiting to be plucked out. Meals probably were served on time. Of course they were, because the fridge was always full, and it always worked.

"All right." Winny scooted out and popped the trunk. Scott twisted around in the front seat.

"How about you let me push this time?" he suggested when she'd positioned herself out there in the June sun.

"If you say so." Then her cheeks flushed and her lips spread into a teasing little smile, causing the temperature of his blood to jump a notch or two.

It was way easier getting the painting out of the car than it had been getting in, but the enormous tearing sound it made, that was new.

"Oh, Scott!" Winny eyed something in the trunk.

"What? Did we mess the painting up?" She had it leaned against the back driver's side door, and only one corner of the frame showed from his spot up front.

"No, but we put a good dig in your car's lining." She bent lower and explored the dark interior with one hand.

"I think it tore a little. And the plastic part over the wheel is dented, too."

Wonderful. Just what he needed. His dad rarely emerged from his alcohol-infused den, so he wasn't likely to discover this, but if he did, Scott knew he'd have some major trouble coming his way. No need to freak out, though. Maybe it wasn't that bad. He scrambled out of the car and around back to see.

It was that bad.

He sucked in a breath, but when he'd had a good long look, he shrugged. "Nobody will notice."

They would, and that rip was destined to get bigger, but he couldn't bring himself to tell her that. It wouldn't do him any good to share his suspicions, and today had been special for her. It should stay that way.

She stared at the damage, chewing her cheek. "Look, if I can help, maybe pay to repair it . . ."

He swatted the offer away. "Like I said, no worries."

Winny stood lingering in the driveway, an arm's length away from him with the sun slanting through the leaves of a cherry tree in her front yard, the light picking up little flecks of glitter in the gloss covering her lips. He'd been about to kiss her back there in the gallery. But that was a terrible idea. He couldn't do that to Becky. Then why was he thinking about it again? Right now?

Winny surprised him by holding up her arms for a goodbye hug. She shuffled closer, and he braced for her sweet scent and gentle warmth. They hadn't hugged that day after the football game. If they had, he would never have been able to let her go.

"Thanks for your help, Scott." Her words vibrated against his shoulder, her breath warming the fabric of his shirt and the skin beneath.

"Any time, Win," he whispered.

"You really saved me today. I owe you one."

"Nah." His words rustled a loose strand of her hair as a breeze shifted the leaves in the cherry tree behind them. "You don't owe me a thing."

"Still, I want to repay you if I can, someday." She pulled back but didn't break the hug. Instead, she paused and pressed a kiss to his cheek. Before she could move away, he leaned in closer, just a tiny bit. And maybe she did, too. Just a tiny bit more. He couldn't say for sure, but her lips touched his, and she drew in a surprised breath, but didn't move. Neither did he.

They were frozen, his heart racing. Her hand lingered on his arm. One of his still rested on her back. His eyes refused to stay open, and his mind shouted contradictory orders peppered with fun facts, like the one about his girlfriend, poor Becky, who in six whole months had never made him feel what Winny was making him feel right now. The conflicting data continued to flood him, but Winny jerked out of his grasp before he could figure it out.

"Oh my God. I'm so sorry, Scott."

Backing up—one step, two steps, three—she made the decision for him, even though he still didn't know if it was the one he wanted.

He focused on the muscles that controlled his lungs and sucked in a breath. "No, it's me, my fault." Of course it was. He'd been thinking of doing this very thing not a half hour before. All she'd needed was a friend, and he'd gone and dragged her into his own drama. She might have blown him off in the winter, but that didn't mean she deserved to have him mess with her head now. Even back then, when she'd turned down his offers to see if they could be more than friends, she did it in true Winny form, sweet as cherry–vanilla ice cream, like she really felt bad about hurting him. For a while, he even tried to convince himself that she meant it when she told him she hoped that they could go out sometime, just the two of them.

His feelings might be all tangled, but he couldn't let any of that mess trap her. Or hurt Becky.

"Seriously. Don't even worry. I'm glad I could help. Want me to . . . ?" He inclined his head toward her canvas.

"No! No, I can get it from here." Though it was awkward, she began dragging her masterpiece toward the front door, and her sheer determination to manage the rest by herself told him everything he needed to know: she couldn't wait to be rid of him. With every faltering step, every readjustment of the canvas, every huffed breath, whatever lingering hope that someday they might try again was gone. Maybe that's what her kiss had meant: goodbye. Hell, she was probably leaving for college soon, just like everyone else. Sure, there'd be parties this summer, and he bet that he'd see her here and there at the café, but this might have been their last time alone together.

He tried to tell himself that it was for the best. Things with Becky weren't great, but more one-on-one time with Winny would ruin whatever they had left.

And no way could he be around Winny and not remember the way her lips had felt against his. Or not wish to feel them again.

So before she could reach the front door, he hopped into the car and drove away into the afternoon, not even bothering to blink against the sun streaks burning into his retinas.

But as he drove, he found himself thinking about Winny again. Not the kiss this time, but of the way she'd wrangled her painting. She was all determination, never giving up. Never backing down.

When he'd gotten back into his car at Winny's, he'd thrown his cell on the passenger seat beside him, and now he glanced at the cracked screen. Had he given up too soon? Sure, his plan threw his parents for the biggest loop of all time, but that had been his goal. They didn't know how dinged up his phone was, and maybe it wasn't as damaged as he thought. Maybe there was still a chance to fix this.

At the next light, he made an illegal U-turn and headed

toward New Haven Avenue and the store where he'd purchased his smartphone. He'd walk in there, and they'd help him. Then, he'd go home, renew his threats to his parents, and things would change. His dad would change. And then Scott could move on with his life. Go to college. Have a career. Something. Anything but stay here and throw his life away as a busboy at Café Flores.

This would work. This *had* to work.

25

SCOTT

One Hour and Twenty Minutes After Closing

The door shuts behind the three of them—Winny, Ryan, and Toto. A car starts somewhere farther along the street, and when it passes the café, I race to the window, parting the blinds and pressing my face between them for one more look at her.

I'd promised I'd keep her safe, and now she's out there. Alone. With them.

"Scott." A warning darkens Oscar's voice, but our remaining captor hasn't taken any notice of me. He's engrossed by the phone—my phone—which he's working like a hand-held video game.

Guess he got something good to work on there after all.

I make my way back to wait with the others. But I can't stand the silence. Minutes tick by so slowly. Where is Winny now? Is she okay?

Suddenly, it's like I'm at home, where everything sucks

all the time, and no matter how hard I work, no matter what I try, I. Can't. Fix. It.

It hurts in my stomach. Not where my dad punched me, but somewhere deeper. It hurts in my chest, where my heart is beating too fast to be okay. It hurts in my bones, my knuckles. And I look at that guy, sitting there in the corner, enjoying a timeout with my phone. Playing a *game*, even though there's a dead body in the basement. As though this is any old day. And I want to pummel him. I want to make the ache inside me go away by smashing my fist into his face. It may not erase that pain at all, though. And it might start a new one, one that's more than just my bruised knuckles and strained muscles.

Maybe that's why my dad lays into me—creating new pain erases one that's worse. One from his years of humiliation, of being unable to care for his family. Being unable to find work in a field where he's an expert. Maybe that new pain helps, except maybe not enough, because he keeps coming back for me. Coming back for more. Or it could be that, like Twitch with his meth, my dad has developed an addiction to it.

Is that what will happen to me if I start to give in to the lava trying to burn me up from the inside?

Do I want to risk that? Becoming like Twitch? Like my dad?

No.

I ignore the feelings surging in my body. I ignore the pull to do something—anything—and I sit still, like Sylvie and Oscar asked me to do. But it gets harder every minute.

And then the phone rings and they let Winny talk, and for the first time in ten minutes, I can breathe. But then Twitch hangs up, and the clock starts all over again. And I wonder how I'm going to get through the next ten minutes.

And the ten minutes after that.

And the ten minutes after that.

Please, God, bring her back soon. Bring her back safe.

Please.

"Okay," Oscar says. "The clock starts now. We have ten minutes."

"Ten minutes for what?" Pavan asks.

"I have a plan."

"I'm in."

"Scott," Sylvie says. "You don't even know what it is."

"I don't care."

26

WINNY

Six Hours and One Minute Before Closing

When Winny saw Scott, she had to pause and look again, just to be sure it was him.

Scott had come. He'd remembered.

Her mind blanked, refusing to compose words to send to her frozen tongue. And if she didn't say something soon, he'd be gone.

"Scott?"

He spun at the sound of her voice, settling his eyes on her and sending her heart up into her throat, where it fluttered like hummingbird wings. Her head threatened to float away at the first tentative curve of his smile.

"Hey! There you are. I thought I missed it."

"Well, the showing is kind of over."

"Yeah." Frowning, he shifted his gaze to his feet and shoved his hands in his pockets. "Sorry."

The silence around them was broken only by the soft notes of "Für Elise" playing in the background.

Stupid! Why did she say that? He'd taken the time to show up—the only person who'd come to see her work except Janey—and she had to be rude about it.

Too much had happened today. The weight of it all settled over her shoulders and for the tenth time that day, she wondered how she'd manage to get the huge-ass canvas home. She had no idea the gallery would be taking the student artwork down right away.

"Sorry," Scott said again, and she blinked several times. She'd gotten so swept away by her pity party, she'd almost forgotten he was there.

"I guess I'll go, then. Let you get on with . . . whatever you've got to do." He turned away but paused and gestured at the painting. "I almost forgot. Congratulations. It came out incredible." Then he walked away.

The sound of her ears clicking as she swallowed was deafening even through the chatter of the people who still lingered in the room. He'd nearly passed the threshold to the gallery's small lobby before she managed to get her mouth moving: "Wait, Scott. Stay. Please."

Smooth. Now she was ordering him around.

"If you want to," she quickly added.

He turned back to her, and the smile spreading across his face erased all the awkwardness from a moment before.

"I don't think I saw your painting when it was all done. Close, but not one hundred percent."

"Yeah, they had to collect it almost as soon as I finished. The paint was still wet. I guess they needed all the student projects here to figure out the layout."

"Anyone else from our school have a piece in the show?"

She shook her head. "Just me." She shifted her attention to her abstract interpretation of the Tree of Life—not super original, but it had inspired her. Still, she couldn't focus, not with Scott so close.

"Nice music," he said.

"Yeah?"

"Seriously. It's . . . classic."

She choked back a laugh. "It *is* Beethoven . . ."

He laughed and bumped her with his shoulder, and he was so warm she shivered. She wanted to move closer to that warmth.

For the millionth time, she heard the apology she'd rehearsed play in her head. It would be so easy to tell him she was so sorry if she'd given him the wrong idea. That stupid EMT class that would never do her any good anyway had taken up all her free time. That, and all the other things her parents talked her into signing up for.

Her brain dragged her back to that day in early February. It had been the coldest one of the year. After Scott had asked her out a third time, she'd waited and waited for him to try again, but the days added up one by one, until nearly two weeks had passed. She'd seen him at school plenty of times. They'd even hung out at a couple of basketball games, but he hadn't raised the topic.

"Do it yourself, then," Janey had suggested. Despite the nearly twenty-four-hour pep talk, Winny still hadn't been sure she could go through with it. She'd rehearsed all the way to school that Friday morning, but when she'd arrived at Scott's bank of lockers, just around the corner from hers, he hadn't been alone.

Scott had been there all right, leaning against his locker with a pair of arms wrapped around his neck—arms that belonged to a different girl. She'd leaned into him, and he'd pulled her closer.

Winny had waited too long and Becky had seized the moment.

Scrambling back and out of sight, Winny had scanned the students moving past her, milling around their own lockers. It felt like all eyes were on her, like everyone had known what she'd been about to do, knew what it meant that Scott was over there with another girl.

"Hey, Win."

Winny had jumped, unaware that Becky and Scott had rounded the corner. She'd looked from Becky to Scott, wondering if they'd known Winny had seen them. Becky was smiling, but not in a smug way. Winny hadn't even realized that Becky liked Scott. When Becky leaned in to give Winny a hug, she'd been too stunned to even lift her arms to return it.

Becky had whispered, "I asked him out and he said yes!"

Winny hadn't thought there could be anything worse than seeing one of her friends wrapped around the boy she'd been pining for for months.

And then this morning happened.

And now Scott was here. Without Becky. And Winny wanted to tell him how sorry she was, but the apology didn't matter anymore. What good would it do to tell the guy she'd turned down not once, not twice, but three times—the guy who'd found someone else—that she really had liked him back then?

And she still did now.

She'd look pitiful. And desperate. And he'd still be with Becky.

Winny and Scott would never be anything more than friends. It was better than nothing, mostly.

But right now, alone in the gallery, it was everything.

"I guess we should get out of here, huh?" he asked.

She scoped out the room, which was now empty except for them. "Yeah, definitely." She sighed, preparing to thank him for coming, to usher him out so she could suffer her latest humiliation alone.

And then what?

"Scott, can you do me a favor?"

"Any time."

"Think you can give me a ride home?"

He looked around the room. "You mean . . . ?"

She let her whole body sag and nodded. "Janey was supposed to come back, but I haven't heard from her, and the gallery really needs us to clear out and—" She grimaced. "Pathetic, huh?"

"What? No! Not at all."

The tears had been waiting all day. After her mother's tirade, getting through the show alone, and then the guilt of how she'd funded her piece . . .

"Hey, don't, Win. Come here." The shock of Scott's arms encircling her startled the tears right out of her body. She couldn't do this. Becky was her friend, and she wouldn't betray her. But Scott was her friend, too. And friends hugged.

Besides, Winny really needed a friend right now.

She wrapped her arms around his back, and they stood there, his heart thudding against hers, faster and faster. Or was that her heart? She couldn't tell anymore. His scent— musky styling paste and clean laundry—mixed with the fragrance of linseed oil from her canvas and the aroma of slightly burnt coffee from the reception table. For a moment, everything was okay. She was safe.

Scott looked into her face, parted his lips, and snuck a tiny breath as if he were about to tell her something.

Or maybe do something . . .

"You almost set there, Winsome?"

They jumped apart as Jackie, the gallery owner, approached. "I'm sorry to kick you kids out so soon, but that Impressionist show starts tomorrow and there's just so much to set up."

"Of c-course," Winny stammered. "Scott and I were just leaving."

"I saw Dean Hollis speaking to you earlier." Jackie lightly dug an elbow into Winny's arm. "Told me he's thrilled you're taking a spot in his program. He thinks you'll be brilliant in his media arts seminar."

"That was nice of him."

Scott furrowed his brow. "But I thought you were doing premed."

Winny shook her head at him, wondering where the heck he'd heard that. "I'm still figuring out college stuff," she said, finally.

"Any school will be lucky to have you, Winny," Jackie said.

"Thanks, again."

After a little more small talk, Jackie finally left them alone.

"Art school, huh?"

"Apparently everyone has an opinion about my plans for next year."

"And that means?"

"Nothing. It means nothing."

"Okay . . . Well, you need a ride, and I have a car."

Jackie's assistants were already toting paper-wrapped canvases into the space and leaning them against the wall.

"That would be great. There's one thing, though. You got room for a huge-ass canvas?"

27

WINNY

Ryan pokes his head between the driver and passenger seats of Toto's SUV. "Ten minutes."

It's not even midnight yet, but so much has happened, my muscles think it's hours later than it actually is. The new-car smell is overwhelming and between that and the fear, nausea takes hold and grows worse with every bump and turn.

I expected them to blindfold me. That's how they always do it in the movies, but I guess real life isn't like the movies. At least, not entirely. I try to block everything out, pretend I'm somewhere else, but Toto's driving won't let me.

"Call them." Toto says as he guides the vehicle along the streets.

Next to me, Ryan rests his gun in his lap, so he can dial. "Stay put," he tells me.

Like I'm going to throw myself from a moving vehicle.

"Make sure you hear everyone's voice," Toto says over his shoulder.

Ryan nods, phone to his ear. "Everything okay over there, Twitch? Let me talk to each of them."

We're in a residential neighborhood, not the kind where I'd expect to find a gun shop. I scan the street ahead for the out-of-place glow of a neon sign. Would it even be open at this hour? My stomach and throat turn sour, and I have to swallow so I won't puke. What if they're planning on robbing the store, and they make me help?

"All right," Ryan says. "Put Twitch back on." A pause. "Hey, we'll call again in ten minutes. Don't screw anything up."

"Here we are." Toto pulls the truck into an empty driveway and cuts the ignition.

A three-story Victorian rises before us. So, not a store at all. At least I won't be an accessory to a felony, or whatever kind of crime stealing weapons is.

"I'll stay here," Ryan says when Toto cracks open the driver's door. "I'm not Rochelle's favorite person these days."

"We all go," Toto says. "I'll need your help to carry the merchandise."

Ryan rolls his eyes. "Fine, but don't say I didn't warn you when she won't let me get two steps past the front door."

The wooden porch creaks as we plod up the steps, and Toto leads us to a pale lavender door with a dried flower wreath on it. How can an arms dealer live in a house with dried flowers hanging on a purple door?

The bell buzzes under Toto's finger, summoning footsteps from deeper within.

"Darrel?" a woman calls from the other side of the peephole.

"Yeah, baby. It's me. I brought some friends."

Darrel? Of course, his real name couldn't be Toto.

She says something in Spanish and the door bursts open. Even though I get all A's in that class, I can't make out her words. That part of my brain won't turn on. The woman's expression is stunned as she takes us in, which is exactly how I feel. She's my age. Maybe a year older, no more, and something is super familiar about her.

"Are you for real with this?"

"Come on, let us in, baby. We have some business with your dad."

The line of the woman's back straightens. "He's not here."

"Then I guess we'll have to deal with you instead."

"Whatever it is you're doing, I'm not getting involved." She darts her gaze back and forth between my face and Toto's.

Does she recognize me? Scott's note is still in my pocket; maybe I can give it to her. Maybe she can help.

"And will your father approve of that?" Ryan asks.

"You shut up. I don't want you around here," she snaps before turning back to Toto.

"Told you," Ryan mumbles, earning a glare.

The woman catches sight of the gun Ryan is digging into my side and she takes a step back. "What did you bring to my house?"

"Just let us in, Shell. It's not safe to be talking out here like this."

She closes her eyes for a second, then mutters a swear. "Fine. But only for a minute. Then you have to go," she says to Ryan. "And you can take her with you."

She holds the door open as we file in. Once it's closed, and she turns back to the room, Toto's waiting. He pulls her into a hug and kisses her, but she stands like stone.

"What?" he says.

"I thought you had one fast job to do tonight, and then we would . . ." She darts her eyes to Ryan, like she doesn't want him to hear, then tugs Toto farther inside. "One fast job, you promised. And then you show up on my doorstep with . . ." She waves her hands in my direction. "What's she supposed to be?"

"Look, Rochelle," Ryan says. "Things didn't go exactly according to plan."

"Not from you. I don't want to hear anything from you. What's going on, Darrel?"

The doorway to the kitchen is to my left, and from the corner of my eye, I spot a familiar red and blue image—a box of Cap'n Crunch tucked away in a little countertop niche next to *The A to Z of Cupcakes*.

These are real people, just like me. Toto has a birth certificate somewhere and a driver's license in his wallet that says Darrel. This girl eats Cap'n Crunch, just like I do. She bakes cupcakes, maybe puts sprinkles on them, the rainbow kind.

And she helps killers get guns.

It's too much. The argument in front of me begins to fade, but I can't let myself shut down. I need to stay sharp in case I get a chance to run.

"We just need some firepower, okay?" Toto says to Rochelle. "I know your daddy has some inventory around here. Are you gonna help us, or what?"

"And if I don't?"

"First off, your daddy's gonna be real pissed that you cost him five grand plus more later. Second"—he shrugs—"without these guns, we maybe need to cancel our trip."

She rubs her forehead, and when she speaks next, her voice has lost some of its bite. "You're really going to lay that on me? I thought you were done with all this."

"I am done." He moves closer to her, tries to tilt her head so she'll look at him, but she twists her head and retreats a step.

"Don't touch me."

"Hear me out, Shell. I am done. Tonight. Once this one exchange is wrapped up, I'm finished. I just need to get us some money and get these guys off my back."

206

Ryan is shaking his head, his mouth pulled into a smirk. Rochelle doesn't see this, though. She doesn't see a lot of things.

A door opens somewhere deeper in the house, and a voice calls out. "Shelly? You home?"

Toto steps away from Rochelle, and she swears under her breath.

"Yeah. In the living room." She glares at Toto. "And we've got company. Customers."

The man's footsteps head down a hall toward us.

"Shell," Toto says, voice suddenly urgent. "Take the girl out of here. I don't want him to see her right now. It might complicate things."

I look from Ryan to Rochelle to Toto. My head spins at the ease with which these people control my every move.

Firm fingers tipped with bubblegum-pink nails wrap around my arm. "Come on. We'll wait in my room." Rochelle tugs, and stumbling, I follow her down a hallway to the door at the very end.

Everything around me starts to go fuzzy, like it's not real anymore. Like I'm not real. My mom may have limited my choices, but she never took them away one hundred percent. All I wanted was a chance to figure out my life for myself. But now, my chance at a future is getting farther and farther away with every breath I take.

28

SCOTT

Six Hours and Forty-Five Minutes Before Closing

The cops were out of the question and so was home. That left . . . nothing, so Scott decided to just drive. He turned the car stereo on and then off twice. And then did it again. Everything that came out of the speakers jangled his nerves, but his brain didn't have enough reserves to focus on finding something better.

He made a left turn, a right, and another left, moving easily through the quiet residential neighborhood. Without meaning to end up there, he parked in front of Becky's house. Shadows watched him from behind the windows of the large Cape. Both her parents should be at work, and Becky was off . . . where? Her car wasn't parked in its usual spot.

What the heck did she do with herself all day now that school was done? He searched his brain for any mention from their phone conversation the night before but came up blank. Something must seriously be wrong with him if he was that clueless about his girlfriend's activities.

He had no idea what he'd have said to her if she were home, anyway. They didn't exactly have a drop-in kind of relationship—not that he'd invite anyone to drop in at his house. But now that he considered it, she'd never given him an open invitation at hers either. He could count on two fingers the number of times he'd eaten dinner at her place in the six months since they'd started dating. She'd been interested in his family at first, but he'd brushed her off so many times, she'd stopped asking about his home life. Maybe she'd stopped caring, too.

What the hell kind of relationship was that?

It didn't matter. They had this one last summer to enjoy before she went off to school and he either left too, or didn't.

His time with Becky had been his only chance he had to unplug, to laugh, to be a regular senior. It was when he got to forget everything else—bills and work and college offers he was too afraid to accept—and let his guard down for a little. Even if she had been here right now and they had the kind of relationship that came with unannounced visits and a spot at the table for Sunday barbecues, he wouldn't screw up what they had with his drama.

As he drove away, a breeze blew through his windows, loosening a scrap of bright paper that had been tucked in the passenger visor, dropping it to the floor. Keeping one eye on the road, he snatched it up and turned the sheet over.

"Shit," he said. "I almost forgot."

He'd be cutting it close. The little gallery on Howe Street was only about ten minutes away, but with early rush-hour traffic, it was taking way longer than it should have. Luckily, there was a spot right in front, and he pulled up to the curb as the clock passed 4 p.m. He'd just make it.

Sunlight streamed through the huge Victorian windows, playing across the exposed brick of the gallery's entryway. The reception area opened up to the main showing room, which, though small, felt spacious with its gleaming white walls.

Gleaming, *empty* white walls.

A handful of people still milled around, but he'd clearly arrived too late for the main event. He turned to beeline back out to the street when a small gasp caught his ear.

"Scott?"

Pivoting, he scanned the room again and smiled. "Hey! There you are. I thought I missed it."

Winny stood on the far left, next to her canvas. "Well, the showing is kind of over."

"Sorry."

She stood with her shoulders slumped, and a flat expression on her face, not at all what he'd expect of an artist on the day of her debut. Not at all like Winny. Maybe it was him. Maybe he shouldn't have assumed that she'd be okay with him coming unannounced, and only sort of invited. He'd been with their friends when she told everyone about the show at school, but that didn't mean she wanted *him* here. God, he couldn't get anything right today.

He shook his head. "I guess I'll go then. Let you get on with . . . whatever you've got to do." He turned away for the second time but paused. "I almost forgot. Congratulations. It came out incredible."

He was two steps from the doorway when her voice made him freeze.

"Wait, Scott. Stay. Please. If you want to."

That was all he needed to hear.

29

SCOTT

One Hour and Twenty-Seven Minutes After Closing

T his is our chance," Oscar whispers. "While he's distracted, maybe we can sneak out back."

"Oscar, he has a gun," Sylvie says. "He killed Maggie, and he's clearly unstable. What are you thinking?"

"We can't just leave," I add. "They've got Winny. If they call, and we're not here . . . You heard them. I won't risk her life that way."

Oscar shakes his head. "I'm not talking about running. I'm talking about going for my gun."

"Yes. Let's talk about this gun." Sylvie crosses her arms.

"Here it comes," Oscar mumbles.

"I thought you got rid of your service weapons after your discharge."

"I did," Oscar says.

"Since when do you have a gun, then, and what on earth moved you to bring it here?"

"Since last week. Look, Ryan has been showing up here, twisting your arm about selling the café. What *is* that?"

"You know I'd never sell."

"Yeah. Everyone who knows you knows that. So why is he all gung-go about this restaurateur friend of his? And where does he get off brokering offers for a business that isn't his?"

Suddenly, something that made zero sense to me a few weeks ago is clear. Ryan and Sylvie arguing about this very thing, selling the café. Only, the dishwasher had been running, and it was loud in the kitchen. I thought I must have heard wrong. Then there was Ryan's comment about bringing Sylvie a deal that would have set them up good. And what Toto said when I was hiding behind the counter: *Why do you think they've been all over you to get your sister to sell this place? We were raking it in back then.*

"Ryan uses our property as a front for his drug ring, then he tries to sell it off? You tell me that's not sketchy as hell. So yeah, I got a gun. I wanted to be prepared."

"Good thing, too," I say, but that only earns me my own scowl from Sylvie.

"I was going to tell you, I swear. And teach you how to use it. I just never had a chance."

She nods her head in Twitch's direction. "And what if he finds it?"

"Don't worry," Oscar says. "It's hidden. There's a secret shelf underneath my desk."

"I don't want firearms in my café."

"We can discuss the security plan for *our* café later, after the armed gunman is gone, okay? Right now, we need to do something. I'm going to see if I can—"

"Are you kidding me?" Sylvie's voice grows louder.

"Shh." Pavan throws a worried glance over his shoulder at Twitch, but he's still in a state of digital hypnosis.

"You can't even stand, Oscar," she says, quieter. "How do you think you're going to just nonchalantly waltz through the door to the office and back here?"

"I'll do it," Pavan offers.

Sylvie shakes her head. "I can't let you."

"Sylvie, my dear," Pavan says. "I appreciate your concern, but you are my friend, not my mother."

We can't sit here arguing over this. I'm done waiting.

Dropping to a crouch, I crawl back around the counter to reduce the amount of time I'll be exposed. Hopefully, Twitch hasn't noticed that I've snuck away, and since he's still quiet over there in his corner, I don't stop until I slip through the swinging doors into the kitchen. A peek through the window tells me Twitch is the only person in the room unaware that I'm missing. I need to get back out there with the gun before that changes.

Oscar said it's hidden in a secret compartment under his desk. Probably would have been good to find out where the hell that was before I came back here, but it's not like I can just pop back into the café for instructions.

The space is tight and dark, and I have to roll the chair aside so I can squeeze in to kneel between the wall and the desk. I grope around on the right side. No sign of the hidden compartment, no suspicious groove or button or anything. What if I find it, but there's some special code? I could be here all night.

Why did I storm back here without waiting for the details? *They call, and you jump. Your mom. Your boss. Everyone except me. You don't even ask any questions. You just do it.* Becky was right. I just risked my life—their lives, too—and it might be for nothing.

I can't find any hint of a hiding place on the back wall of the knee hole either, but when I slide my hand along the left side, my fingers brush against cold metal. The handgun's weight surprises me, but it's also kind of reassuring. Okay, I've got the gun. Now to make it back into the café without Twitch noticing.

Back in the kitchen, I scope out the scene through the window and immediately duck, my heart racing and my limbs going numb.

Twitch is no longer in his corner. He's pacing the room, carrying on a conversation with thin air, waving his gun like it's his car key fob and he can't remember where he parked. *Does he know I'm gone? Oh, shit. What if he comes looking for me?*

Or hurts someone else.

"Get it together, Bradley," I say, imitating my cross-country coach. "You've got the gun now. If you need to, you can defend yourself." Except, with my lack of experience, I'm more likely to put a hole in Oscar and Sylvie's wall or shoot myself in the foot.

My best bet is to get the pistol to Oscar.

I inch up to peer through the window again. Twitch is still in the middle of his freak-out. Ready to drop again, I notice movement by the counter. Sylvie ducks as the gun points in her direction. Pavan winces. Then Oscar turns. But he isn't focused on Twitch. He's looking my way. At me. Before lowering his gaze, he holds up one finger—*stay put, not yet*—then brings his attention back to our captor.

I move out of sight again. I can do that. I can wait. For a change. Too bad we didn't have time to discuss a contingency for this scenario before I got the bright idea to come back here.

But if the asshole realizes I'm gone, why hasn't he come to get me?

Twitch keeps groping his pockets like he's looking for something, and when he comes up empty, he resumes delivering his rant.

I might be able to sneak out of the door and at least get behind the counter, a little closer to Oscar. The only problem is, Twitch isn't pacing in anything like a predictable path. It's more like he's wandering aimlessly around the room, but at top speed. The only way I can tell when to go for it is if I look through the window, which means I need to be standing.

I watch the guy for another full minute. Oscar motions again for me to wait. Are they planning something? It's hard to tell. My view of Sylvie and Pavan is blocked by Oscar's back and a rack of fair-trade chocolate bars on the counter, but it looks like they're whispering.

After a fast, heated exchange, Pavan stands and shuffles in Twitch's direction. "Young man, excuse me," I hear him say.

Twitch spins around, freezing right in my line of sight.

For a second, I swear we make eye contact.

"Shit!" I hiss and hit the floor again. "Damn it." He could have seen me, could be coming this way right now, sweaty gray face turning red. I need to know what's going on out there, but every time I think about standing up again, my muscles feel as though they've been replaced with marble. Then I catch snatches of Pavan's words.

If they're still talking, Twitch can't be closing in.

Most of what Pavan says is muffled. ". . . okay, young man? . . . help you . . . any way?"

He didn't really go up and talk to that guy?

"They know!" Twitch shouts. "About the inversion control. They found out, and now they're coming. Who told them? Did you?"

Sylvie gasps, followed by Pavan's gentle voice. ". . . nice cup of coffee? Come, my friend. Have a seat, and I'll brew you a perfect espresso." From the clarity in Pavan's voice, he must be facing this way now.

I have to look again. I need to know.

Twitch's hand hangs by his side, the gun dangling like a dead weight. Pavan snakes his arm around Twitch's shoulders. The dude's actually letting Pavan lead him to a table and seat him with his back to me.

Pavan is my new hero.

This is it. I may not have another chance. I hit the floor and crawl through the swinging double doors, only opening the gap wide enough to squeeze my body through. The soothing tones of Pavan's voice guide me.

"Everything will be just fine, son. You'll see." I make it to Sylvie's feet and stand just as Pavan turns back in our direction. "One espresso, coming up."

Twitch is still on his tirade, but now only mumbles reach my ears.

As I shove the gun into his hand, Oscar takes my shoulder and gives me a shake. "If you ever do that again, I'll kick your ass."

"Sorry, Dad," I grumble.

Sylvie grabs me, too, but instead of shaking me, she throws her arms around my neck, almost knocking me to the floor. "And if he doesn't, I will." It's the first real smile I've seen from her all night.

"Wait a minute," Oscar says. "Where's the ammo?"

Sylvie's smile disappears.

You jump.

"Ammo?" I say.

Don't think twice.

"Scott, please tell me you grabbed the box of shells?"

The room tilts under my feet and little black spots dance in my vision. "Shells?"

Oscar lets out a stream of Spanish that cuts through my gut.

"So, the gun's not loaded?" Sylvie asks.

"Oh, God." Not loaded?

"Okay, everyone." Pavan whispers to us as he comes around the counter with Twitch's coffee. "Just calm down. Those guys will be back soon. If you're saying we're still defenseless, we'd better come up with a way to remedy that."

I'm such a stupid, useless ass.

Everyone's martyr . . .

Except it's the martyr's job to die. With my rash decision, I may have killed us all.

30

WINNY

Six Hours and Fifty-Eight Minutes Before Closing

I hope they get here soon, Winsome," Jackie, the gallery curator said. "There's only an hour left before we have to shut down the exhibit."

Winny forced a smile and checked the door again. "I'm sure they'll be here soon, if they can. Things just come up with work, you know. Weekdays can be hard for them."

"Oh, I'm sure they'll make time. They've got to be so proud of you." Janey rolled her eyes, but Jackie didn't catch it. She was too busy beaming at nothing in particular—the room or the day or life, maybe. "There are so many talented kids in our area."

"It's a very nice show," Janey replied. She'd put on a dress for this special occasion, something she hated unless it was Halloween or a dance, but she didn't even complain when Winny told her she couldn't come in her usual jeans.

So far, only a couple of the other exhibitors' parents

had commented on Winny's work, both with expressions on their faces that said, *Poor girl. No one here to support her.* After only a few minutes of small talk, they'd returned to their own children's sides to gush about how proud they were. A couple of local art bigwigs were here, too. They gave Winny her fair share of sincere admiration, but of course they had to devote an equal amount of time talking with the other artists.

When Jackie moved on, Janey said, "You didn't tell her that your parents don't know about this?"

"Actually, my mom found out."

"No!"

"I have no idea who said something. She said someone from school this morning, but yeah. I knew it would be a problem when Mrs. Simms announced it in class. Word was bound to spread."

Before her ride arrived, Winny had knocked on her mom's office door, all dressed in her suit and her black patent leather pumps, so much like the ones on her mom's feet. "Hey, I know this didn't all go down in the best way," Winny had said, trying to ignore the expression on her mom's face that said she was in the middle of something important despite her midday sojourn home. "I know I wasn't supposed to be in this show, but I am. And since you're already here, you know, not at work, it would be really nice if you could drop by the gallery. I mean, it would really mean a lot to me if you'd come."

Winny got a full thirty seconds of silence before her mom answered.

"They're expecting me back by one-fifteen. Maybe next time."

The rejection sizzled her throat. "Sure. Of course. I understand."

The underlying message hadn't been lost on Winny, either. Next time. There wouldn't be any next time if her mother had her way.

Still, Winny hadn't been able to keep from scanning the face of each person who entered the gallery showroom. After two hours, she realized how deeply she'd tricked herself into thinking that her mother was going to surprise her and put in an appearance. By the time Janey arrived half an hour later, she'd given up all hope.

A tall, balding man in a blue suit approached them from across the room.

"Ahh!" Janey whispered in Winny's ear.

"Stop it."

Janey ignored her and continued tugging on Winny's arm. "But check out the old-school 'stache."

"Shh! That's Dean Hollis from the Connecticut Art Institute."

"Oops. But you have to admit, that Selleck job he's got going on is incredible."

Janey was right, but Winny couldn't say any more because Dean Hollis was standing in front of them, one hand extended to shake Winny's. "Congratulations, Ms. Sommervil. I had a sneak peek of the projects, you know, and I'm immensely impressed with what you've accomplished here. I'm still waiting for your acceptance letter."

"It's . . . I'll be sure to decide soon."

He clapped a hand on her shoulder. "Good. Enjoy the rest of your debut afternoon. You've earned it."

"You're going to that school?" Janey asked, eyes wide. "What did your parents say?"

"Nothing, because I haven't told them yet. And I haven't decided yet, either. Not really." She blew out a frustrated puff of air. "They're going to say no, I know it."

"But that's where you want to go?"

"It doesn't matter. If I don't pick a school from the parent-approved pile, they'll disown me."

"Don't be dramatic." Janey took a sip of her sparkling cider. "This is flat, you know. Must have gotten a dud batch." The foot of her plastic champagne glass kept falling off, but Jackie's attempt at festivity was still nice.

"I'm not being dramatic. My mom basically said as much before I got here."

"For real? Yikes."

"Yeah."

"Shit," Janey said as her cell went off. "Here. Hold this."

Winny took Janey's glass and the disk fell off again. She didn't bother to pick it up.

"It's from my mom. I have to go and grab Zach from daycare."

"Of course. It's no biggie."

"I'm so sorry, Win." Janey pouted and threw her arms around her best friend's shoulders.

Winny, not used to standing for hours in two-inch heels, nearly toppled over. "Seriously, it's fine."

"Look, I'll get him, then circle back here so I can bring you home."

"You sure you don't mind?"

"Not if you don't mind maybe getting whatever rug-rat germs he's spreading."

"Sounds . . . risky."

"You don't even know. I'm not kidding. The zombie apocalypse is going to be caused by the preschool generation. You watch." Janey waved as she backed away, leaving Winny standing alone at her debut, feet throbbing, and with a heart as flat as the fizz-less cider in Janey's impostor glass.

31

WINNY

Cool air greets me, chilling the sweat that coats my skin, but in a good way. I can breathe in here. Maybe it's the sea blue walls or the warm glow of the old-school light bulb in the bedside lamp, but it's a relief regardless.

"You can sit." Rochelle gestures at her bed, which is covered by a clean white blanket and topped with plain white pillows. It gives the whole space a spa-like vibe. On a tall dresser, a picture frame catches my eye, the exact replica of the one my school gives to every graduating senior, the pics inside snapped at the moment our diplomas were placed into our hands.

"I've got that same frame." I freeze, leaning closer to take in the image, then jerk my gaze to her face. "We went to the same school." I snap my fingers, but I can't pull the info from my memory. "You graduated last year, right?"

"So?"

Shelly what? I keep coming up blank, but I know her. We were in choir together for a semester last year, but we didn't sit near each other—I'm a soprano and she was an alto.

I can't let myself get comfortable. The space is cozy, but far from safe, and this girl, though familiar, is no friend of mine. I perch on the edge of the bed while Shelly moves to stand before the open window. We've unintentionally positioned ourselves so our backs are to each other. Well, for me it was unintentional, but maybe that's what she wanted, so she won't have to acknowledge that all of this is real.

That I'm real.

Forced here, among people who don't know me or care to, I'm no one. I get smaller and smaller until I'm a non-person, just a tool kept around to serve the needs of these strangers. The familiar structure of home and school and the rules that made me who I am are gone now. How simple it would be for these guys to kill a person like that, a no one. For a moment, I feel like I'm floating away in a dark, empty void, cut off from the world. Anything could happen.

"He's not a bad guy. Not really."

Shelly's voice brings me back to this peaceful prison.

She's turned back to face me. "Darrel, I mean. He's . . . It's complicated. He's got this family—his mom—they put all this pressure on him, so he has to help . . . he has no choice."

"They killed a woman."

She flinches like I just punched her. "Darrel?"

I shake my head, and she sighs in relief.

"But he's in charge. And there are more of us back there. Four others, and he shot one of them." I shrug. "I'm sorry." And I am, and not just for Oscar and Sylvie, but for Shelly, this girl who's almost my age and who maybe bought that cupcake book so she could make birthday treats for her boyfriend.

Shelly collapses into a honey-colored wooden chair that sits in front of a vanity table. And then she sits up straight. "He had no choice, but after tonight, he's done. With all of them, his family, too. He promised."

"You love him?"

Her eyes answer for her.

"I love Scott, but he doesn't know it. I couldn't say anything because he was going out with my friend. Maybe he still is, but I think they broke up. Now, maybe we're going to die, and I'll never get to tell him, even though I could have told him any time. Maybe he and Becky were together, but I still could have said something. And maybe it wouldn't have mattered, but at least he would have known. I wasted all this time I could have spent doing the things I wanted. Things just for me. My mom thinks I'm afraid of the future, of challenging myself. She doesn't get that art terrifies me, but I love it so much that I don't even care. And now it's too late. For all of it."

"Darrel won't let anyone kill you. He couldn't."

I shake my head, but I don't argue with her. "Please, help me. Help us." I point to an iPhone sitting on her nightstand. "Let me call the cops. They can stop all of this. The two of you can run away now, tonight. Instead of loading the truck with guns, you and Toto—" I catch myself. "—Darrel can pack it with your things. I'll even help."

She shakes her head. "They'll catch up to us, arrest him. Put him in jail. I can't do that to him."

"What if that happens anyway? I wish I could wave a magic wand and make it not real, but the devil will eat you whether you greet him or not."

"I hear that. But at least Darrel will have a chance this way."

"It's going to get worse. I heard him say so to Ryan. Why do you think they're buying guns? They want to get some guys, Aaron and the Chef. Or maybe they're the same guy, I don't know."

"No. Darrel promised me."

"I heard them make the plan."

"No."

"What if Darrel and Ryan don't win their fight? What if the Chef or Aaron or whoever wins, instead? And you could have stopped it? Darrel may not be a killer yet, but if you don't help us, that's exactly who will come home to you tonight. If he makes it."

Eyes wide and unseeing, she gets to her feet and backs

away until she strikes the window. "He isn't *like* that. You don't *know* him!"

How can this girl be so blind? The evidence is right here in front of her.

If you cover a fire . . .

"Then give me a weapon. Something we can use to protect ourselves. Please, help us." She can't say no. I have to make her understand. I take a step closer, but she skirts me and circles around so she's blocking the door.

"I can't with my dad here."

"A knife, anything. You don't get it. People are dying. There's blood on the floor, and on my dress and my shoes." I point my toes, but she doesn't look at my silver sandals. "There's going to be more. You can't just pretend this isn't happening because you don't want it to be true."

She stares at the wall behind me for a minute, gnawing on a bubblegum-pink fingernail. A second later, her head snaps up. "Wait here and don't make a sound." Before leaving the room, Shelly grabs her phone from the nightstand.

The house feels huge around me. No voices. No TV or radio. I try the door after I'm sure she must be gone. The knob turns and it opens—*It opens!*—but only a little. Something catches. A gap, maybe an inch thick, gives me a view of some kind of latch. Shelly locked me in from the outside.

I want to cry, but if I lose it now, I'll never get it together again, so I breathe instead. *Think. Think.* The door to the hallway isn't a great option, anyway. Even if I do get the door open, how will I get through the house without being seen?

Hurrying to the window, I try to calculate how high we are here on the third floor. Below me, the dark rectangle of the driveway stretches into the night. I could jump. The windows are new, and the screen slides up easily enough. A warm breeze promises freedom and safety, but when I lean out through the opening my head starts spinning.

No way.

What if I break my leg or arm, and they catch me anyway? Then again, what if I make it to the ground and I'm fine? I can't think, can't decide.

I hear footsteps in the hall. It's too late now. I waited too long.

I slam the screen down hard enough that it bangs, and the door opens before I make it back to the bed, but it doesn't matter. It's only Shelly.

God, what's wrong with me? Only Shelly? Like she's safe just because we went to the same school and she hasn't threatened to kill me yet?

"Why do you have a lock on your bedroom door?" I ask.

"It's from when I was little. My dad holds meetings in the house sometimes. He didn't want me getting in the way. Here." She holds up a black vest. "This is the best I can do. It's bulletproof."

"But won't they see it?"

"It's a size small. That's why my dad has it around. No one he deals with can wear it. Put it on under your dress, and button your sweater all the way up. You'll be a little hot, but unless they're really paying attention, they won't notice it. And since men never really pay attention to stuff like that—"

"—they'll never know." I laugh, and though it feels wrong, it feels good, too. It feels like me, the real me. That's something. "Thanks."

Shelly turns her back so I can slip off the bodice of my dress. It just about fits over the vest. With my cardigan buttoned to the top, my reflection in the full-length mirror is a little bulkier than usual, but she's right, it's not super noticeable.

"You sounded good, you know," Shelly says from behind me. I watch her smile in the mirror. "In the choir. You had that pretty little solo at Christmas, right?"

"Yeah. That was me." As I study the new, Kevlar-enhanced Winny, my smile fades, leaving behind a grim face. "That *was* me," I whisper again.

32

WINNY

Nine Hours and Thirty-Five Minutes Before Closing

Barefoot, Winny descended the stairs as though she were being walked to the gallows. She adjusted her robe, trying to block out the AC-chilled air and the cold soaking through the soles of her feet from the hardwood boards.

"Mom. You're home. How nice." She tried to smile, but her lips felt too stiff.

"Did you get my message?" Jeannette Sommervil waited for her daughter at the foot of the staircase, hands on her hips, one black leather pump telegraphing her impatience.

"I heard part of it." The floor boards creaked out the moan Winny was struggling to suppress. Her mom coming home in the middle of the work day had to be about the exhibit, no doubt about it. "I was showering."

"Going somewhere?"

There it was.

Winny didn't answer. Her brain whirred, but she couldn't come up with a response that wouldn't implicate her, so she kept her mouth shut and waited. There was no point in resisting the incoming tidal wave of her mom's wrath.

"I was under the impression you didn't have any plans today," her mom went on. "At least, you never mentioned anything."

"Mom—"

"I just heard from one of your school friends about the art show, Winsome. Why would you deliberately disobey our request?"

Was she for real? "Because you guys gave me no choice. I seem to recall your disapproval of all things art." Winny stormed past her mother and into the kitchen where she ran the tap to fill a glass of water.

Her mom's heels clicked behind her. "We've talked about this. You said you understood."

"Yes, I understood the words coming out of your mouth, but that doesn't mean I agreed with you." As Winny raised the glass to her lips, her hand trembled. "The only thing you guys approve of is stuff that will look good on a med school application. And, in case you don't remember, I'm not even in college yet."

Her mother inhaled one long slow breath through her nose and let it out in a rush. "Art is a wonderful hobby, but not a career path. It can't possibly give you a future."

"You don't know that! Maybe I'm good, really good. You wouldn't know, because you've never seen my paintings."

"I'm sure you're good." Her mother's expression softened, and she actually smiled. "You're good at everything you do. You have an incredible life ahead of you. But you need to see that and not limit yourself or your goals."

"But it's okay for *you* to limit my goals?"

"You have the next three years to create the kind of CV that will get you into a top tier medical school program. After that, it's too late. Now isn't the time to waste on frivolous pastimes."

"It's not frivolous to me!"

"Let's not forget the facts of the world," her mother continued on as if Winny hadn't spoken. "Medicine, engineering, business, psychology—those are all valid career paths with earning potential. You're not always going to have your dad and me to provide for you. *Ou wè sa ou genyen, ou pa konn sa ou rete.*"

"Right. I have no idea what I'm in for out there in the big, bad world." Winny didn't even need to listen. She'd heard this speech from her mother countless times before. "Why can't you just trust me to pick for myself? You always said I could be anything I wanted."

That was why they'd come from Haiti, or at least that's the line her parents had fed her all those years. Her dad would plop her on his lap and talk about all the opportunities open to her that he never had. Why it was worth it to them to leave the home they loved, their family. He'd launch into his dream of her joining his practice, father and daughter physicians, working together, side by side. Winny used to love that, and she'd wanted nothing more than to follow in his footsteps. But what her parents hadn't understood was this aspiration was more fantasy than reality. Winny's five- or eight- or ten-year-old brain hadn't understood what medical school would be like. Or a law career. It did understand nights eating dinner with only her mom or her dad. Or the nights spent at the Forans' house next door, or Janey's, because both her parents got stuck at the office.

"Of course you can be anything you want to be, but I don't want you to let fear lead you."

"You think I want to pursue art because I'm afraid of a real career?"

"All I'm saying is that I want you to choose wisely. A career with stability that lets you use your potential."

"Even if it makes me unhappy?" Even if she didn't faint at the sight of blood, her parents' life was not the one she wanted. There was no magic there for her.

Her dad would define magic as a dead heart coming back to life or the destruction of malignant cells in the face of pharmacological advancements. For her mom, it was helping a deserving person get justice. But for Winny, magic took the form of color and light on a dull, blank canvas. Color and light she created with her hands and her brush and her pigments. Depth coming out of flat nothingness.

Life breathing through a still image. Beauty born into the world.

"So, are you saying I can't go today? My ride is coming in like twenty minutes. I should call and tell them not to bother." Winny glared at the wall behind her mom's shoulder as she awaited the pronouncement. "And I have to call the gallery curator, Jackie."

Eyes closed, her mom sighed. "No, that's not what I'm saying. Your name, our family name, is attached to this event now. You won't dishonor that by shirking your responsibilities."

Winny turned to her mom. "What? Really?"

"But," her mom said, holding up a finger, "we're discussing this matter further tonight. And remember, Winny, your father and I have worked hard to support your education. We expect to have a say in it."

"What's that supposed to mean?"

"We don't have to continue to pay your way, you know."

"You're threatening me? Threatening to cut me off?"

"You have a wonderful future awaiting you."

"If I do what you say."

"Winsome—"

"I can take care of myself, Mom." But her voice held no confidence.

"I'll be telling your father about this." With that, her mother spun on her heels and headed out of the room and down the hall to her home office.

33

WINNY

ONE HOUR AND FORTY MINUTES AFTER CLOSING

The guns come wrapped in blankets, but I don't know if that's to keep them from bumping together in the car or to keep them from being noticed by the neighbors or any cops, if they happen to stop us.

The bundle I'm given is way heavier than I expected.

"Don't you drop that, girl," Shelly's father says.

Our bundles make quite the mound in the SUV's cargo area. Where did these even come from, and who buys them, if not us? Other criminals? White-collar Everymen just trying to protect their families? Gun enthusiasts who want to see what an assault rifle can do at the shooting range? Probably not. Those guys probably buy their guns from fancy stores. Maybe that's where these originally are from.

They all have to come from somewhere.

"Winny."

It's Ryan. I didn't even know that he knew my name. I wish he didn't. "What?"

"There's one more, back in the kitchen."

I give him a wide berth as I pass by.

Once we're loaded up, we climb back into the SUV. Shelly doesn't say goodbye. She's been in her room ever since Toto knocked on the door to get me.

"Aren't you gonna wish me luck?" he asked.

"I think we're done talking." She shut the door on him, and he hadn't moved for several moments, making me wonder if he forgot I was there.

Unfortunately, he hadn't.

"I think it's time to check in on our friends," Toto says before we pull onto the street.

"All as it should be over there?" Ryan asks.

I strain, but can't catch Twitch's response, only the hiss of the SUV's air-conditioning and the gentle hum of the engine.

Everything must be fine, though, because Ryan nods. "Talk to you in ten."

"We good?" Toto asks over his shoulder as he pauses at a stop sign halfway down the block.

"Right as rain." Ryan pockets the phone.

At the house on the corner, a car's lights go on in the driveway.

Before Toto can pull through the intersection, we're blasted on all sides by screeching tires. Two vehicles come at us from the cross street, and the one in the driveway just ahead careens our way, stopping nose-to-nose with Toto's car.

"What is it?" I ask. "Who are they?"

Ryan leans between the seats. "Shit. Not good. Do you think it's . . .?"

A tall, slender guy exits the car to our right, and Toto sighs. "Aaron. I should have known the sneaky bastard would be tailing me."

"You mean they were just waiting for us? They knew you'd be back here tonight?"

"Must be."

"Are you kidding me? Toto!"

"Just shut up."

The guy comes around to the driver's side and taps on the window with his knuckles, three sharp raps. "Mind joining me out here, gentlemen?" he calls through the glass. When he ducks to peer into the back window so he can give Ryan a wave, he spots me. "Oh, gentlemen *and* lady. Interesting."

No more no more no more.

I can't take any more tonight. My throat goes so dry, it clicks when I try to swallow. Whatever it is that can scare these awful, terrible men has got to be bad, and suddenly all I want to do is crawl onto the floor, curl into a ball, and cry.

"Out here, please," Aaron says. "All of you." The tall, black-clad man runs his hands through his dark hair, the streetlight spotlighting his sleeve of tattoos. More ink winds around his neck, where it disappears out of sight.

Three other men join him from the cars on either side of us, all smiling like we're just running into a few friends at the mall or in line for a froyo at Pinkberry. The car blocking our path sits motionless, headlights off now, its tinted windows revealing no clue as to who lurks inside.

"We have more than two hours before our meeting," Toto says. "What the hell's this about?"

I try to stay behind the men, but everyone's shifting from foot to foot, and Aaron circles us.

"What, no handshake? And who's this little lady?" He leans close to me, a grin slicing his thin face. "A friend of yours, Toto?"

I catch a dark shape in my peripheral vision and reflexively I jerk my head up just as his fingers brush my cheek. "Keeping some good company these days, Toto. I approve."

"She's nobody."

"Really?" Aaron's smile deepens. "She doesn't look like nobody to me. What happened to your last girl?"

Toto pushes between us, and I gasp for breath, my whole body shaking. Ryan's hand on my arm is almost comforting.

"My girls are none of your business."

Aaron holds both hands up. "Okay. No worries. I get it. Besides, that's not why I'm here. Where's our money?"

"Stop playing around." Toto stomps, crunching gravel

under his high-top. "We just talked to you barely an hour ago."

"Let's just say that the Chef started having second thoughts when you suggested a change of venue. You know the Chef doesn't like surprises."

"Like you ambushing us here isn't a surprise?"

"Touché."

"Listen, you go back and tell the Chef we're straight so long as you give us until three, like you said."

Aaron and the Chef. The guys they're planning on attacking with the very firearms we just loaded into Toto's truck. My heart races as I take him in, trying to imagine what it will be like when I'm holding one of the guns wrapped up in blankets in the back of Toto's truck. Holding it and pointing it at this man. Or one of his friends—who appear to have vanished. I startle at the scuff of feet on asphalt. They're still here, just in the process of surrounding us.

"Like I said, I'll make good. Some other business came up that we had to take care of first, but now we can turn our attention to our dealings with you."

"And explain again, why do we need an alternate meeting spot?" Aaron's voice sounds bored and a little snobby, like he's a patron at a glam hotel and Toto is his servant.

"The original place won't work. I caught wind that a few other guys are going to be around there tonight. This new place I found is quiet."

"Sounds romantic, especially if this little one will be

there." Aaron pushes Toto aside like he's going to talk to me again, but Toto shoves him back. When one of Aaron's men, a blond guy, launches at him, Toto doesn't see him coming. They collide with a grunt, and Aaron is immediately on him. Another man, his shaved head gleaming in the street lights, gets up in Ryan's face, and I'm suddenly free while my captors grapple with their enemies.

I run, not knowing where the hell I'm going, only that I need to be anywhere but here. My sandals slap the pavement, but I don't even clear the beam of the streetlight before a hand, carrying the scent of garlic, grips my shoulder.

"Well, hello there," says the hand's owner. A woman's voice. "You can't leave yet." She spins me to face her. The light forms a halo around her head, adding dimension to the honey highlights in gentle curls that frame her face, which have escaped from a knot at her neck. "Tell me, is there something I should know?" She taps a foot while I struggle to come up with an answer.

I suck in a breath and try to wet my lips, but my tongue is so dry, it sticks to the roof of my mouth. I have to swallow a few times just to clear my throat.

"That's answer enough." A line creases her smooth brow, and she flicks a quick glance at the men who are still brawling, oblivious to our conversation. She leans in close to whisper in my ear. "What are they planning? Tell me quickly."

Toto and the blond guy are rolling on the ground now, and Aaron delivers a ferocious kick to Toto's back. Ryan tries to jump in, but the bald guy seizes him by both arms.

If I'm going to do this, I need to do it now, but I still can't get my mouth to work. Then I remember: I have the note Scott gave me. "Here." It comes out in a hoarse rasp, but at least it comes out. The folded page is still there, and I slip it into the woman's hand.

For the first time, I read what Scott wrote. Just three lines, seven words: *Gang fight. Café Flores, Unionville. Call 911.*

"They're going to use us, the hostages. Help us. Please."

She gives the little green and white slip of paper such a fast glance, I doubt she even read it. She shoves it into her pants pocket. "Well, I always did like to be fashionably early." She throws me a wink, pivots, and clears her throat. The men freeze. Toto rolls on the ground, clutching his stomach and groaning. The bald guy still has hold of Ryan, clearly intending for the blond to land another punch on Ryan's already bruising face, but he lets his hand fall to his side.

"Enough," the woman says. "Let's let these men be on their way. After all, we do have business to take care of later tonight. We need to keep them in decent shape. For now."

When the bald guy lets go of Ryan's arms, Ryan totters. I expect him to crumple to the ground, but he plants his feet and locks his legs, standing firm with an expression of defiance on his face.

"Later." Aaron flutters his fingers in a goodbye wave, and he and his men slip into their cars, while the woman jumps into the one blocking our own.

Before she closes the door, she pops her head out. "Three, you say? We'll be there, just like we planned."

Ryan and Toto are in such bad shape, I have no idea how they'll carry on, or if they even can, but I don't care. I need to get out of here. The nearest houses are only twenty feet ahead. The one with the yellow roses—I'll aim for that one. If I can get there and slip into the dark between the houses, I'll be out of sight in seconds.

"Don't even think about it. I'll shoot you right here," Toto says.

As if I'm some wind-up toy with a dying motor, I slow and stop, frozen. Chills streak up my back and my knees shake, but I can't turn around, either. Can't face Toto's gun pointed at me. All I can see is the family portrait from our dining room at home, now with one empty spot where the image of me used to be.

"Bring her back over here, Ry."

Ryan's moans of pain and the crunch of gravel behind me is all the warning I have, but at least I'm ready for his grip on my arm.

I swear, if I make it out of this, I'll never let another living soul grab me this way again.

34

SCOTT

Scott drove around aimlessly, brain whirring, barely seeing the streets as they stretched out before him. Hot June air blasted from the open car window and his mother's voice echoed in his head: *Maybe when you get out of here he'll be better.*

He slammed his palm against the steering wheel. It was bad enough when he was the victim, but now he was the cause, too? No way. He refused to let them lay that on him.

Who did you show this to?

He hadn't intended to show the video to anyone. He'd just hoped it could maybe knock some sense into them if his dad could see what he looked like in one of his rages, could see the fear on his wife's face, on his kids' faces . . .

The pain.

Maybe then his dad would . . . what? Scott wasn't so naive that he expected his parents to get down on their knees and beg his forgiveness, but he'd hoped it would trigger . . . something, even just an acknowledgment that their situation was seriously messed up.

But he could show someone. Child and Family Services. Or the cops. He shivered and sweat sheened his skin as his head went spacey, the way it did whenever Oscar forced one of his espresso supremes on him. He could do it if he wanted to. No one was stopping him from calling the police right now. His hands trembled so hard he couldn't grip the steering wheel, so he coaxed the car to the side of the road. The scent of greasy fried onions filled his nose from the burger place halfway up the block and his stomach protested with a nauseous gurgle.

If Scott went to the authorities, they'd arrest his dad for sure. Little chips of sunlight fell on the sidewalk, filtered by the swaying leaves of the maples lining the road; he stared at them until they blurred together. All he'd have to do is call them, and the police would be knocking on the door of their ranch. His mom would answer with that rabbity look in her eyes.

"Is Jack Bradley here, ma'am?" they'd ask.

She'd gape and shuffle back a step, but never let go of the door. No way could she lie. She might be willing to bullshit her son, but she couldn't pull that with the cops. Even if she did, they'd force her to turn her husband over. Who knew, with all the voices, maybe his dad would stumble from the living room on his own, his white toes sticking out from the bottom of his two-week unwashed jeans like pale fish.

They'd take his dad away and then Scott would be free. He could go to Florida or New York. Hell, he could do the progressive program right downtown and live at home. His mom would tell it like it was then. She'd apologize for taking her husband's side and express her gratitude that she and her children were finally safe.

Scott dragged his gaze away from the sun-dappled street and focused on the phone in his hand. A two-inch crack spanned the screen, and behind that his reflection regarded him, that angry slash falling over the mirror image of his pale lips like a grin.

Scott hit the little green icon to open the telephone app, leaving a smudge of sweat behind. He didn't even need to look up the local police number; he could just call 911 and report a case of domestic violence occurring at that very moment, one he'd only just barely escaped.

The familiar sounds pierced his eardrums as he dialed. One tone. Then a second. But his trembling finger froze over the screen before the third.

Was he really doing this? Once he hit the final digit, he couldn't go back. Nothing would ever be the same.

But nothing was the same now. His family had been a mess for two years and it probably always would be. His house would forever be haunted by the memories of all those shouted words and the bruises that left Scott lying in bed, pain-sweat gluing his skin to his sheets.

What had Mrs. Sommervil said this morning? *You better not wait too long. Opportunity has a way of escaping us if we don't act.*

He'd never get back the happy family they once had been. The dad who coached little league, even though Scott couldn't play for shit, was dead. Same with the guy who'd surprise him at least once each school year with a hooky day just so the two of them could mess around all afternoon.

Something lodged in Scott's throat, and the image of his dad's tear-streaked face from earlier that day surfaced in his mind. He'd never seen his dad use his hands to hold back tears before, never seen him cry before. Those hands had been for teaching Scott to hold a baseball bat and tie his shoes. "Screw that," he said. Screw the guilt and the nostalgia. There was nothing nostalgic about the days he had to miss school because he was too much of a mess to show his face in public. And all the guilt, well, that belonged to them, to his parents. His dad for causing those bruises and his mom for permitting them. It was a wonder he even managed to get good enough grades to graduate, let alone earn financial aid offers.

But the hot lava anger was gone. All he wanted to do was put his head down on the dash and sleep for a thousand years. If he did that, though—gave up, gave in—they'd win, and Scott would be stuck in this same hell for another year. *Opportunity has a way of escaping . . .*

He thought of the video's brutal images, and it almost brought a sense of comfort. The video was his way out of this mess. He groped in his lap for his broken cell and swiped the screen to wake it up. It flickered once. Then again.

"Not good."

A second later, the familiar grid of cheerful icons settled into place.

He jabbed the screen until he found the gallery icon, but the video folder was empty. "What the—?"

He closed it and tried again, then tried going through the folder icon directly. Still nothing. He ran a check of half a dozen other apps; some worked, some didn't. He couldn't access the video.

Opportunity has a way of escaping us if we don't act.

His evidence was gone.

35

SCOTT

O ur plan sucks.

First, we wait for the last call—assuming there is a last call. Then, once that's over, we make our move on Twitch. With an unloaded gun.

As if fate is on our side, for once, my familiar ring tone interrupts the silence.

"Who is this?" Twitch narrows his eyes as he looks at the closed blinds. "Who gave you this number?"

Now that he's no longer distracted with his espresso, Twitch is freaking out, all paranoid, again. Ryan's response is a *Peanuts* squawk on the other end.

"What? Ryan? Is that you?" Twitch laughs. "You had me scared there for a minute. Yeah, they're here."

We go through the now familiar routine, each saying a version of "hello, this is blank," like we're at some messed up meet and greet. All except Oscar; when it's his turn, he says, "Bite me," earning him a smack from Sylvie.

Twitch reclaims the phone. "Okay, see you in a few." He turns his back to us and whispers, but too loudly, "And be careful who sees you. They know, Ry. They know about the introversions and extroversions. Don't let them see you."

Twitch is right back on his mumbled monologue as soon as he cuts off the call. The finger-tapping, too.

"This is it," Oscar whispers. "As soon as we get him to drop his gun, Scott, you grab it. Sylvie, you run for the shells. We need to have two working weapons by the time those guys come back through that door."

Sylvie shakes her head. "I still don't like this. Your gun isn't loaded, and what if he shoots you? And look at him."

We all do. Twitch's fists are clenched, one around the cellphone and one around the gun, which is aimed at the ground. For now.

"What?" Twitch shouts at us. "What are you talking about? Did you tell them? Are *you* the ones?" He screams this last question right in Oscar's face.

"Young man," Pavan says.

"No!" Twitch lets loose a string of numbers in some kind of chant: "Nine-one-seven-six-five-seven-seven."

"What the?" I mutter.

"They have the elixir and they won't tell us where it is!" He grabs me by the shirt collar, somehow fisting the fabric along with my phone still in his hand, and pulls my face up to his. "They have the *elixir!*"

I blink against the spit and clamp my lips shut so none of that shit gets in my mouth. Twitch's breath is sour mocha.

His other hand comes up, and the cold metal of the gun massages my cheek. Suddenly, there's no more air in the room. No more in the universe. My head floats above my body, and my stomach muscles convulse. I'm about to puke. Twitch shifts his grip on the gun, and the metal digs into my neck.

"God bless you all," someone says behind me, but I can't say who. The statement is long and low and slow, like when I used to put the wrong size record on my dad's old player as a kid.

"Young man!" the too-slow voice says.

Then Pavan is at our side, his hand groping in my waist-band. For a second, his frantic motion pushes me closer to Twitch, who's still shouting.

". . . introversion control . . ."

"Oh my God. What's he doing?" someone says, but my brain can't latch on to who it is.

Pavan wedges himself between Twitch and me, then throws his elbow into my gut, right where my dad's punch landed earlier. The jolt shocks my lungs back online. Gasping so hard my throat closes in on itself, I stumble backward.

Twitch's eyes are locked on mine over Pavan's shoulder, tracking my retreat, which means he totally misses the movement of Pavan's right hand. Pavan clutches the scissors from Winny's first aid job—which he just tugged from my waistband—and in one motion, he streaks them right at Twitch's chest. The blades sink in with a meaty slice, a sound that will never leave my head as long as I live. And Twitch is screaming, shrill and loud. And I think I may be screaming, too, but I can't tell. Our cries cut off the twang of the metal shears hitting tile when they slip from Pavan's fingers, the horror on his face a reflection of the horror unfolding in front of our eyes.

"Oscar!" Sylvie shouts.

He's already wobbled to his feet, his bad leg doing a poor job of supporting his weight, but he never gets a chance to raise his useless pistol before the report of Twitch's shot echoes around us.

Pavan's body jerks and his eyes lock on Twitch's. Twitch blinks several times, then he gapes, his bottom lip trembling. Pavan places a hand on the guy's shoulder, gives a small smile, and topples to the ground.

"Scott, move!" Oscar shouts. "Twitch, drop your weapon now."

But I don't move, and Twitch doesn't drop his weapon. Still fighting to keep the bile down, I'm surprised to find the scissors in my hand. I try to remember when I grabbed them, but time isn't working right. Neither is my brain.

Distantly, I hear Oscar shout for me to get out of the way again, but it's too late for that.

I aim the scissors at Twitch's gut and draw my arm behind me as a million images flash through my mind: the three of them standing here in the café earlier, Ryan with that smirk on his face; the flash of cold, gray metal and the stink of those first few rounds of gunfire when they went off; Maggie on the floor of the basement, my apron tied around her head; Oscar's stricken expression when I came back with the unloaded gun; Mom's exhausted fear when she pleaded with me earlier not to wake up my dad. And my dad, the constant mask of fury he wears on his face all the time and the stench of alcohol on his breath. The power in his bicep, the iron of his fist when it lands. The emptiness in his eyes when it's all over. It's the same emptiness I've seen in Twitch's eyes all night.

I channel it all into my muscles. In a moment, I'll unload the years of pain and fear onto this man, this murderer. Who deserves it.

I take a deep breath. In a moment, when this is over I'll . . . what? Will killing Twitch remove the bullet from Pavan's body? Will it rewind the clock to the moment these guys walked into the café and make them decide to go to the movies instead? Will it erase the pain in my stomach where my dad hit me this morning? Or delete—permanently—the images on the video only recently retrieved on my phone? Will it give my dad his job back?

If I give this murderer what he deserves, only two things will be different: he'll be dead, and I'll be a murderer, too.

What will I deserve then?

My stomach clenches, but this blow comes from the inside. I have to stop myself from retching. I have to let go of the scissors. I have to let go of everything.

Metal clangs on tile as the scissors slip from my wet fingers. I stumble back and trip over someone or something. Pain explodes in my cheek as my face hits the counter.

All the strength runs out of my legs. If I don't do something, I'll end up on the floor with Pavan.

But Sylvie is right there, her arms strong around me. "It's okay, Scott. It's okay."

Nothing will ever be okay again, but I don't know how to say that, so I nod and don't complain when she hugs me even tighter. A moment later, she pulls away to study my face.

"You're not going to pass out on me, are you?" Her voice is light, but her eyes are full of fear.

"I don't think so," I say, "but I'm not making any promises." My head buzzes from the impact of bone against granite.

A groan comes from the floor.

"Pavan." Sylvie bites her lip, looking at him, then me.

"Help him."

She squeezes my elbows, then dives to the ground, where she pulls Pavan into her lap, cradling his head. He smiles up at her, but the smile turns into a grimace, then a cough that brings up stringy, bubbly ropes of phlegm.

"Shh," she urges.

The room blurs around me as tears fill my eyes and I kneel at his side. "I'm so sorry. This is my fault. If I had waited. Gotten the bullets, not just the gun—"

"Quiet, my boy," he whispers. "I made this choice. Only I have responsibility for my actions, and I'm proud that my end is in service of friends."

Twitch is still ranting, but I can't think about the gun or the orders Oscar is barking or the bell ringing on my left. I can't look away from the old man's face, not until a voice jars me out of my daze.

"What the—?" Toto shouts. "Ryan, get in here. Close that door!"

Toto's voice is too loud, and Twitch is too close to the edge. He shrieks, and the gun in his hand goes off, the bullet striking Toto in the shoulder.

"Shit." Ryan gapes and Winny struggles against his grip on her arm.

"Scott!" she shouts.

I crawl, then stumble to my feet, trying to get to her, but Ryan's already raised his weapon, and I freeze even though it's not trained on me.

"I tried to stop them, Ry," Twitch wheezes. "I—"

The shot silences him. A final breath eases out of Twitch's chest with a long, gurgling sigh that seems like it will never end.

36

WINNY

As Winny emerged from the bathroom, towel wrapped around her and water still dripping down her legs, she heard her mother's voice. At first Winny thought her mom was actually in the kitchen, but then realized it was the answering machine.

". . . be home in a few minutes."

That couldn't be good. Nothing short of an absolute emergency would compel her mother to leave the office during work hours.

A drop of water slid down Winny's back, and she shivered. "Crap," she muttered, running to her room to get dressed.

In less than forty minutes, her ride would come to bring her to the gallery. The only reason she agreed to be part of the art show was that it had been scheduled for a work day when her parents would both be busy, so she could sneak

257

out of the house without them ever discovering she'd defied their wishes. Not only would they freak if they found out she was wasting her valuable time on painting—time she could have been spending building up her list of extra-curriculars to beef up her med school application, never mind that she hadn't even started college yet—but they'd wonder where she got the money for art supplies since she sure hadn't asked them for it. They weren't dumb; they knew how much canvases and oils cost, and there was no way they'd ever let her get a job. Or keep the one she got behind their backs.

Holy crap, did her mom know about the art show? No . . . no way she could know. Winny had been so careful to avoid giving the house phone number to anyone involved—the gallery curator, the other kids. She'd made sure to remove every tiny blob and splatter of paint from her hands before coming home. Her parents were well aware that they weren't covering painting this semester in art class, so they'd ask about any traces for sure.

Yet Jeannette Sommervil was on her way home. Right now.

As the moisture evaporated from Winny's skin, her mouth went dry. "So not good." She still had to get ready. Her suit, the one her parents had gotten her for her college interviews, hung over the white bi-fold closet door, and Winny hadn't made her bed yet, either. "Double crap!"

Dropping her towel, she slung on a robe and pulled the

lime-green and turquoise duvet into place. Not perfect, but good enough. All she could do was get ready as planned. Maybe she could do her makeup and hair, but leave off the suit, so her mom wouldn't notice. That might not give her quite enough time to dress when her mom left, though. She'd hoped to put on some mascara today, to give her eyes a little extra oomph, but with an ambush coming any minute now, there was no time. Sticking to her usual routine—blush and lip gloss—was probably safest, anyway.

Eyeing the clock, Winny calculated how much time she had left. If her mom didn't get here soon, she'd be busted for sure.

Just as she secured the last section of her bun with a pin, the front door opened, and her mother's voice echoed from the entryway, bouncing off the Brazilian cherry floors.

"Winsome, come down here this minute and tell me why you thought it was okay to lie to me and your father for months."

"Triple crap," Winny whispered, leaving the safety of her bedroom. "I am so busted."

37
SCOTT

Two Hours and Six Minutes After Closing

The checkerboard tile digs into my knees, sharp pain like skewers shoved into my joints, but I can't move. My left eye leaks a steady stream of liquid that I hope is only tears and not blood, but my cheek is on fire where it bounced off the counter. Blinking, I try to move my jaw, but something grinds in there.

"You need to get to a hospital," Ryan says to Toto.

"Oh, hell no! No hospitals tonight. Not for you or me. Not for any of you." He sweeps his arm in our direction, then starts pacing, one hand clasped over the bullet wound in his shoulder.

"Missed the heart," Winny whispers.

Toto hasn't stopped spouting curses since shaking off the initial shock of being shot. He hasn't sat down once, either, which I hope is because of the adrenaline, but I suspect it's actually because his wound isn't very serious.

Ryan, for once, sits quietly on a stool, not even trying to calm Toto down.

"What the hell happened to those guys?" I whisper to Winny, who kneels by my side and rests her cool hand on my back. Even before Twitch shot him, Toto had to be in bad shape. I don't need a mirror to know his face looks worse than mine, and his white tee is covered in dirt and blood.

"Fight—" she says.

Toto lunges at us. "I ought to kill your asses right now." Then he paces away, but I don't feel any better. He's like a caged tiger, getting more and more worked up, more frenzied. Soon, he'll pounce.

"Fight with the Chef's men," Winny continues. "Some guy named Aaron. There were others, too."

"What?" Oscar glances over to make sure Toto and Ryan aren't listening to us.

"You mean the dudes who are coming here?" I ask, but Winny doesn't answer because Toto is glaring right at us.

This is it. Forget their plans and the weapons they got for us to use. This is the moment when Toto throws all of that out the window. Even if his crazy idea had any chance of working before, it's fucked now. He knows it, we know it. He has no more use for us.

But he spins and unleashes his fury on Ryan, instead. Beside me, I feel Winny's shuddering breath of relief.

"So are you just going to sit there all night?" he says,

getting into Ryan's face. The guy is still slumped in a chair. "We have work to do. Unless you're just going to take a beating and not retaliate."

"Those guys kicked our asses. Don't you think we'd better—"

"What? You got a little hurt, and now it's too real for you? Don't want to hang anymore?"

"I'm just saying—"

"There is no *just saying*. Those guys are coming here for us. We still owe them money."

"Right. Money we don't have." Ryan doesn't shift a muscle; it's as though he might never move again.

"They don't know that. And we have our army. Even if one of them *is* down." He glances at Twitch's body.

"Two," Ryan says. "Don't forget the old man."

"You don't think I see what's right in front of me?" Toto bellows. "Come here." He tugs Ryan into a corner to talk away from us.

What does it mean that I don't even try to listen this time?

Winny fixes her gaze on Twitch's still form. "Is he dead?"

Between the bullet wound and Pavan's scissor strike, the guy has lost a ton of blood, but the flow has downgraded to a trickle. Oscar blots at Twitch's slow-oozing wound with some of the discarded towels from his own first aid session.

"I think so," I say. God, it hurts to talk. "He killed Pavan."

Not like I'm glad Twitch is maybe dead, even if he did shoot two people . . . it's just that after everything, I don't have enough emotion left to worry about what happened to him. Not if I want to stay focused on keeping myself going.

"This whole thing is so messed up," Winny says.

I chuckle, then wince. "That was exactly what I was thinking."

"Come on. See if you can get up, get to a chair. I'll bring you some ice."

"Those guys won't like it," I protest.

"I don't care if they like it or not," she says.

Then I remember how much the floor is hurting my knees, so I let Winny ease me up.

I want to thank her, to ask her how she can be so brave right now when all the world has fallen apart, but the energy to do those things is gone. I settle on giving her hand a squeeze as I settle into a chair.

Sylvie has been sitting by Pavan in a stunned silence this whole time. Once Winny gets me set up with some ice for my face—our captors didn't even look twice in her direction when she rounded the counter to the freezer—she kneels by Sylvie's side and whispers into her ear. Whatever she says, it works, because Sylvie joins me at the table.

Winny squats and takes Twitch's wrist in her hand. "Oscar, you can stop now. He doesn't have a pulse, and you're bleeding again."

He looks down at his thigh. "Shit. Okay. Yeah."

"Guys . . ." Winny says in a small voice.

She stands, addressing us as if she's a CEO running a board meeting, her palms pressing against the tabletop. Who is this Winny with the blood stains on her dress and that intense glint in her eyes and that grim pressing of her lips?

"Listen." She takes a deep breath. "I might have made things worse. Or better. I don't know."

"What do you mean?" Sylvie asks.

"Your note, Scott."

"Yeah?"

"Wait!" Sylvie says. "You had a chance to give it to someone? A cop?" Like a kid about to tell Santa what she wants, Sylvie leans toward Winny, her expression crossing from the threshold of excitement to hysteria; but Winny shakes her head and Sylvie deflates.

"No, not to the police. To one of the Chef's men. A woman, actually."

"Wait a minute. What? One of the gangsters?" Oscar asks. "And how did you figure on that helping us?"

"I had to try. I couldn't come back here without at least trying. 'Greet the devil, and he eats you.'" She shrugs. "'Don't greet him and he eats you, anyway.' There were no other options." But her voice is suddenly less certain.

Oscar lays a hand on Winny's arm. "No, you're right. And I don't see how anything can make this situation worse at this point anyhow."

"If they know that we're not involved with these guys," she goes on. "If they understand what Toto's plan is—"

"Maybe they'll focus on Toto and Ryan, and let us go?" I finish for her.

"But we can't let them get Ryan," Sylvie says.

"Sylvie," Oscar says, "are you for real? He's involved in the death of three people. If it means you stay safe—you, and Winny, and Scott—God forgive me, then I'm all for seeing that guy with a bullet in him."

Sylvie buries her face in her hands, sobbing. I wonder what it must be like to have someone you love do something so horrific. My father's face swims in my mind. Good old Dad isn't such a nice guy these days, but I can't imagine him ever doing this. Then again, how can I really know? Could he be pushed to it? Maybe if his depression gets worse or the financial hole we're in gets deeper?

Even so, if Mom's life were at stake, or mine, or Evie's, would anything hold me back from doing what I needed to, even if that meant taking down my own blood?

Sylvie is still crying, and I can't look at her. I agree with Oscar. Ryan may be her brother, but hell, he chose to associate with these maniacs, so he gets whatever he gets. What did Winny say a minute ago? *Greet the devil and he eats you . . .*

"All right, kiddies. Break it up." Ryan's got a bruised temple—funny, the darkening smudge is just about the same spot where Dad got me the night of prom—but other than that, whatever injuries he's suffered are invisible. "They'll be here at three. We need to get ready."

Toto slips in and out of the café, returning with a rolled-up blanket. He swipes an arm across the tabletop, and an explosion of glass makes us jump as the vinegar tang of Heinz's ketchup fills the air. Another pop of shattering glass goes off when Toto swipes the salt and pepper shakers to the floor, making room for whatever he's got in those blankets.

"One more load. You go," he tells Ryan, then collapses to a chair, wheezing. He looks like shit. One eye is totally swollen shut, and the other is nothing but a slit. His face is bruised and covered with blood, and the white tee he wears is the perfect backdrop for all that red coming out of his bullet wound.

Winny's trying to get our attention, but we can't talk freely. Not now.

Toto and Ryan busy themselves unfolding the blankets, and when I first see what's resting inside them, it's like a cold stab of ice down my neck. So much matte black metal, the barrels, like half a dozen eyes, boring into me. The pair loads the magazines like robots, the bullets snapping and clicking into line, then they slap each magazine home.

When they're done, eight automatic assault rifles lie on the white, linoleum-topped tables I've cleaned almost daily for the last two years. Coffee splatters and cupcake crumbs, dabs of cream cheese at breakfast and stray shreds of coleslaw in the afternoons; all that's gone now, replaced by eight tools of mechanized death.

"Scott. Are you listening?" Winny asks.

"Huh?" I rub my temple. "Yeah. Sorry. Yeah, I'm with you."

"I don't think we have until three." From the way Oscar and Sylvie gape at her, I'm guessing I missed this bit the first time around.

"So," Oscar asks, "what time do you think they're really coming?"

She swallows. "Soon."

"Did you re-lock the front door, Ryan?" Toto asks at the same time.

"Damn it." Ryan lays down his box of bullets. "I'll get it."

The jingle of the bell stops him dead.

"Well, well, well. Looks like quite the party at Café Flores tonight, huh, boys?" Aaron's lanky frame fills the doorway. At his back, a throng of men and one woman line up, ready for us.

Ready for war.

38

SCOTT

Nine Hours and Fifty-Six Minutes Before Closing

W hat the heck are you doing here on your day off,
Scott?" Oscar asked.

Scott laughed. "Just can't get enough of this place, I
guess."

"Want anything?"

"Whatever's freshest."

Oscar filled one of the green Café Flores mugs with
the house blend and placed it before Scott. "Something's
wrong." He narrowed his eyes. "I can tell."

Keeping his focus on his coffee, Scott shrugged. The
steamy brew turned his mouth bitter, matching his mood.
He wasn't sure if it was his conscience or fear; he just knew
he was close to losing it.

"I'm fine," he said after another swallow from his mug.

"Uh huh. If you want to talk . . ."

"Yeah, I know."

Café Flores thrummed with the daily hustle and bustle—the chatter of patrons, the hissing gurgle of the milk steamer, and plinks and clinks of glasses and dishes. Soon it settled his nerves. Becky never got how he could be so okay with his work schedule, but the little restaurant was the only place where he truly felt relaxed. School was . . . well, school, and at home he was always jumping out of his skin. But in the café, where the air was scented with vanilla and mocha and herbs from the lunchtime sandwiches and the simmering soups in the kitchen, he could let down his guard.

The bell jangled and he heard the click of heels on the black and white checkered tile.

"One large latte, please," a woman said, her French accent converting that everyday word—*latte*—into music.

"Mrs. Sommervil, right?"

She turned to survey him, an eyebrow raised.

"I'm Scott Bradley. I go to school with Winny. I met you back in the fall at the science fair."

She smiled and nodded absently. But now her gaze fell on him, scrutinizing his face. Why had he even spoken to her? Because he needed a distraction. Maybe he was looking for an excuse to bail on the whole plan. He'd been agonizing over it for more than a week, and he'd sworn to himself that one way or another he'd find a way to put an end to his dad's reign of terror. It wasn't enough to get himself out from under that iron fist—he had to make sure his mom and sister were safe, too. But nothing had gone as he'd planned.

They were all still in the exact same place as before. Worse, maybe.

Mrs. Sommervil was still looking at him and he cleared his throat, scouring his brain for something to say. "She's got that art thing today, right?"

"Art thing?"

"At that little gallery on the north end of Howe."

Mrs. Sommervil's brow wrinkled and her smile deepened. "That little gallery, right."

"Her piece looks awesome. You must be so proud." God, he sounded like a fifty-year-old at a PTA meeting. Real smooth.

"Yes, we're very proud of our Winsome. She's going into premed, you know."

It was Scott's turn to squint. "Oh. Yeah? Cool. I'm sure she'll kill it."

"Here you go." Oscar placed Mrs. Sommervil's cup on the counter.

After she paid her bill, she turned to Scott. "Take care, Mr. Bradley, and good luck to you. Where are you going to school next year? You were in Winsome's grade, yes?"

He ducked his head, fiddling with the handle of his mug. "Yeah. I'm still mulling over my options." He glanced at her and saw a slight tinge of smug satisfaction there. Heat spread from his palms, which were snugged around his coffee cup, and surged right to his head, where it flooded his face.

"You better not wait too long. *Wè jodi a, men sonje demen. Live today, but plan for tomorrow.* Opportunity has a way of escaping us if we don't act." She clicked her way across the café and out the door into the June sun.

"Whoa." Oscar stared at the door and the retreating form of Winny's mom on the other side of the glass. "She's kind of intimidating, huh? Nothing like her daughter."

"Yeah." Scott knocked back the rest of his coffee, scalding his throat, but he barely felt it. "Intimidating, but she's right."

Oscar shrugged. "I guess."

"See ya later. I've got to run."

39

WINNY

Aaron's voice mixes with the memory of new-car smell and garlic, and I gag.

"You don't mind that I brought a few friends, do you?" A leather jacket covers his tattoos now, except the one on his neck, which peeks out from under his collar.

Pairs of stomping feet clad in leather boots or retro Vans or fluorescent Nikes carry his crew inside. They line up at his back. The woman from before is there, too, her hair loose over her shoulders, which are bare aside from the straps of her black tank top.

They're here early, which means the woman believed Scott's note. I just wish I knew if that is a good thing or not.

The woman and how many men? One, two, three . . . seven. Eight in total.

Eight against six.

Toto and Ryan weren't too far off. If we still had Twitch

and Pavan, we'd be perfectly matched. Still, we might have a shot.

"How sweet," Aaron says. "Your little friend is here. Hey, honey." He winks at me.

"What the fuck?" Scott whispers.

"Not now."

"You're early, man," Toto says. For the first time, his voice carries a hint of doubt, and I want to shout *Ha! See how you like it?* He moves in front of the gun buffet as if he can shield the table from Aaron's view and wipe the memory from his brain.

Aaron shrugs. "Yeah, well, change of plans. Sorry. We'll take our money now. Nice bullet wound, by the way. Is it new? Looks great on you."

"I told you we don't have the cash yet. Now, we had a plan, you and me. I can't follow through if you go changing the rules without giving me notice. Call the Chef and tell him that we need more time."

A creak of wood makes me turn my head. Oscar's on his feet, plastic wrap gleaming from shin to mid-thigh, though what he thinks he's going to be able to accomplish in his state is beyond me.

"More time to assemble your iron?" Aaron nods toward the table and its array.

"Those?" Toto throws a glance over his shoulder and pulls an expression that's supposed to be all innocent, but he's not fooling anyone in the room, not even himself.

A slight grin twitches at the corner of Aaron's mouth.

"That's got nothing to do with you," Toto says. "This is for a different deal."

"Really?" One of Aaron's eyebrows rises and his slight grin grows into a full-on smirk. "Or maybe you need more time to train up your army there." He points our way.

"Look." Barely under control, Toto's voice comes out as a growl. "If you just call the Chef and ask him—"

"No need." The woman's voice slices through Toto's next words.

He squints, trying to see past Aaron. "Lady, you stay out of this."

She shoves past the line of men, then levels her gaze at Toto, shaking her head almost as if she feels sorry for him. "You really thought you were something special, didn't you, Darrel? Some little punk like you with some ludicrous plan." She extends an arm in our direction. "Using this beat-up peanut gallery to defend you? Two kids, a chick, and Mr. Saran Wrap over there? Some army. As if they aren't just waiting for a chance to kill you."

"They'll do what I tell them to do," Toto says.

"And who's this?" The woman strolls over to Twitch's motionless form and nudges his shoulder with her foot. "This one's out of commission, I think. But I guess I know who gun number seven was for. Number eight was the old man, huh? The girl was right. Unbelievable."

Toto tenses. The woman pauses a few feet in front of

him, her gaze steady on his face. "When I read the note, at first I thought there's no way these fools would try something so ridiculous. But here we are, and the evidence suggests our little doe-eyed friend was telling the truth."

"What note?" Ryan asks, looking from Toto to the woman then to me.

"Lady," Toto says. "I don't know who you are or what you're talking about, but if the Chef wants his money—"

"*Her* money."

"Oh, fuck," Ryan whispers.

Toto's eyes widen. "Excuse me?"

The woman takes one more step in his direction. "I said *her money*. And let me tell you, Darrel, she does want her money. She wants it very badly. So, what should she do? Put a bullet in you? Another one, that is?" The woman reaches behind her into the waistband of her pants and pulls out a gun.

"*You're* the Chef?" Toto takes her in again, head to toe to head.

She makes an *afraid so* face, gun never wavering. "I don't usually make a personal appearance at these little soirees, but after what I found out from our run-in earlier, I just had to come and see for myself."

"Bullshit!"

"Toto. It's over." Ryan's voice is flat, dead, like he's already taken a bullet and knows his fight is lost. "How'd you find out?"

Toto throws an arm across his chest. "You shut your fucking mouth!"

"Why, your girlfriend," the Chef says, strolling in my direction. She grabs my arm and pulls me away from the others, parading me in front of Toto like some old mystery movie detective showing everyone who the real killer is.

Her hands still smell like garlic and celery and something I can't quite place. I gag again but manage to swallow down the sour bile.

"I have to hand it to you," she says, addressing me now. "That was a ballsy move, even if you don't have any balls to speak of."

"I don't care who you are." Toto spits at the Chef's feet. "You lied to me. This is one big freak show. I don't owe you anything. We're done here."

"Toto!" Ryan barks.

"You're right, my friend," the Chef says. "It's done. You're done." Saliva flies from her lips, and a foamy fleck lands on my forearm. I want to wipe it away, but I'm too afraid to move. She's still got that gun. It's aimed at Toto, but I'm closer to her. Way closer.

This wasn't how it had played out in my head. I was supposed to be with the others, with Scott, and the Chef and his guys—no, *her* guys—were supposed to tell us we were okay. We had nothing to do with this. That we'd be safe.

"So," she says with a new jauntiness, "this is how it's

going to go. Since it's clear you can't get my money, I'll forgive your debt to me, but only because we're going to kill every last person in this room. Or..." She raises an eyebrow.

"Or what?" Ryan's voice is desperate now. He reaches out, almost grabbing the woman's arm, but thinks twice of it at the last moment, letting his hand drop to his side. "Or what? We'll do anything."

"There's one way you don't *all* have to die." She grins and turns to, of all people, Sylvie. "I believe Ryan brought you an offer from me a couple months back."

"What?" Sylvie asks.

"She'll make the deal!" Ryan says.

"Sell me the café, and everyone can go free. I'll even make you a good offer. I did a little research on this place after Ryan here got himself fired. I've always had a soft spot for small business owners, especially when said business is food-related. And even more so when the owner is a woman. And this is a very choice location."

"You mean, you're the restaurateur Ryan told us about?" Sylvie asks.

"You're actually a chef?" Scott asks. "Like, with food?"

"Quiet, Scott!" Oscar warns.

"What kind did you think I was?" she asks.

"Uh, the kind that cooks meth?"

She laughs. "I have people for that," she says, turning back to Sylvie. "So, what do you say? If you *really* wanted to make good, you could work for me. I could use a new employee. Aaron over there will have his own restaurant soon, and I'll need some extra help with my side ventures. Middle management stuff. Very desirable."

"She'll do it!" Ryan practically shouts the words this time.

"What?" Sylvie gapes at her brother.

The Chef drags me in front of Sylvie. "I'll front you some product, spread the word that we've got a new outpost for our customers. Added flexibility. Shop at any of our convenient locations. A chain, just like Planet Fitness. I might even cut you in on the profits. What do you say?"

"You want me to sell drugs for you?" Sylvie blanches. "Out of my café?"

"Come on, Sylvia, you and I know how hard it is these days for small businesses in this state. And small business owners who are women have it even harder. You can't tell me you haven't struggled. Thinking about keeping the doors open, worrying about when this bill is due or that one. Dead days when it feels like you can't sell a cup of coffee to save your life. What about the dead weeks? And dead months. A business like this is always sixty days away from closing its doors. Why do you think I started my side ventures to begin with? There's plenty of honor in going legit. Profit, on the other hand, not so much. But having my own restaurant was my dream. So what's a girl to do?" The woman shrugs. "And now I have three. If you join me, that will be four."

During her speech, the Chef's fingers loosened on my arm, and I try to slip out of her grip, but she readjusts her hold and smirks at me. "Not so fast, sweetie."

Ryan is at his sister's side, lips practically in her ear. "Say yes, Silv. Just do it. You know she's right. You know what it's like around here. Feast or famine."

Sylvie puts her hands to her ears. "For once in your life, Ryan, just shut up!" She shoves him away and turns back to the Chef. "My answer to both of your offers is no."

"Are you sure? You'd be set for life. And you'd have protection." The Chef gestures at Aaron and the others.

I try to imagine what it would be like stopping in on Wednesdays after choir for a scone and macchiato and seeing Aaron hanging around the café. Would I always hear the sounds of his feet driving into Toto's stomach and back? His taunting words to our captors? His total creeper comments to me? Then I try to think about what it will be like to come here, knowing hidden somewhere in the back is more of the stuff that destroyed Twitch—the stuff that took a kid with a career in front of him out of college and put him in Café Flores on a Friday night after closing, holding a gun.

I don't want that to happen to Sylvie and Oscar's place, but I also don't want my life to end tonight.

"Sylvie, just for once, do something for me." Ryan's voice is a growl, and his eyes have this blank, frantic look.

Everyone waits. The clock ticks loudly. A gurgling hiss comes from one of the machines behind the counter.

"My answer," Sylvie says, "is no."

"Then you all die, I guess."

Aaron laughs, and the sound is like a hundred spiders crawling on my skin.

"Wait!" I shout. "No! You're supposed to help us. We don't have anything to do with this."

The Chef spins me to face her, amused pity playing over her face. "I appreciate your faith in me, I really do, but did you think I'd take care of your friends here and just let you walk out that door? That would be signing my arrest warrant, wouldn't it?"

"Let her go!" Scott shouts.

I try to look at him, but the Chef grabs both of my wrists and twists them hard, forcing me to stay where I am. Her grip is strong, and images from all those TV cooking shows, chefs slicing produce with lightning speed, flash through my mind. Constant kitchen work has given her incredible upper body and hand strength, though she stands only a few inches taller than me.

"Let her *go*," he repeats.

Oscar takes a stumbling step forward. "You heard the kid."

The Chef rolls her eyes. "I'm so over this whole place. All right, time to clean up and get out of here." She shifts her weight and angles her head to talk to the men behind her.

"Now!" Oscar shouts, and three bodies come flying our

way, colliding with us, forcing the Chef to break her hold. I hit the floor a second later, covering my head against the trampling feet around me.

The first gunshot goes off, but I have no idea who fired, not until Sylvie pulls me beside her. Toto has his weapon out, and he gets one of the Chef's guys. Scott and Oscar have grabbed guns from Toto's cache, and although Scott doesn't hit a thing with his next three shots, Oscar gets four guys in a row, only missing on shot number five.

"Shit," Scott says.

"Shit!" The Chef surveys her fallen men, one squirming and groaning on the ground. Three others doing nothing but lying there.

Tables crash to the floor with an ear-piercing clang, and more bullets echo off the brick, granite, and tiled surfaces.

It's so fast. Our enemy tally goes from eight men to three plus Toto and Ryan. Then it's just three plus Ryan, because the Chef trains her gun on Toto, waiting only long enough for comprehension to settle over his features before she fires.

I can't move. Can't think. I can't tear my eyes away.

"Winny!" Scott's voice jolts me out of my daze. He and Oscar are on the ground behind the barricade of tables they've created.

I shove Sylvie in their direction, and she drops onto her belly to avoid the bullets still flying. I'm about to do the same, but something catches my eye.

Twitch's body, not two feet away. With Scott's cell lying wedged partly under one leg. In the commotion, Ryan and Toto must have forgotten about it.

I dive for the phone.

"Winny, what the hell are you doing?"

The phone comes free with little effort.

Stray bullets lodge in the wall at the foot of the plate glass windows. Another wild shot, this one disappearing into the ceiling, sends a fine dusting of plaster down to powder my arm.

"Hurry!" Sylvie shouts.

A second later, I'm behind the table blockade. So is the last of the Chef's men. Oscar grapples with him while I work Scott's phone. The battery is down to ten percent, but reassuring tones sound when I hit those magical three buttons. When the operator comes on, I say, "We're at Café Flores in Unionville. There are men with guns. People are dead. Come now." Then I lay the phone on the floor, shielded by the tables, so the dispatcher can listen in on all hell breaking loose around us.

The Chef watches her guy fight her battle, then raises a hand, flicking it in Aaron's direction. "You come with me. We'll have the guys out back finish this off. We can't be found here." Without another word, she and Aaron flee into the night.

Scott stands at Oscar's back. "What do I do?"

"Get them out of here." Oscar drives a knee up into his

opponent's gut, but it's Oscar's bad leg, and they both fall, Oscar landing on top, the guy's gun clattering at their feet. "Try for the back door," Oscar grunts through the effort it takes to keep the guy down. Meanwhile, Sylvie snatches the thug's gun. Oscar moves to his knees, blood collecting behind his plastic dressing. "If that doesn't work, take them downstairs, or the kitchen. Anywhere but here. Now, Scott, do what I say. For once, just listen."

"Okay. Okay." Scott rushes to us, just as Ryan streaks at me and Sylvie, his eyes crazed.

"You couldn't just give me the money?" He seizes his sister by her throat and thrusts his face—so red, white splotches stand out on his cheeks—into hers. "Now look what you caused." His whole body shakes as what can only be pure hate rolls through him.

"Hey!" Scott shoves Ryan's shoulder, getting his attention before ramming his temple with a fist in the same bruised spot from the scuffle with Aaron and the Chef's guys out by Shelly's house.

Ryan staggers back, but then lunges at Scott. "You." Ryan aims his own blow, but Scott ducks away easily and shoves him. Ryan can't keep his feet. He goes down, and that's when I catch the red seeping from his stomach.

"He's been shot," I whisper.

"Shot?" Sylvie tries to go to her brother, but Scott gets in the way, shoving us toward the back of the café, toward the employee door.

"Go!" he shouts.

"No. Wait!" Sylvie cries, but Scott has her hand and tugs her out of the room with me on their heels.

I throw one last look at the brawl behind me. Oscar is still wrestling with one of the Chef's guys. The door swishes in my face and we're standing in flickering shadows.

"Winny!" Scott urges. "Now."

I let him pull me into the belly of the building, though I can't drag my gaze from the door. On its last inward swing, I catch a glimpse of Ryan as he struggles to stand.

The door has stopped moving for now, but it will open again, because for Ryan, this fight isn't over.

Any second now, he'll be coming for us.

40

SCOTT

TEN HOURS AND SIX MINUTES BEFORE CLOSING

S cott sat on his bed, three sheets of paper clutched in
his hand, though his brain wasn't registering the meaning of the words printed there. Three sheets, each with
the best news of his life. There was sunny Florida, where
he could study psychology and maybe even get into their
grad program later on for another five to seven years of
higher education. That would be a full decade away from
this place.

Then there was the huge school in New York, the most
expensive, but they'd also given him the best package—
half of his tuition and room and board covered. That still
left a hefty chunk to make up on his own, but Scott was no
stranger to skimping and scrounging. He tried to imagine
himself walking the streets of the city, popping into trendy
coffee shops with his laptop—

The fantasy cut off there, because Scott didn't have a laptop. While all his future college friends would do their papers at the local Starbucks or the Village Blend, he'd be holed up in the cave of the computer lounge. Hell, he barely even had a cellphone after the fiasco with his parents. Scott dug his thumbnail into the sizeable crack now adorning the screen of his only real piece of tech. It was the story of his life these last couple of years.

Shuffling the sheets of paper, he read the third letter. The best news of all.

And the worst.

A full ride for four years. No work study. No student loans. Just a solid education. He could get his undergrad degree with only the relatively small expense of books and materials, with one exception. Nowhere on the letter did it say anything about room and board. The local commuter college—perfect for the non-traditional student with plenty of online and blended classes for added flexibility, particularly helpful for the working parent—didn't have dorms. He could go to school for free, but he'd be stuck here for another four years.

His mom's footsteps in the hall warned Scott that the torrent he'd unleashed this morning hadn't dried up yet. It had to be her, because his dad never put on shoes anymore these days. His bedroom door slammed open, the little coil spring on the baseboard letting out a *ting* of protest.

"What the hell is wrong with you?" she fired off before

she'd even crossed the threshold. "Why would you behave that way toward your father?"

He bolted up from the bed. "What's wrong with me? How about what's wrong with *you*? The evidence was right there on the screen in front of your face. How can you still defend him?"

"You know the strain he's under—"

"Him? We're all under pressure. Face it, Mom, he's not getting better on his own. It's not just his temper, either. He's more and more depressed every day."

Tears overflowed her eyes, and she had to look away. "You can't stop loving him just because he's had problems these last couple years."

Right, because turning into a drunk only recently made it okay. Never hitting your son in the first sixteen years of his life meant you could do whatever the hell you wanted to him after that. Like saving up a lifetime's supply of ass-hole points to use them all at once.

"I can be angry with him for hurting us. Literally hurting us all."

"Maybe when you get out of here he'll be better."

"Are you kidding me? Are you trying to say this is *my* fault?" What did she think would happen if he left home, took away their family's extra income, and his dad didn't have good old Scotty to torture? Who did she think would take the brunt of his anger then? "I'm doing everything I can to help out here. Do you think I like working so much?

Giving up most of my pay?" He waved his busted phone in the air. "Here's more money down the drain. You can't pretend this isn't happening."

"He'd never hurt me or Evie." Her voice lost steam as a flicker of uncertainty flashed across her face.

"You really believe that? Fine. I'll leave. Right now."

"Scott—"

He didn't stick around to hear more. Storming down the hall, he stuck his head into the kitchen where he found his dad with a tumbler full of amber liquid on the table before him. "I'm taking the car." He reached to pluck the key ring off the hook on the wall.

"Like hell you are." His dad started to rise, but Scott was already through the front door.

41

SCOTT

TWO HOURS AND THIRTEEN MINUTES AFTER CLOSING

W e'll get out through the back. Stay behind me."

"But, Scott." Winny chews on her lip. "The Chef said something about guys back there."

"They're long gone. Hell, maybe she was bluffing." But I slow my pace. What if Winny's right? Every step along the way tonight, I've just jumped into things, risking my own neck and everyone else's in the process. Not this time.

Sylvie's not paying any attention to our debate, too focused on every bump, crash, and shout coming from the café. "I can't leave him in there." I don't know if she means Oscar or Ryan, but I don't ask. Maybe she doesn't know herself. She tries to return the way we came, but I grab her.

"Sylvie, you can't go back out there."

"Oscar wants you outside and safe," Winny says, and I'm transported to class the last week of school, when she blew everyone away with her abstract art project. The

289

calm authority she gave off, the way she addressed each class member, one at a time, as she discussed her work. She brings that same calm presence to the chaos now. "The cops are coming. I called them. You'll only get hurt back there. At least this way, you have a chance, and you might be able to help us."

Sylvie nods and lifts the hem of her polo to wipe her face.

"Besides, you've got the only gun." I put my arm around Sylvie's shoulder and draw her toward the tiny vestibule off the hallway that leads to safety.

"Huh?" Sylvie raises her hands, both clenched around the pistol grip, and looks at them as if she's never seen them before. "Holy crap. You're right. Scott, you take it."

I shove back when she tries to press the gun into my hands. "No, you keep it. I'll take the lead. Sylvie, you guard our backs."

There's no window in the back door, so the only way to tell for sure that the coast is clear is to open it. The lock twists easily enough under my fingers, but the click has my teeth on edge. I wait an entire count of thirty, but the door remains still and shut. "Okay," I whisper. "Sylvie, get ready with the gun. We'll stay behind the door so we can shut it if we need to. Okay? Winny?"

She nods. "Be careful, Scott. Please."

"Go easy. Just an inch or two." The knob turns as silently as the motion of the hinges—thank God I didn't forget to hit *these* with the WD-40. I start by easing it open just an inch. And then another. I pause for a couple of deep breaths. We're feet away from either freedom or more torment. I almost don't want to know which.

Winny nods at me.

Time to do this.

"One," I mouth, "two, three. Now." I pull the door open a good two feet, catching surprised cries from the other side. The men at the foot of the short set of stairs come racing at us.

"Shut it, Scott!" Winny's right there with me, adding her weight to mine, and we slam the door in their faces just before they hit it with the full force of their four-hundred-pound combined weight. I throw my shoulder against the steel door, absorbing their attempt to ram it open. "Shit!" They manage to nudge it, but weren't expecting even that small success, and we bang it shut before they can redouble their efforts. Winny is ready and twists the lock before they can land a second blow, and this time, all they get for their efforts are bruises.

"Downstairs!" Winny heads the way we came, but a second later, she freezes. I collide into her back, nearly sending her flying right into him.

Ryan.

I catch her before she can tumble forward and shove her behind me. "Ryan, man, come on. They're gone. It doesn't have to be this way."

"There is no other way. It was always going to end like this. When you got out of bed this morning, Scotty-boy, it was already too late." His face is cast in flickering darkness, but he extends one arm, and the weak spill of light coming from the tortured halogens is more than enough to make out the gun in his hand, and it's aimed at my chest.

"Tonight was set in stone twenty years ago. You should have thought about it before you ran out on us."

"Huh?" I say.

"Enough, Ryan." Sylvie is right at my back.

"Almost, big sis. Almost, but not quite."

"Put it down."

"In a minute. This will be over fast."

"Don't you think you've killed enough people tonight?"

"I don't know what you're talking about. That wasn't me. Those guys—" He waves his gun hand behind him, where the struggle continues, but is maybe losing steam. "They did this."

When he turns back our way, his hand remains at his side. It's not a big improvement, but my breath comes a little easier without that weapon pointing me in the face.

"And whose idea was it to come here?" Sylvie asks. "Whose idea to prey on your family? The only people who ever tried to stand up for you?"

"Scott," Winny whispers in my ear. "Do you hear that?"

I close my eyes and strain to listen past Sylvie's and Ryan's raised voices.

"Sirens," Winny says.

My eyes snap open. She's right. If we can hold out a little longer . . .

"Are you kidding me? You can really stand there and say that? What did you ever do for me, Sylvie?"

"When are you going to grow up and stop thinking everyone owes you something because life treated you hard? I left, okay. I admit that. But Dad was the one who did the rest. Dad. Not me."

"The screwing up of Ryan was a group effort."

"We're all screwed up, Ry. But about what you did here tonight? All the steps you took to be out there, storming our restaurant at ten after closing? Do you see it? Picture it in your head. You, at six years old, on a path that led you to my door tonight. Look at all the times you could have chosen something different. Every chance life gave you. Dad—hell, even me—we might have put you on that path to start with, but you were the one who walked it and ignored the signs that could have led you someplace other than here, with a frickin' bullet in your stomach and two kids cowering in front of you. I've tried to fix you way too long. It's over. No more. You're on your own."

He scoffs. "Yeah, just like I've always been." He raises his gun.

This is it. The corridor is so narrow. There's nowhere else to run. Just like at home, there's nothing to stop this weapon from getting me.

It's inevitable, and it's a fight I won't walk away from.

"Scott, move!" Winny shoves in front of me.

"No!"

"I said *move*. Now!"

I pinwheel my arms to keep from going down on my ass. "Winny, don't—"

Gunshots silence my sentence. First Sylvie's from behind, and a split second later, Ryan's from in front of me. Twice. It happens so fast and so slow. I have time to feel the breeze of the bullet tickle my cheek as it passes.

"Winny!"

Is she shot? Am I shot? I'm pretty sure the first bullet zipped by us. But Ryan's second, where did that one go? I get my arms around Winny so she won't crash to the linoleum. For all I know, Ryan's second bullet is lodged somewhere in my body; I can't feel it, not yet. Just Winny's warmth against me. Why did she do that? Why'd she put herself between me and a madman with a gun?

The sirens roar on the other side of the café wall, followed by new shouts. The cops are here. It's all over, but they're still too late. Lights dance in my vision as I wait for Winny's muscles to let go, for her weight to pull at me. Or for the pain to blossom somewhere inside me. For us both to crash onto the floor. No matter who took the bullet, I'm not letting go, so if one of us falls, we're both going down together.

Then Ryan crumples to the floor.

A clatter of metal at my back makes me jump, and Sylvie's gun slides into my foot. She runs past her brother to the café. "Oscar!"

"Silv?" he answers. His voice is weak, but he's alive.

Winny and I are alone, except for the dead man, but still I don't let go of her. One arm firmly around her waist, I move my other hand to the spot over her heart and press her to me while I wait for reality to crash in on us with the force of an automatic handgun. "Are we hit?" My breath brushes her neck. I clench my eyes shut against the pinpoints of light—like fairy lights—dancing in my vision to the drumbeat of my pulse.

Winny hitches a breath and brings a hand to rest over mine, holding me closer to her. "I don't think so." She spins, struggling to maneuver, because my arms are still wrapped around her, and runs her hands over my arms, my chest, my shoulders, my neck. "You're okay too, Scott. We're okay."

I take a huge gulp of air, like I just jumped into a cold shower. Instead of growing brighter, the pinpoints of light recede.

"I think Sylvie got him first and he missed. Both shots missed."

"You're okay? We're okay." I lift her up and spin us around.

She's crying into the crook of my neck, and slowly, I ease her to her feet. "You're sure you're not hurt?"

She's laughing. "Yes! I'm fine. I'm great!" With both

hands twined around my neck, she stretches to her tiptoes and places a kiss on my lips.

I inhale in surprise, cherry vanilla, but this time, her sweet scent is tinged with salt. I don't know how it's possible, but I pull her more tightly against me, lifting her again, trying to feel as much of her as I can. We stared death down moments ago, and now I feel more alive than ever before.

"Who's in there? Identify yourselves."

The lights are back, but instead of fairy twinkles, I'm assaulted by a blinding LED.

"Put down your weapons," the officer shouts.

"We don't have any," I call.

We turn, hands up, and I never imagined that move would feel so cheesy even with a dead man lying only a few feet away. "We're unarmed," I say. "I work here. She's a customer. We got caught up in . . ." I can't begin to think of what to call this. "He . . ." I point to Ryan. "He attacked us."

"Holy Jesus! Are you kids okay? Come on. We've got a fleet of ambulances on the way. We'll check you over. But go the other way, through the kitchen, so you can avoid the . . ." He inclines his head toward Ryan.

I nod and reach out for Winny's hand. Her fingers curl around mine, and we follow the officer's orders, heading through the silent and gleaming den of stainless steel before facing what lies beyond the doors in the café. Suddenly, I'm afraid to go out there, to see any more carnage. I turn to Winny. "You ready?"

"No, but . . ." She laughs.

"What?"

"If he thinks we couldn't handle walking past Ryan, wait till he hears who carried Maggie downstairs."

"Right. And wait until he sees the café. It's dead bodies galore in there."

Winny's fresh giggles mix with a new flood of tears.

"I think you've lost it, Win."

She sniffs. "Yeah. I'm totally gone." After one more deep breath, she nods, smiles, and takes my hand.

We push through the doors, ready to confront whatever awaits us out there.

42

SCOTT

W hat is this all about, Scotty?" his mother asked.

"Just come in and sit down, both of you," he said.

His dad was silent as he settled onto the sofa, stealing fast peeks across the room to the hallway and the entry to the kitchen, where the fridge stood in plain sight with his dad's cavalry of aids atop it: Johnnie Walker, Smirnoff, and a bottle of premium Bulleit bourbon. Good old Dad was already itching for his morning pick-me-up.

Scott needed to act fast, before the lure of the first shot of the day became too strong for his dad to resist.

He'd rehearsed this plan when they'd both been asleep, and now he walked through the steps without a hitch. The TV flickered to life. He got the Blu Ray player going, purchased just before his dad's company started the series of layoffs that kicked off this two years of hell, and opened the app that would let him stream the video from his phone to the screen.

His friends had been bugging him for years to cave and get a new smartphone, but they were so damned expensive. So, when the starter phone his parents bought for him back when he was twelve finally died, Scott went without. Until things got really bad, and the idea came to him. *This* idea.

"Here we go," he mumbled. The image of a box of generic rice puffs filled the small flat screen. Scott hit play, and Dad's slurred voice emanated from the outdated, but still functional, surround-sound speakers.

"I told you I'd take care of the bills," his on-screen dad said, while real-life Dad sat transfixed as he took in the drama from nearly two weeks ago. He turned to Scott, who stayed a safe distance away from the sofa. "What is this?"

"But Jack," his mom said on the screen. "I had to take care of it today, or else they would have shut off the lights."

No matter how many times his mother had denied how messed up his dad was, she gave herself away on the video. Scott had been struck the first time he watched it—one of many private screenings—how she always managed to keep at least a full arm's-distance away from her husband, and she never turned her back on him, not once, during the whole exchange. Even if her conscious brain was in denial, her unconscious survival mechanism had kept her vigilant. So far, it had worked to keep her safe.

Not so much with Scott.

"What is this?" his dad asked again.

His mother couldn't tear her eyes away from the screen as she relived the scene of domestic terror.

The confrontation, filmed ten days ago, had started over breakfast and continued as his mother had tried to clean up. It had lasted three-point-four minutes. No matter how many times Scott had watched this two hundred and four second replay of his life, it never failed to sweep up every dark and ugly feeling within him and mold it into a condensed ball of pain that lodged right where his heart should be.

He'd suffered—hell, he'd suffered. Now it was their turn.

On the screen, his dad's temper jumped up a notch. Scott found himself mouthing the words as they rang through the sound system. On cue, Evie started to cry, and his mother rushed to the table to snatch her out of her highchair. The towel she'd been using to dry the dishes fell from her shoulder where she'd slung it. His dad grabbed the rag so he could first wave it in his wife's face, making Evie cry harder. When that wasn't enough, he smacked her with it, and caught Evie, too.

That was the part that had kept Scott up, wrestling with indecision, for three straight nights. He kept replaying the way his nine-month-old sister flinched and blinked her tiny eyelids, with their fine fringe of baby-soft lashes, as that towel flapped in her face. It couldn't have hurt much. It was just a towel, after all. But it scared her, and what would happen the day it wasn't a towel, but the remote, or a bottle, or his dad's fist?

"You taped us?" the bastard asked, the cords of his throat strangling the words so they came out in a rasp. His face crumpled and his lip trembled.

He was actually going to cry?

What the hell *was* that? His dad buried his head in his hands and rocked back and forth on the sofa, and for the first time, that self-righteous burn that had become so familiar to Scott began to cool.

Had this been a huge mistake?

"I'm sorry. God. I'm sorry," Scott's dad mumbled from behind his hands.

"Shh, Jack." His mom rubbed her husband's back while glaring at Scott. "It's fine, Jack. No one got hurt."

"Speak for yourself," Scott said, returning her glare. No, it wasn't a mistake. He was done letting her hide in denial.

The recorded image jostled. To catch this footage, Scott had propped the phone against a bowl of overripe bananas that never made it into the shot, and all the movement caused it to slide a bit. He'd tried this setup on several other occasions, but nothing had gone down. Instead, the fireworks had flared unexpectedly, at random moments when Scott wasn't prepared. But he'd known that all he had to do was wait and keep trying and eventually he'd catch his dad in action. Scott's reward continued to play across the wide-screen.

Enter the hero of this show. Scott appeared on-screen, trying to wedge himself between his parents, but his dad responded by shoving him into the counter, causing the cell to topple onto its side. The camera kept recording.

His TV mom shouted his name. His dad turned his attention back on her, shaking her by the shoulders and jostling the baby still in her arms.

"No more," Scott had bellowed, jerking his dad away by one elbow. That's when his dad had hit him, a kidney shot, a bright explosion of agony. The memory of that pain still caused his skin to sheen with sweat, though the spot was now only a yellow ghost of the original bruise.

"Who did you show this to?" his mom asked.

"No one. Yet."

"What?" His dad lifted his tear-streaked face to take in his son, a familiar twitch seizing hold of one corner of his mouth. "What? You're going to show someone? You mean . . . you'd blackmail me?" Rage was drying the tears on his cheeks. "Your own family?" Standing, he brushed away his wife's hand and came at Scott. Instead of unleashing his fury, he slapped Scott's new smartphone from his grip, sending it flying across the room. It ricocheted off a lamp and smashed to the tile laid out around the fireplace hearth.

"I just got that," Scott gritted out.

"Jack, please, sit down." Scott's mom tried to pull her husband back to the sofa. She wrapped her arm around his shoulders while throwing a livid look at her son. "I think you'd better go somewhere else for a little while."

"Fine." Scott snatched his phone from the floor and thundered out of the room.

He had no idea what he'd expected from this stunt, but he imagined he'd feel better, maybe even have some kind of resolution. He didn't feel better at all. If anything, he felt worse. "Well, I guess anything's possible," he muttered as he slammed his bedroom door to block out his parents' shouting.

As he stood there, back to the door, his gaze settled on the three sheets of paper on his desk. God, he had to get out of this place. But how could he go? No matter how angry he was at his parents right now, there was no way he'd leave his mother and baby sister alone to fend off that monster.

He was just as stuck as ever.

People at school liked to talk about the zombie apocalypse, almost wishing for it, as if a worldwide disaster would be preferable to whatever they didn't like about their lives. That was the most ridiculous thing Scott had ever heard, but today, he'd almost welcome a disaster if it meant he could get out of this hellhole for good.

43

SCOTT

When the paramedics finally leave me alone, I close my eyes and lean my head against the wall of the ambulance. I can't believe it's over and everything can go back to the nightmare it was before this new nightmare started.

I check outside the rear doors, but everyone seems distracted, so I scoot farther inside and fish my phone out of my pocket. No one saw me snag it from the floor where Winny left it after she made her life-saving call. I need to get it to the cops. They've been looking for everyone's devices, and they'll want this one—the phone the 911 call came from, the one Ryan and Toto used to stay in touch with Twitch while they took Winny on a firearm shopping spree.

But I need to hold onto it for a little longer. The battery is staying at seven percent. Scrolling through the apps,

I find the photo gallery icon. The retrieved video is still there, safe and sound.

I think about Ryan and Sylvie's conversation at the end of all this mess, there in the hallway. Ryan's sense of betrayal. Sylvie doing everything in her power to save him. I see so much of me and my family in their story. All the parts we play are clear. I'm Sylvie, the martyr. They call, and I jump. Saving my family, keeping us going, even though it means putting my life on pause, trying to save us hostages from the bad guys.

So, if I'm Sylvie, that means Ryan is my dad. The person who blames everyone for his problems. The one who uses violence to vent his own pain. The monster.

Or am I Ryan? I seem to recall playing the blame game myself. Laying fault in the lap of my mom for hiding behind me. For letting me take on a little more and a little more and a little more after that. There's more blame to sling at Dad for turning into the villain he's become. At the world, for being the kind of place where a loving father could mutate into someone so utterly unrecognizable.

But the part of tonight's drama I can't get out of my head is how they were both sort of right—Ryan and Sylvie. Ryan, alone, was responsible for his choices, all the things he did to get himself wrapped up with Toto and the Chef, and all the things he did before that. And before that.

The part I find hardest to face is that Ryan was right, too. He was just a kid when Sylvie left home. What would it have been like if the current version of my dad was the one around when I was seven? Who would I be today? What things might have I done?"

Maybe Ryan would have been exactly the same if Sylvie had stayed home to keep him safe, but maybe not.

That's the problem. No one knows. No one can ever know.

I look at my phone's display, that little triangle that hovers over the image of a box of generic cereal, and I know that I don't want to be any of them. Not Ryan. Not the Sylvie who could have stayed nor the one who ran away. Whatever happens, holding the pieces together by myself isn't the answer. The status quo is over, but I can't completely abandon my family, either. Not my mom or Evie. Or even my father.

The truth is, I love them all.

Tears well up in my eyes for the first time since Dad lost his job. Sobs tear from my chest, and I shove my fists into my eyes until it hurts and I see flashes of light.

"You need anything in here?" The EMT pops her head in, and I scrub my face with my shirt.

"No, I'm good." I clear my throat and speak louder so I can hear myself over the ringing in my ears, the only wound I took from tonight's gunfire. "Just give me a minute, okay?"

"Sure. I'll be right over there if you need anything."

I nod, the phone still clenched in my fist.

What did Mrs. Sommervil say this morning? People talk, but don't act. Well, I acted, and I got results, just not the ones I expected.

My screen has timed out, so I tap it, bringing the video back up. Three options are highlighted at the bottom of the display: SHARE, EDIT, and DELETE.

I'm not keeping quiet or letting him hurt us anymore, and I'm done putting my life on hold, but shaming him more is not going to help. His shame is what started this all in the first place. Sure, the video might be evidence to convince the cops what's going on, but if I'm honest with myself, I was never worried they'd doubt my story. And yeah, I hoped things would change at home because of it, but my true motive for catching the drama on film was to make my parents suffer, plain and simple.

I did it for my own satisfaction.

Dad will either get better or he won't. If he does, then he'll know what he did, and he'll feel it. If he doesn't, then nothing I do or say will ever give me the satisfaction I'm seeking, and I'll be stuck carrying this lava around, letting it burn me up—like it burned up Ryan—forever.

Nothing good will come from this video.

I hit DELETE.

The cereal box vanishes, replaced by a new text message. From Becky.

OMG, I heard there was a holdup at Flores! R u okay? Please let me know ASAP. I'm freaking out over here.

I key in a quick reply as I hop down from the ambulance floor.

"Oh, hey, officer."

The cop stops on her way to whatever she was about to do. "You okay? Can I get you anything?"

"No, but I realized, I did have my phone after all. Everything got so confusing in there, I forgot I put it in my pocket."

"Thanks. You sure you're okay? Maybe you should just sit and rest."

I shake my head and scan the street for the ambulance where the paramedics took Winny, and I spot her, highlighted by the light spilling from the rear doors. "I'm going to be fine."

44

WINNY

I want to get lost in blue and red swirling lights, but my brain keeps throwing me back inside Café Flores. Snippets of scenes from the last three hours flash through my mind, especially the final showdown with Ryan in the back hallway.

My latest memory reel is cut short when fingers wrap around my hand, and the back of the ambulance bounces as Scott hops up to sit next to me with his feet dangling over the edge, like mine.

"You okay?" he asks.

I take a deep breath and give his hand a squeeze. "I guess. I mean, no. I'm not, but we made it, right? That's all that matters."

"We made it, yeah." Someone has bandaged his cheek. "But that's not all that matters."

"Huh?"

"It's just, surviving can come at a cost."

"Like the things we saw?" I shiver. Once more, I'm in the back hallway of Café Flores staring down the barrel of Ryan's gun. I still can't believe I jumped in front of Scott like that. "And the things we did?"

He nods, releasing my hand and scrubbing his palms up and down the legs of his jeans like he's trying to wipe away something nasty. "Or the things we almost did."

That dark tone tells me not to ask, and I don't expect him to say any more.

"I was really going to do it, Win. Kill Twitch. There's still a part of me that wishes I did, like that would make the shitty parts of my life better somehow."

"But it wouldn't have, would it?"

"No." His answer comes down like a judge's gavel. "I think my dad is still trying to figure that out."

"What?"

He shakes his head. "It's not important right now." His hazel eyes are fixed on mine. "Why'd you do it, Win? Get in front of me like that?"

The weight around my torso triples. "I'll show you." With fingers that aren't trembling as much as they were five minutes ago, I undo the buttons of my cardigan, revealing the white bodice of my dress beneath.

"You're taking off your sweater. Why are you taking off your sweater?"

"Wait for it." Shedding the cardigan, I twist to give him

a good view of the Kevlar poking out beneath the straps of my dress. "Bulletproof."

"Where'd you get that?"

"Shelly . . ." Unbidden, her last name surfaces in my mind, finally. "Shelly Olvarez."

"Now you've lost me."

"I'll explain, but not right now. Okay?"

"You were going to take a bullet for me? I can't believe I just said that."

I shrug. "I figured I was protected."

"Yeah, your torso, but what about the rest of you? Even if it hit the vest, the bullet might not have killed you, but you probably would have ended up with broken ribs at the least."

"I wasn't thinking about that then, but I am now. Believe me." A crazed Ryan stares me down, and he raises his gun again . . . A lump of terror lodges in my throat.

"Win?"

"What? Yeah. Sorry. Zoned out there, didn't I?"

"A little. Did you mean what you said? About explaining the Shelly Olvarez incident later on?" He yawns and rubs his eyes. "Or maybe tomorrow, after we sleep? If we can sleep. I'll be honest, I don't want to let you out of my sight. Ever. Your parents probably wouldn't let me come home with you though, huh?"

"Definitely not." Like sugar in a steaming mug of tea, the lump in my throat dissolves; warmth floods my body. He leans in closer, and I'm lost in him, heat rising to my cheeks. Without meaning to, I brush the bandage on his cheek with my fingers. "I see they decided to forgo the Saran Wrap on this dressing."

My nervous laugh is cut off when he takes my fingers and brings them to his lips. "Thank you, Winsome Sommervil, for standing up for me like no one else ever has."

My breath hitches, but for the first time tonight, it's in a good way.

An officer crosses the street, two figures at his heels. I blink back tears, tears that don't come close to the flood streaming down my mother's face.

I'm up and running to her, not even knowing how I cover the distance between us. All I know is her arms and her scent and the petal-soft silk of her dress against my cheek. Her voice—the one that resounded in my head through the terrible hours since I left home.

"We could have lost you." She can't decide what to do with her hands. They're on my cheeks, my head, my shoulders. "When they told us what happened . . . and I wasn't there to protect you." She shakes her head and closes her eyes.

I laugh through my tears. "But you *were* there. The whole time, bossing me around, just like always." She pulls back to check me again, a confused expression playing on her face. "I couldn't have done it without you, *manman*."

She strokes my hair over and over, and my dad, who has stood by, shuffling from foot to foot, finally throws his arms around us both.

"We need to get these kids to the hospital," the officer says. "EMTs think overnight observation is best."

"Of course," my mother says. "Winsome did EMT training last fall. She did wonderfully. She's going to med school."

"Mom, I passed out at the first sight of blood."

She sputters. Finally, my mother is struck speechless. When she regains her composure she adds, "And she's an incredible artist."

"Oscar couldn't have survived without you tonight. You saved him," Scott reminds me.

"Yeah, I guess I did." The paramedics tended to him first, and he and Sylvie are probably already at the hospital by now.

"Damn right she did." My dad wraps me in a hug.

"Scott," the officer says. "Your mom was going to come here, but we told her to go straight to the ER."

"What about the people who did this?" my dad asks.

"We'll place an armed guard on each of their rooms, of course, but we've got a good idea who to look for."

"Oh God. The Chef and Aaron. I totally forgot they're still out there." I grope for Scott's hand.

"Don't worry," the officer says. "We'll do whatever it takes to keep you two safe, Mr. and Mrs. Flores, too." The officer pivots to return to the café but turns back a second later. "Oh, and Mr. Bradley, thanks for handing your phone over. I understand it was the one used to call 911."

Scott nods.

"We'll need to keep it for now, as evidence, you understand, to corroborate everyone's testimony. When we get it charged, that is. You don't happen to have a cord handy, do you?"

"Check under the register," Scott says, laughing.

"Please, kids," the officer says. "If you'll return to your ambulances now. Parents, you can follow along."

"I'm going with her," my mom says but pauses and turns to me. "That is, if you want me to."

"Yeah." I nod. "That would be good."

"Can we have one second?" Scott asks, holding up a finger. "Just one?"

"Fine," the officer says, "but we want to clear the street."

Scott reaches out his hand to me, and I take it as we round the side of the ambulance for a little privacy.

"What is it, Scott?"

He kisses me before I can draw breath. Blue and red lights bathe us in their glow, but not in warmth. That comes from Scott. From his hands, from his lips. From his heart.

When the ambulance driver calls for us to get a move on, we break apart.

"I'll see you there," he whispers as though he needs to catch his breath, and maybe he does. I know I do.

"You think they'll give us rooms on the same floor as Sylvie and Oscar?" he asks.

"Sure. We can have a Café Flores post-shooting party. We'll play charades."

He laughs and holds up two fingers then tugs on an ear-lobe. "Two words. Sounds like *charmed bun-pen*."

"The most messed up game of charades ever."

He holds me in his gaze, and I shiver. As I watch him make his way to his medical transport, the EMT comes to help me into my ambulance.

"Crazy night you guys have been through." She holds the door so my mom can climb in.

"Yeah."

"So," the EMT says as we pull away. "You're joining our ranks?"

I consider for a moment, very aware of my mom's eyes on me, though I don't look at her. "Yeah, I think I am."

"Premed, huh?" she asks as she checks my pulse. Again.

"No."

She starts, but raises an eyebrow and smiles. "No?"

"Nope. I'm going to art school. I sent in my acceptance letter today." Now I do look at my mom, who is working very hard not to say anything. Maybe it's low, telling her about art school at this very moment, but she had to find out sometime, and I can't imagine a scenario less likely to get me grounded. Again.

Mom rolls her eyes and shakes her head at me.

"This EMT thing is just a hobby," I tell the paramedic. "Plus, it's nice to have some handy skills. You know, in a pinch. *A foreseen disaster does not kill the fool.*"

"You sound like my mom."

"Yeah. Mine, too," I say and smile at her as tears well up in my eyes. What does my portrait look like now? No longer that blurry smear or a replica of my parents. Not empty, either. There is still so much to figure out, but it doesn't scare me anymore.

The night spins past us as we race toward the hospital, toward the future. This time, I'll be ready for it.

ACKNOWLEDGMENTS

One day I started writing, just for fun, and now my life has changed forever. I can't believe I get to do this, that I have the privilege of writing these words right now, and I wouldn't be able to if not for the support of many people.

I want to start by thanking my endlessly patient and relentlessly passionate agent, Dr. Uwe Stender of Triada US Literary Agency. Uwe, I can't imagine a better partner or advocate on this journey. Your belief in this book, my writing, and my future career has meant everything. And I'm just so proud to be a member of Team Triada. Also, a big thanks to Brent Taylor for lending your expertise back in the pre-submission days.

To my editor, Alison Weiss, thank you for helping to make this book the best it can be. I never thought I'd meet someone who loved it as much as Uwe, but apparently, I was wrong. You *got* it, on every level, and I knew right away that my book was in the best possible hands.

To editor Nicole Frail, thank you for all you've done for *Ten After*, particularly for your endless patience as we navigated the details during pre-launch and production and for always being available to answer my questions—my many, *many* questions.

I'd like to thank the rest of the Sky Pony Press team, people who gave *Ten After* its face, style, and helped shepherd it out into the world including, Joshua Barnaby, Kate Gartner, Johanna Dickson, and Jill Lichtenstadter. I also want to thank the artist, Kevin Tong, for his beautiful and creepy cover art.

Next, I must thank a group of very special ladies. To the novelists, Cristina Dos Santos, Juliana Haygert, Ginger Merante, and Ghenet Myrthil. Without you, I literally wouldn't be here. You all came into my life at the perfect time, and your friendship was exactly what I needed. We're a writing group, but we're so much more. I've never shared so many rental houses, hotel rooms, Facebook posts, cups of coffee, or pumpkin cookies with anyone in my life. I'm so glad we're in this together.

To my critique partners, the talented Emily Colin and Dana Mele, I'm so lucky to have found two fabulous CPs who are willing to take time out of their busy schedules to help me and who write books I can't wait to get my hands on to critique in return. And to Jean Chery and Steve Myrthil, thank you for reading and sharing your feedback on my early draft.

To the Electric Eighteens, I'm honored to be among so many fabulous middle grade and young adult authors. Sharing this experience with all of you this year has been so much fun and so rewarding. And it doesn't end in 2019. Here's to the next phase of all your careers!

To all the readers and bloggers out there who have supported me this far in my writing career, thank you, thank you, thank you. No writer can do it without readers, and there is nothing as satisfying as when someone enjoys the work we do.

I must also thank my family and friends. I was sure that everyone would think I was out of my mind to start this writing thing after spending a decade becoming a psychologist, but not once did anyone respond the way I feared. You've all be so supportive, even more excited than me at times, and that has meant the world to me.

To Dad, thank you for your unceasing confidence in my success no matter how arduous the process might be.

To Mim, there's nothing like getting a call from you while you're reading one of my books or after you finish one and are still thinking about it. I'm so lucky to have a mom who believes that everything I do is amazing (even when it isn't).

Lastly, I want to thank my husband, Eric. You're always there for me in every way. Your plotting help, your emotional support, your belief that I can do this. You always know what I need to keep going. Thank you for your patience, too. You roll with it all—those long days I spend on the computer, the garden that hasn't been weeded in longer than I can recall, and all the other ways that writing has impacted our lives. Thank you for your excitement, which is often the thing that takes me out of fear mode and lets me live this experience with my whole heart.